Short S

Jim Cunningham

MICHELLE,

BEST WISHES,

JIM CUNNINGHAM

CCP

Coyote Country Publishing

To Gene

Contents

A Sad Stretch on Chromosome 11*

Blind from birth, she could tell the difference between the odor of chrysanthemums and tulips and remember her first whiff of both. She could identify the scent of her brother in a groping group of sweaty brutes. She knew her nose was her biographer collecting memories, visions her eyes could not.

1

She studied biology only to discover her compendium of smells originated in a space infinitely smaller than a fly's eye—a few molecules devoted to identifying ham, the rich smoky meat of her first Easter. Another clump to help her hold the faint smell of perfume which lingered in the room hours after her mother passed.

And who knew what atoms, what cells, what curse of chemistry forced her to recall, most of all, the sweet scent of her newborn's hair, the few seconds she held him, after his heart stopped, and they took him from her and placed him in a smooth, cold box, where sight, sound and smell were locked forever.

*A section of chromosome 11 has been determined to be responsible for the development of much of our sense of smell.

For me, the creek may as well have been the mighty Mississippi. Too shallow for canoe. Mostly carp and crawfish called it home.

No great novels were penned about adventures there, though I had my own tales to tell: sand squishing between my toes on a sultry August day, a water moccasin I decided to let live, the time my grandfather taught me how to clean the catch, fish guts given back to the sluggish current.

Most of all, the arm I found on a Sunday afternoon, one attached to a body who turned out to be a man who had cheated my grandpa and vanished only days later—assumed to have absconded to avoid John Law.

My uncle the sheriff fished him out and planted him again without a doc's scrutinizing eye. Never was the man mentioned again, even by his kin. Whipped white trash. Such was Texas in 1940— questions not answered because not asked.

Drought dried the creek to fetid puddles the year my grandpa passed. The very spot I found the arm, one of the last places to dry. A stagnant pool with minnows and memories colliding in death throes, and my grandfather buried spitting distance from the man I had found. Both now above the creek where it joined the river Brazos, it too a victim of the sun's relentless sear, though not so willing to give up secrets, to cast doubt on legends, or let ghosts rise from the mire.

Feeding the Holier

Teresa climbs on the bus before the sun, if she has the fare to get there, where she makes the bread. She's done this labor two of her nineteen years. Yet she has fears they will come for her, green card or not.

Though they like her rolls. Teresa kneads the big balls, pulls, pinches—a sculpting of dough, a laying of trays, one after another. Then, from the Iglesias, they come, decked in their finery, though she does not see. She only hears the litany of language she can't comprehend, a clanging of trays, laughter. Then the urging of the jefe to work faster, bake the bread. The communion wafers did not fill them.

Now they are here, breaking fast, forgetting the words they just heard, the songs they sang. Teresa does not complain; she is glad to feed the worshipers, though they will never know her name. Nor will they stop for her in the pouring rain, the blistering sun. Teresa never wavers. Next Sabbath will be the same: dawn, the dough, the oven. It is the work. Her hands which make the bread others break, the grace granted to serve. Holy, holy, holy...

I walked through torrents, shivering not from the burden of the flesh, or the earthly winds, but from the vision of my footprints disappearing before they were even made.

I woke in the cabin and remembered the dream—walking in ankle deep water, freezing though it was July's finest hour. I beat you to the cook stove and fried bacon. I used the grease for the eggs, the way you liked.

Quiet. Interrupted only by thunder and the few words we spoke. I don't remember what we said. Did we talk about when we would die? Did we talk about who had already died? Your father? I don't remember. The storm was fine.

The eggs were good. And the walk after breakfast. Clean, cool after the rain. Puddles pocking the ranch road. Your dog sloshed through every one of them. When we came to the Cimarron, it was swollen. We had seen the Rio Grande that way. We swam across it at the border levee, forty-five years before. I remember that day on the Rio. After the swim, we went to Mr. Taylor's house. He put towels on the couch, so our sopping shorts did not mud stain the fabric. I remember being hungry. And the barbeque place we found later. And the wrinkled old man who ran the place. Probably the only black face within twenty miles in that corner of the state.

I stopped to take pictures of the Cimarron. Digital. Not like you with your Canon F-1. Each image you got was precision framed and f-stop perfect. I snapped a hundred of the Cimarron in the time it would take you to capture two of the surf at Bodega Bay or a tall Ponderosa Pine in the Sierra. You always had more patience with things.

I took crisp shots of the current. I got a good one of the place where it happened. Where I was helpless. More helpless than on the killing fields when I was nineteen and holding my thumb on Pete Garcia's femoral that was slashed by the same mortar shrapnel that got me a purple heart. But I was "the doc." I was going to save Pete, just like I had Tom the week before when a mine took his leg to the knee and I had a tourniquet on it the minute he hit the ground. Back in base camp, "the doc" got lots of beers for that, even though almost nobody liked

Tom from Peoria, Illinois. But the beer was for saving them later—insurance, I guess.

Everybody liked Pete from Fresno. I was going to save him for sure. I didn't though. And I didn't get any free beer that night in base camp. I drank my own. You knew the stories of Pete and Tom. And maybe you thought I could save you.

I saw your spaniel jump into the current, trying to get to the other side to chase steers. You liked coming there to let her run free. But that water was deep and swift, and her legs were getting old. The mile we hiked from the cabin was two miles of circles and sniffing for her.

When she went under, I watched you wade in after her. The steers all started running, kicking up dust even after the rain.

That was the last I saw of you—chest deep in chocolate water, the small herd behind you running as fast as the current that sucked you in. I jumped in and felt the weight of my running shoes. Your hiking boots must have been heavier. And your 357 magnum and that ammo. And your flashlight and knife. And your body. All disappearing. And I was swimming after you, kicking to keep myself from being pulled down.

The cattle disappeared into the salt cedar where we found bear scat the previous autumn, when the river had been a mud hole with some puddles. I swam not until the river dammed a half mile down, where I expected to find you, and the dog, waiting for me, but only until my head started sinking and my eyes started clouding with the muddy water. Only until I found some rocks that would give me a handhold.

My legs ached as I walked to the dam, looking for you, for the cattle. Thinking if they reappeared so would you. Thinking of how we made it across the Rio Grande. Thinking you chased that damned dog. Thinking you loved to let her run free.

You were there, stuck in the roots that helped form that dam. But I didn't see you. Not until I walked back to the ranch, and the rancher called his son in law, the sheriff, and the other folks who would help me find you. It was dusk when we did. The rancher's grandson, only seventeen, spotted your hand between two limbs. I didn't see it until I was directly above, staring down at your palm that looked like it was waiting for something to drop into it.

I still wonder if you thought I could save you. If I would save you. I wonder if I tried or just took a hard swim in a river, knowing you were already lost to me and I just needed to keep kicking my feet, flailing my arms. I still wonder about Pete.

I spent another night in the ranch. I got your things together and drove your jeep to your sister's. The rancher followed me and carried me back to the ranch for my SUV. That night, there was lightning on the mesas again, and the smell of rain. I walked back down to the river the next morning; the sun was making a gold shaft on the water. The Cimarron had forgotten about the storm.

I saw the footprints I made into the river after you. We never found your dog. Maybe she made it to the other side and chased those cattle.

The Eyes of a Blue Dog, a Thumb Tale

That summer, "Born to Be Wild" and "Mrs. Robinson" were on AM. A & W Drive-Ins served frosted mugs, and Tet's blood had not long dried black on Saigon streets. I was sixteen, going on sixteen.

My father had dumped me with Uncle Roy, Colonel Roy, to "rehabilitate me." That lasted forty days and forty nights. Would have lasted longer, I suppose, but my thumb took me from the green tipped tongue of western Kentucky across the wide world to a café in Santa Rosa, New Mexico, where I spent my last eighty-five cents on a white bread tuna sandwich and chips at the café that was also the bus depot.

A bench was waiting for me when the restaurant closed its doors at 12:10, the old waitress giving me a generous extra dime of time, knowing I had to face the night and the bench, or the New Mexico road. I chose the latter and headed south under a coal dark sky.

Only eighteen-wheelers passed, their screaming lights robbing me of the quiet vision night's monotony would have granted. They saw my thumb, but not one stopped. They did not know I had walked a dozen dark dead miles and had not closed my eyes in sixty hours; nor did they care about me or my shadow on Highway 54.

The mesas were dotted with pinons and cedars. I spoke to them as they moved about like mournful buffalo, stirred to life by a sound or a scent, perhaps my own foul road bouquet. They were mute, though, even when I asked them if I was seeing god in their measured marching across my desert dream.

Long before the dawn I had begged to come arrived, I saw him, dead center on my highway, so black he was blue—his eyes hanging like two emeralds in some ethereal space, staring at me. The rest of the absent world unaware he was there, growling, the rumble so low I tasted it, as he might taste me. I felt our nostrils flair, as his would when he devoured me. I saw the blood feast through our eyes—the final morsel of me a pale art form on the asphalt palette. As he swallowed the last of his meal, an eighteen-wheeler came, its high beams bouncing off the beast only long enough for me to see his mouth was dry and his belly empty, before he vanished into the blue night.

An old man in a '54 Ford came over a rise with the sun, picked me up, and told me he did only because he thought I was a girl. He asked me to lay my head in his lap. I told him no. I didn't tell him the Colonel and my father both taught me to break a man's neck, and I don't know if I could have that summer morning. I also didn't tell him I had seen the rooted trees move on the mesas, or that I had been devoured by a beast and resurrected by a simple beam of light. I could yet see through those eyes and knew I was safe, even when the old man propositioned me a second time.

Deliverance

I found a skeleton of a bus so far into the pines, I knew it had been dropped from the sky to save me. They had to be far behind, the other side of the stream, where those hounds lost my scent. Jed and Tonto didn't follow me across the shallows, and I'd bet all the money I ever stole those curs and posse ate them up.

There was almost half a moon, though inside the bus was black. Outside freezing drizzle was pattering on the roof. The coat I filched was soaked, and my trousers too—nobody told me Alabama got this cold. If they had I wouldn't have believed them, until that night.

I curled up in a ball behind the driver's seat and shoved my frozen hands in my shirt; then I heard that hiss and saw those eyes. I stayed quiet, quieter even than when I hid from John law.

The cat growled, deep, slow, but I kept watching her eyes: emerald and still, still in the place I first saw them. Then we were both silent. I'd pee my drawers before I'd move. Freeze outside—get ate inside.

The hours passed fast. I drifted, dreamed a little about being back inside, and woke when the sun hit the cracked windshield. She was still there, with two cubs nursing, now used to my smell, I suppose, since she didn't jump.

When I slid down the bus stairs into the frosty grass, I saw a doe, chewing forbs to the roots. Lucky the lion had her babes stuck to her teats. Lucky I was between the cat and prey. Lucky the bus was in that grove to deliver me from a cold death.

Alabama, Jackson County, 1952

Sea Breeze*

That summer, Paul would sit in his chair in his shorts and let the curtains blow over his knees, tickling the hair on his thighs. The breeze was always there, but the warmth was not. Long were the months when the shore and his cottage were battered by winds, rain, and sleet. Those times, he could only watch his windows be pelted and imagine strange creatures and landscapes in the trails the water made on the panes.

Once, during a November gale, Paul saw a pattern on the pane that reminded him of two rivers that became one, making a "Y" from the cockpit of his plane—the place he flew with a combination of trembling trepidation and exhilaration until he was shot from the sky and crashed into the banks of the river. Paul's crew perished, but whatever gods ruled the skies and earth left him alive, legs shorn off to his knees.

Now Paul's world was his room, his cottage, and the books in which he would travel to lands over which he once flew and others he never knew. Before he took to the skies, the sea had been Paul's blank page where his adventures were recorded with the bow of his skiff and oars in his two strong arms. Paul would row and watch his wake, wondering what it looked like from the sky, or what the creatures below would make of his hull and the tugging of his sculls in the surf.

The Atlantic was now a taunting vision, and the sky borne view of the earth a lump throat memory—Paul was in the chair. Few were the days when he could find comfort in the soft fabric's pendulous dance on his skin. All the time, he missed her more than flying or being on the sea. Yet she was there, his wife, Lorraine, sleeping in the next room, walking past him, like another breeze, silent save her footfalls which sounded more feline than human.

Lorraine would take her own journeys on the sands and in the waves. Whenever weathers would permit, she was gone. Paul would watch her walking through the tall grass to the beach. He would see her strip to her nakedness and walk into the waves, sometimes swimming so far from land Paul could barely see her golden hair. The "Lorraine pain" he would think—a special ache, not as sharp as the one he felt when his legs were shredded in the crash. But Paul would gladly exchange the transient agony of that day in the war for what he experienced now, a year later, in the cottage he had built for her and the children who would never be born.

Often Paul recalled the last night they made love, only hours before she dropped him at the train station. He remembered her expression—what he saw through the window as the train pulled away from the platform. Then, he could not decipher it. Now he knew it was resentment that would become incalculable indifference when he returned, less than whole.

Loraine had begged him not to go. One phone call, one telegram to her father, and Paul would have a posh assignment stateside. Paul knew marrying a Senator's daughter could provide such power and privilege, but Lorraine knew if she had made the call, Paul would never feel whole in his own way. And Lorraine knew Paul would never forgive her. He said as much over dinner, on their first anniversary. Paul remembered the exact moment he told her: the flickering light of the candle at their table, the voices of the other patrons, the taste of the lamb he was chewing, the smell of mint sauce, the feel of his fork in his hand, and the tears he saw in her eyes when Paul said, how can I possibly trade my wings for a desk in DC when all the men with whom I trained will be putting their lives on the line? Lorraine did not say it, but Paul knew what the tears and her expression meant that night. What about me? What about us?

Now, on this sun baked afternoon, with a warm salt breeze filling his room, there was no us. Lorraine was with her parents in Boston, to return by dinner time. But it did not matter. Even if they ate at the same table, which they rarely did, they would not utter more than the prosaic phrases necessary to complete the meal—pass the butter, pass the peas, please, and yes, I would like coffee.

Paul looked at his watch for the hundredth time that day. One-thirty. Lorraine would not be home sooner than six, seven if she caught the later train. The maid was off. Today would be the day. At least that is what Paul kept telling himself. Today. Paul rolled himself to the chest of drawers where he kept it. Loaded. Loaded with the same shells he put in its cylinder a week after he came home from the hospital. Loaded with the shells he thought he would use to kill Lorraine's lover if he could somehow make it the mile down the lane to where the lover lived. His name was also Paul, and before the war, Lorraine had called him arrogant and a drunk.

The truth was Paul would not have shot the man if he walked through the door. He could not blame the other Paul. Lorraine was beautiful, and Lorraine had a gaping hole he himself had made in her. Any lover would be glad to fill it. But nothing filled that space. Paul had seen Lorraine's lover drop her off one evening after what was likely an afternoon of lovemaking. But the post coital contentedness he saw on her face after their own lovemaking before Paul went off to war was not there. Now, only a scalding brand of burning indifference. Apathy with a scarlet A, perhaps.

The gun fit well in his hand. The barrel reflected the light streaming through the windows. Paul looked again at the time. Two. Where had thirty minutes gone? Paul switched the gun from one hand to the other, as if deciding which one to use to commit the act. As a child, Paul discovered he was ambidextrous. His father, a surgeon, convinced him to major in pre-med and told him the best surgeons were ambidextrous. But upon graduation, though accepted at Johns Hopkins med school, Paul took a job working for the Congressman in his District. His college roommate was the Congressman's son and Paul and he took jobs in DC in the summer of 1940. It was there he met Lorraine while she was visiting her father. It wasn't love at first sight since the Congressman and her father belonged to different parties. During Paul and Lorraine's first conversation, they argued about Roosevelt, but Lorraine's beauty and wit forced him to cross the aisle and walk her down another aisle six months later.

That was a forever three years ago. More than a thousand days. Enough days Paul had decided. He looked through the window at the surf—small white caps, a yacht in the distance, and a few whiffs of clouds far to the east. A calico cat was coming across the lawn towards the cottage. Its presence was unsettling to Paul. He felt the animal was an interloper in this scene—an audience of one without a ticket to this play about to reach its tragic denouement. The cat jumped onto the sill. It swiped at the sheer curtains as they swayed to and fro in the breeze. Paul began to laugh, and his eyes filled with tears. He lifted the gun and looked down its barrel. He looked back at the cat. No, Paul thought, not in front of you. The cat jumped back into the grass and was gone. Paul looked at his watch again. Two thirty. Another half an hour?

The phone rang. Paul did not answer. Seven rings and it stopped. He again stared down the barrel of the gun. He pointed it to the window, then back toward his face. The muzzle only six inches from his mouth. Both hands began to shake, the way Paul remembered they had the first time he had flown solo, and every time they did when Paul was flying while his bombardier was releasing incendiary bombs on German cities.

The phone rang again. This time it did not stop. Paul thought of the bells of the church that seemed to chime interminably. He wheeled himself to the phone, picked up the receiver and said nothing. Paul, Paul, is that you? He recognized his mother's voice. Three o'clock, his mother's favorite time to call, after her Monday bridge game. Yes, Mother. Paul, just calling to remind you about Saturday. How are you? Did you finish that dreadful Joseph Conrad book? Two o'clock Saturday. Remember. Yes, Mother. He hung up while his mother was saying your father and I look forward to seeing you and Lorraine.

Paul again laughed and again his laughter turned to tears. Lorraine was a consummate actress in front of his parents. They never knew of the despair between them. Perhaps they saw but did not allow themselves to think their damaged only child could endure such a burden. Maybe Paul's pain of losing his legs *and* Lorraine would have been too much for them.

Paul wheeled himself back to the windows. The wind died down and the sheer curtains were still. The cat jumped onto the sill again. He pointed the gun at it. No, he would not shoot it. No, he would not shoot the "other Paul." Killing hundreds of women and children from a mile high, yes, but the calico, no. Still he found himself cocking the gun and pointing it at the cat. Paul pulled the trigger, but his aim was, intentionally, over the cat's head. The calico did not move and the round from his '38 revolver landed somewhere in the surf. He fired four more times. Each time the cat startled but remained crouched on the sill.

Paul imagined the rounds sinking into the shallow shelf off shore. He imagined the fishes, the same ones who once saw his hull moving above them, now watching the descent of the bullets, darting about, sending whatever signals fish did among themselves. The cat, his mother, the fish. All these living things. Paul placed the hot muzzle against his forehead. The salt sea breeze picked up again and the curtains swayed. The cat swiped at them, its claws snagging a bit of the fabric. Paul placed the gun in his lap and rolled to the window.

Get out of here! Lorraine made those curtains. Go away. The cat jumped from the window and ran across the grass.

Paul rolled back to the chest of drawers and replaced the gun. Three-thirty. Paul wheeled himself back to the windows. He watched the cat disappear over the edge of the grass, down the slope and to the shore, out of his sight. The wind gusted, lifting the curtains to a horizontal position. One drape brushed across his shoulder on its ascent and again as it came back towards the sea. Paul closed his eyes and saw Lorraine, smiling. He opened them, and she was gone. He returned to the chest of drawers and placed his hand on the brass handle, but he did not retrieve the gun. Instead, he returned to the window and waited for the next breeze.

*Inspired by David Larkin's painting, Scarborough Sea Breeze

Doorknob

Gold, round—it has felt a thousand hands in sixty years. Tomorrow it will be replaced, the dead door along with it.

The old brass globe knows nothing of gentrification, its desecration of memory: the carpenter who bore its hole; the first child to turn the knob to go out to play; the last man to yank it in anger when he felt the bowels of defeat, the bane of bankruptcy, and the effluent epiphany of eviction.

How many tales began with the spinning of the circle, the opening of the door, letting in the light? Tomorrow, and tomorrow, and tomorrow, the door and the handle will rest in the landfill, the graveyard of myriad doorknobs. All with their own stories of auspicious beginnings, mysterious twists and turns, and plots thickened by the hands of time.

Shelters, Thursdays

Hypodermics lined up like firing squad rifles, loaded with Morpheus' mortal brew, at this "humane" place, where we stare in the face of every critter we "put down." Felines, canines, by the score. There will always be more.

We do it Thursdays; each gets its own black plastic bag for a trip to the incinerator courtesy of the county's grandest crematorium, which has donated the friendly fire for our four-legged friends. We watch the smoke trails fill the night sky.

There is no Zyklon B to fear. Not here, where we use shots instead of showers and while away the hours scratching the ears and petting the rumps of those we slaughter with sleep.

Where the Mountains Meet the Plain

They could see the Rockies on most clear days, though their ranch was as flat as any Kansas cornfield. The slopes cursed them with wicked storm now and then, but other than a few shingles off a roof and a steer or two struck by lightning, their place was no worse for the wear.

Father and Son ran this place as did two generations before them, and after chores one eve they watched a Texas flood they thought only a vengeful God could command. They flipped a coin to decide who would take a truck of supplies and who would stay to tend to the herd. The boy won the toss. Just as well, the old man reckoned; his spirit was not as ready for the road as it once was.

He helped his boy load all the pickup would hold and his only son left on a clear dawn, headed for the wake of some monster named Harvey. The son sliced the Oklahoma Panhandle while most folks were still eating breakfast. Amarillo was in his rearview by lunch and he had a hunch he could make it all the way there by sunrise the next day. Odds are he would have, had a fleeing Houstonian not fallen asleep at the wheel and pulled into his lane under a midnight sky.

The doctor from a small Texas town with a name the father wouldn't want to remember assured him his boy went fast. His son didn't suffer. So the doctor said.

Once the father got his son's mangled body in the ground, the old man took his grief straight to the store, filled up another truck and left his stock to fend for themselves, as he took a journey his boy was not destined to complete. He didn't shed a tear while he unloaded the supplies on a new coastal plain, amid scores who did not lose a son. Though surely, he was not the only one, he thought, who would cry himself to sleep that very night, where wide waters his son never saw receded, far from where the mountains meet the plain.

I am Harvey

I didn't pick my name any more than I asked for all this rain to fall on my streets. I thank the good Lord above Amelia didn't live to see this—me in this chair, a leg lost to the sugar diabetes, her cat disappearin' in the night.

The water's dang near to my waist now, but I ain't too cold—just hungry and dog tired. Last night with Noah's flood arisin' I could have sworn I saw two water moccasins slithering around my one good leg.

I did prayin' a plenty and didn't sleep a wink. Dawn came quiet— guess the neighbor's rooster run off for high ground, if there is any left on God's green earth.

My ears are goin', but I know I hear an outboard. Someone is coming to save me, to pull me from this room turned to toilet. Someone.

The sound of that motor's fadin'. They'll be back. In the meantime, I'll keep calling for that cat. There're high spots where she could be, and I could swear I saw a ray of sunshine through those clouds. And when they come for me, I'll tell them my name. Give them a good laugh.

Dickinson, Texas, August 28, 2017

The Waning Light

She sits by her window to write, ever fond of the morning light. Not a day passes when she fails to pen an epistle to him. She envisions him pulling the missives from his saddle bags and perusing them a second time, a third, admiring her chancery cursive. A year now since she saw him, steady on his steed, his regiment waiting, eager to join the fray, to ride north under his proud command.

Perhaps at eventide, she will write another letter, in case she forgot anything she intended to say this morn, or just to reach out again before the setting of the sun. A cloud passes as she signs her name, another as she folds the paper; soon it seems, a gathering storm. She places the letter in the envelope, its traveling home.

She turns the candle to pour the wax, then presses the seal— another story from her to him ready for its long journey: the stroll from her room to the mantel in the parlor, to the pile of paper that each day grows higher above the hearth. This block of stones, a cold cavern of late, for without him, she eschews all things warm, for she knows he must be freezing in the cruel ground where he fell.

Spartanburg, South Carolina, Winter, 1863

Morning after Walsenburg

Thumb frozen, my ears red in the cold heat. Interstate-25 apocalyptically empty and mute. My northbound shoes making the only sound on the frozen dawn's silent stage. What lone survivor of a sleepless Rocky Mountain night would I encounter? When would I see another face?

The cars came with the sun as it struggled to make white progress in a gray sky. They passed me, again and again, like I was not there, or little more than a faded billboard they chose not to read.

When her brake lights came on, a quarter mile down the road, I ran towards her, wondering if I had been a simple afterthought, an ambiguity. Her black Porsche 911 backed up to meet me. A turquoise bejeweled hand opened the door, extended itself to me in the warm sea of air in her tiny cabin.

Hi, I'm Myra.

Denver? I asked, as I shook her hand.

No, just the Springs, but we'll see what he can do.

And Myra and I flew by the cars that had passed me. I gave each a haughty stare, those slower vessels that had left me there to freeze on the Colorado high plains.

"Escaping" from Santa Fe she said, from a bar on Canyon Road, where "he" had turned on her, spilled their sacred secrets like beer on the tavern floor. She made her exit when he was in the john, pissing or puking, or both. Now, at ninety miles an hour with a stranger half her age, she was spilling her own secrets into my eager ears. Her black mini skirt and tight red sweater spoke to me as much as her words: she was there for the taking, precious flesh ready for greedy consumption. Her stone heavy hand touched my leg, punctuating her story with breathy exclamation points, plaintive question marks and prescient, pregnant pauses. I wondered where she would take me or if she would take me.

Denver? she asked. Mind a little detour?

It didn't matter where. Thumb time is not measured in minutes or miles, and Denver was as cold as the road from which she plucked me.

Her house was a wall of glass, with Pikes Peak framed perfectly by her bedroom window. And when we finally swam smoothly on the waves of her waterbed, she cried out that all was beautiful again, now that she was home, in the shadow of her mountain, in the arms of a stranger, whose seed filled her as she moved farther from the New Mexico tavern and whatever truth she chose not to face.

I wanted more of her, but the intoxication of strangers lasts only little longer than full blooded wine. She called me a cab, and in a black silk gown, glided me to the door, where she laid a hundred in my hand and told me the plane was warm and the airfare was only $39. I tried to kiss her one last time before the taxi stopped on her steep drive, but she buried her face in my chest.

No more, she said. He will be here soon.

The midmorning sun burned the sky blue. The cabbie slapped on his meter, and I was back to measuring minutes and miles. I looked back for as long as I could and saw the perfect reflection of her mountain in all that shining glass, her black silhouette only a curious slice in the reflected portrait of the beautiful fleeting day.

Colorado, January 1970

Squatters

Little remains of my grandfather's house: raw rafters, warped planks with hints my uncle invested in paint. The windows all gone, time and twisters took them, and much of the roof. What is left of that sags, a silent submission to gravity.

A woodstove survives, cold to the touch, with no memory of the fire it once birthed, the precious prairie timber which fed it. Now it knows only mourning doves' song—winged squatters unperturbed by my presence, as if they know I lay no claim to now.

The old boards have stories I will never hear: the birth of babes, reading the Word by kerosene lamps, the last breaths of men. The songbirds may know, but they woo the living in flight. For them, a future of nesting and fertile eggs; they owe no belated dirge to long lost kin.

An Extinction of Frogs

There is silence sandwiched between silence, thanks to the sudden cessation of their croaking. As if a plague took them, but it didn't. I don't know what caused them to stop, but it always spooked me. Like so many things did. There, under a canopy so thick I would swear it was a black blanket rather than lush foliage between us and starry Asian sky.

Bobby from Belton said they went to sleep. All of them dozed off in unison. They weren't asleep. Neither were we. I would never sleep during my shift.

A hunger for sound—that's how Dave B. from Lansing described it. When it was that quiet. It was a hunger for sound and your stomach growling would be welcome. To end the silence. Though we were picky about what song would do this. A symphony of crickets, a whispered lyric, or "Hey, Puckett, it's my shift now." The sweet melody of my brothers breathing, reminding me they were still alive. And I was too.

Though I couldn't see above me, I knew it was a cloudless night. Monsoon long over. That time was better, Sean M. from El Paso believed. The gooks didn't like to fight in the rain Sean said. I believed him.

I believed him until one night on patrol when the rain fell so hard, I worried I would drown just breathing and four VC decided to debunk his theory with enough AK47 fire to grease Frank V. from Brooklyn and hit Terence (Big T) from Oakland twice in the same arm and Sonny from Montana in the gut. I was asleep when the VC opened up on us, but I was wild wide awake when the claymore went off and got three of the four VC and my buddy, Robbie B. from Fullerton, emptied a magazine into the last one as the VC was scurrying up a slippery slope. Got the rat, LT Manson said. Robbie got him good.

That night, before the firefight, we had the hiss of the rain for our song. The drumbeat sound of it on our steel pots. The wash of it through the canopy.

That was our only firefight in the rain. And, since the four VC went up against forty, we decided they just came upon where we were dug in by chance. That was easier than believing they had balls enough to hit us with those odds. But they did.

When dawn broke, the rain stopped, and we reconnoitered the area, examined the dead. Counted the holes. The squish of our jungle boots, our whispers. When we looked at the gook Robbie had zapped, we counted eleven holes. Eleven of the nineteen rounds Robbie fired got him.

We thought that had to be a record, but Fred W. from Steubenville, on his second tour and a survivor of I Drang, swore he knew a bro from California who hit the same VC eighteen times. All from the front, at close range. Took the gook's face off and painted his entire body red, Fred said.

We listened for the sound of the chopper to dust off Frank (bye Frank), Big T, and Sonny. And it came—only minutes after the rain stopped. The downdraft from the blades chilled me as I helped load Big T. He smiled and said, Be cool man, see you back in the world. Big T knew those two rounds in his arm were his ticket home.

It was a dry night when I caught shrapnel in my arm. Another night when the frogs had stopped their croaking. The sudden silence had the effect it always did. My heartbeat. My breathing. I recall thinking maybe the frogs had all died. All the frogs on the planet. No stranger than Bobby B's idea they all went to sleep simultaneously.

Two mortar rounds landed before the AK fire started. The sound of the second bounced off my eardrums the same time the shrapnel hit my upper right arm. I was lucky. I felt the burning of the hot shrapnel and the warm blood coming down my arm, but I could still move my arm. Beside me, Dave B couldn't feel anything. Most of the mortar blast hit him, his body shielding me. Soon, the entire platoon was spraying fire in the direction from which the AK fire was coming.

The exchange lasted a minute—maybe two, and Dave was the only person who bought the farm that night. Other than Dave, only Robbie, who got shrapnel in his knee and thigh, and Tom F. from Austin got hit that night. Tom caught an AK round in his shoulder. Doc took care of us until we were dusted off.

In the silence after the firefight, I heard the frogs again. The swell of their song reached its crescendo when LT had Joe S from Las Vegas pop an M79 round into the trees where the AK fire had originated. When it went off, the frogs again stopped.

I remember, as if it were yesterday, the chopper ride to the 95th Evac Hospital, north of Danang. The sky was turning mauve to the east. Robbie and I were watching it together. Tom F. was in shitload of pain. The morphine that had Robbie and I nodding out wasn't working on Tom. Dave didn't need any morphine. He was there between Robbie and me. Asleep I thought. I still see him asleep—not dead. Otherwise I must ask why he was my shield against the darkness and not the other way around. Otherwise, I feel guilty about surviving that night. I feel guilty about being born. Dave will wake up. Dave will go back to Lansing. I don't know what will happen to me.

Afterword

Yes, in the jungle, we longed for the familiar cadence of the frogs, for their green belched reassurance they would lay more eggs in the mire, the tails would grow, and the swimmers would become singers of familiar verse. But we could not wait for a resurrection we did not know would occur—our duty and the frogs' song would always end at dawn, and by then we could be dead deaf from their silence.

Until We Rise Again in Ribbons of Light*

The entire platoon, lost. Even Leroy. We all said he had the "shield." In this field, he must have let it down—all six foot four of him—on the ground.

Beside him, Tony from Brooklyn, Fresno Frankie. All. The lieutenant, in motionless repose, his head resting on Leroy's ribs, his short blond hair crimson from the base of his skull to his ears, color courtesy of Leroy's shrapnel-grated gut.

Not one sound. Why had they not bayoneted me with the others? I saw one standing over me, leaning down with his AK-47, moving as slowly as the minute hand on a black clock.

Where was the sun, after all these hours among the dead? Hadn't the earth turned, or did it spin into a sky where Helios had vanished, superfluous now on this lifeless plain?

Still, in this darkness I saw, one by one, my sleeping brothers awake. Yet drenched in blood, their arms outstretched, mute as they drifted upwards in ribbons of soft, silent light.

*"Until we rise again in ribbons of light" is a line from Anthony Doerr's short story, "The Memory Wall." This platoon was wiped out in Vietnam before Doerr was born.

On Her Knees

My knees hurt. It is a good pain though, dear. I wish you had this type pain. One that comes from years of kneeling to pick up our children, and now grandchildren, you never got to meet. It is a pain from long walks on the wooded lanes of the neighborhood I was able to spend my years thanks to your sacrifice. It is a pain from standing countless hours in our kitchen, the one you painted pale peach the week before you left. And never came back.

I know it is not you beneath me here in this well-tended soil. Though bones and flesh were placed here, all those sunsets ago, I know what dust remains is not you. But I have nowhere else to go to speak aloud to you, to thank you for the time we had.

When I get up my love, I will return to the house we built. The one to which we brought home our first born. The one our second, your namesake, was suckled with tears rolling down my cheeks onto his fine hair. For you were not there. You were slaughtered in that hot, hellish place two weeks before he clawed his way into this world. This world without you.

He and his brother are fine men, as were you sweetheart. They have families of their own. You have a legacy. I find solace in that notion when I watch their children play and laugh and grow. But it is not the same. If I could rewind the clock, I would not have let you go. Words like honor and duty may comfort some, and I have recited them a time or two myself. But it is not the same. No medal, no flag, no carved stone with your too few years can replace your touch, your voice, or the time you did not get.

It is growing dark now, and they will expect me to leave soon. Just as well. I know you are not really here. I do wish you were and could rise with me now in this fading light and feel the good pain with me. I know your last moments were pain. And not the good pain. I know it hurt when your blood fell on that foul field. I know your pain did not come from the work of living. It came from a brief battle on the killing grounds where you chose to fight. I don't understand why. I don't know if you did either.

Now it seems even darker. I guess I will say goodnight. You know I never close my eyes for the day without saying your name. Tonight will be the same. Memorial Day they say it is. My knees hurt, and you are not here.

(Image, "Dark Homage" created by the author for Memorial Day 2009—the image inspired this reflection, written another year, the eve of another day they call "Memorial.")

The Glint of Light on Broken Glass*

Before 11,11,11, Armistice

My feet are numb in my boots. I have holes in my soles. The brown water rises to my ankles, but it will not freeze, filled with gun oil, blood and dreck.

I am not sure when I slept last, if I ever did. The others are there, their eyes closed. Some sleeping, some trying to sleep, some trying to awake, though they will not.

We have yet to throw their bodies on the heap. All eyes are closed in the trench save mine, and the sergeant, who stands like a statue, more still than the dead. Only his eyes move back and forth.

When I am not looking at the wire, the rutted field, and the ridge where the Germans also sleep, breathing their own foul stench, I close my eyes, though I do not sleep. I think of home, of Irina. I see her eyes, not the sergeant's, and I wonder if they have been closed like Mama's and Papa's and those beside me.

I ask the sergeant if tomorrow will be the white flag, when we and the Germans can retrieve the dead from the wires where they hang, starved naked apes. And when the flares fire the night sky, I see the reflection in their wide-open eyes, like the glint of light on broken glass. I cannot close their eyes.

All is still except for the swimming rats and the pyres that send curling smoke into the gray sky. Neither the rodents nor the fires utter a sound.

The sun is surely there, somewhere, silently making its arc in our pallid sky, but the last time I saw it was two mornings ago, or three, or two. When it rose, I felt it on my face, through the caked mud, and blood from Ivan, who was shot through the neck and fell on me. And I lay still with Ivan on top of me, like a thick blanket. His warm life elixir painting my helmet and face red, him gasping softly, though only a few seconds until more rounds pocked his body. Only a carcass then, but my salvation.

Would I be the sodden sack of flesh that covered another? Would the one who hides under me remember my name, and recall that I was his salvation? I, only a breathless monkey, with holes in my boots and a shit soiled uniform? Would the one I saved someday walk bent over with the blessed cane of age and remember all I had done for him, by simply dying?

*The phrase "the glint of light on broken glass" is part of a quote from Anton Chekov—it has nothing to do with war. For those unaware of the significance of 11/11/11, from the US VA: World War I – known at the time as "The Great War" - officially ended when the Treaty of Versailles was signed on June 28, 1919... However, fighting ceased seven months earlier when an armistice, or temporary cessation of hostilities, between the Allied nations and Germany went into effect on the eleventh hour of the eleventh day of the eleventh month. For that reason, November 11, 1918, is generally regarded as the end of "the war to end all wars."

Mother in Heaven Would not be Pleased...

Though I ate all my peas, minded my masters at school, then learned to march manly, and straight. Straight to these trenches that surely are maps of hell; if there be such a place beyond this dead, grey landscape. This pasture pocked by shells and body parts strewn about like pieces of a puzzle which don't fit.

Father said go, make England proud, but I know he would not wish this fate for me, or any of the children hiding in these pits, waiting for the command to become fodder for the Gatling gun, the cannon. Mother, you would shed cataracts of tears for all of us, if ghosts above yet weep for the living.

We, the damned, will soon join you, though none know when. Surely you will hear me cry your name, the way I have heard them all do, with their last breath.

September 1916, The Battle of Somme

Bobby's Skill

Bobby Belcher was the best coyote killer in the county. To hear him tell it, he was the best in the state. And Bobby made sure everyone knew. He hung the carcasses from fence posts on either side of the ranch road that came into his property. Eight of the beasts were there, most of them skinned—not for the pelts. No, Bobby ripped their hides off just to lay bare their naked, helpless flesh to the elements. Doing the buzzards a favor, he claimed.

Bobby hunted coyote because he was good at it. He had been left a considerable fortune and had no need to work. His daddy, Bobby Sr., as big a drunk as ever tipped a glass, had inherited two sections. On both, drilling brought good crude. The oil was gone, but not before Bobby Sr. had amassed enough money to help nurture his only boy's natural inclination to lassitude. A banker let it slip when the elder Belcher died from cirrhosis in 1945, he had nearly a million dollars in the bank.

Bobby's daddy passed when Bobby was on a ship returning from the Pacific. Bobby would have one believe he was a war hero. Truth be told, Bobby had seen all of two minutes of combat. When his Marine platoon poured onto the beach, a few Jap rounds came from the jungle, one of which hit Bobby in the boot and took his little toe off. The corpsman had him back on the ship before Bobby fired a shot.

The year Bobby came home, he married Duana Peters, daughter of a neighboring rancher. Rumor had it she married Bobby for his money, but she didn't get what she bargained for. Bobby had hired a slick shyster out of Midland to handle the divorce, ensuring Duana got little. After two years with Bobby, who like his father, was given to drunkenness, her severance pay for enduring Bobby was only $5000 and a new Cadillac.

Five years after Bobby's divorce, he was still single, though not for lack of trying to find a bride. Even with his money, three women had said no to his proposals.

The country had a new president and had gotten itself in another scrape—this time in Korea. Bobby had gone, inebriated, to the recruiter in Odessa and volunteered to "go kill those other slant eyes." The recruiter explained he was happy Bobby loved his country, but the Marines would not take a man with nine toes.

Rejected and dejected, in his truck on the way back to his ranch, Bobby finished another six pack—his third that day. Bobby passed out on the county road five miles north of his ranch. He was lucky enough to hit nothing but a sage bush before his new '53 Chevrolet truck slid down a bluff and came to a stop at the bottom. Bobby was asleep with only a small knot in his forehead from where it hit the steering wheel.

A fierce summer storm came from the southwest, pelting the truck with silver dollar sized hail. The hammering hail did not wake Bobby, but a peal of thunder did. Lightning struck not a hundred yards above Bobby on the high point of the bluff. Bobby woke to one of the most ferocious tempests he'd ever seen. Rain came down in sheets after the hail stopped. Lightning turned the midnight prairie bright as day. Thunder roared deep enough for Bobby to feel it in his bones.

Bobby started his truck, but when he put it in reverse and let out the clutch, it went nowhere. Unbeknownst to him, his front bumper was wedged on a boulder. What he did know was the water in the arroyo where his truck landed was fast rising. Soon, it would begin coming over the rocker panels.

Bobby got out and steadied himself against the truck bed. The water was knee deep. He managed to make it to the side of the bluff, hanging on to his truck all but the last few feet where the water was still shin high. As soon as Bobby began crawling up the bluff, the rains stopped. An eerie quiet came with the cessation of the gully buster. Bobby didn't like the quiet. Never had. In his truck, he always had the radio blaring. When stations would go off the air at night, he would honk a tune on his horn.

The sound which broke the silence gave Bobby no solace. Coyotes. Sour howls from every corner of the night. He could see little; only a slither of a moon drifted in the sky. On the bluff, he looked for the road. Still half drunk, Bobby was not sure he was walking in the right direction.

Bobby did reach the county road, but not before falling twice onto the hard caliche. The knot on his scalp hurt and so did his head. Then there were the taunting howls. He thought about going back to his truck to retrieve his Remington from its rack, but he didn't fancy wading through that water again, and he couldn't recall if he had loaded the rifle after he had used it last.

Though too dark to see any landmarks, Bobby had his wits about him enough to know he was headed the right way on the road. South. How far it was, he did not know. The yipping of the coyotes would let up long enough to lull Bobby into a shallow calm, then would start again. Each time, the coyotes sounded closer, louder. Relentless now.

When Bobby saw the ranch road which led to his house, he was exhausted. Still the coyotes sang to him, unnerving him with every note. The eastern sky was turning mauve. Soon the sun. Bobby spoke aloud on the predawn prairie. Keep movin' feet, keep movin.'

Bobby made it to the posts which marked the entrance to his property before he fell. He pulled himself upright—the world now spinning. Bobby grabbed onto the nearest fencepost to right himself. Like the other pickets at the entrance to his place, this one had a coyote's skeletal remains, hung with wire around its neck, facing the morning sun which cracked the horizon just as Bobby's wrist brushed against the coyote's dry bone skull. A chill went down his spine. The howling of the coyotes ceased. In silence, the first rays of the sun shone on sockets where eyes had once been, then on yellowed canine cuspids which had yanked flesh from bone of other low born beasts. Until Bobby. Until Bobby, now panting with his own tongue hanging out, stood on the flat earth and pulled the trigger just because he could.

The Serpent and I

The green grove was a magnet to my eye on these sun baked plains. I entered the glade to take shade with the cicadas and vampire mosquitoes. Then I saw it, Eden's villain, coiled and rattling, red ready to strike. I raised my staff. I too programmed to survive, to do what millennia have taught.

Still we were in this staring standoff. Silent save its rattle. Deaf I was to the chorus of insects. Neither of us moved for an eternity of seconds, until the snake lunged at my feet, where its fangs found a field mouse, and devoured it while I watched, an unwitting witness to expiry other than my own.

The sound of the cicadas returned. I left the spinney, whole, content another creature had, for that day in the sun, taken my place in the bloodletting.

A Wake of Buzzards

A roadkill feast, this doe that met truck bumper the black night before. Now in the Texas sun, talons and beaks make easy work of eyeballs and entrails. The asphalt a convenient griddle, slow cooking dead deer while the ravenous birds dine.

Somewhere in the brush, a childless mother, with no incantation to bring her baby back. This creature without words only senses a void—nipples no longer gnawed and sucked. What mourning for this loss, now attended to by buzzards fast filling their guts?

Until I come upon them, my own bumper approaching at warp speed. My metal beast to avenge this desecration with a twist of my wrist, a turn of tires. Fast from the red road a flapping of blue-black wings. All but one escapes my wrath.

The raptor took too long to take flight, unaware my grill could kill with such impunity. A simple twist of the wrist, a bump, a thump, and one less vulture feeds on the dead. Above him, his brethren wait, riding cool currents, my execution but a brief deterrent to their wake.

The Cat, on the Farm, in Iowa, I Believe

Her husband was not named Schrödinger, though many days she did not know if the cat was dead or alive. I don't believe she thought about it much. Now and then an offering, usually a small sparrow, was found on the porch, and she complained not once of mischievous mice.

From her kitchen window, hunched over a pot, or stirring lemonade, she would spot the black and white creature, (who never was given a name, not even by three farm sons), stalking imagined prey across the yard, under the swing set, or in the corner by the white picket fence.

She could remember the day the neighbor brought two kittens, asking her to choose. It was snowing lightly. She chose the smaller of the two, the civil thing to do. They drank coffee and had some pie. Peach. They watched the kittens play while they finished a second cup of coffee and ran out of things to say. The falling snow was so quiet.

She rarely saw when it lapped up the milk she left, or licked clean the plate with sardines, but she knew it was he, taking a light repast, a sabbatical from great mysterious hunts in the green barn, or by the cellar door.

The boys were all in school then, full of pink color, noise, and often covered with rich dirt. One by one they left. Pneumonia took the youngest a day when the cat sat, statuesque, by their black 1940 Ford. The eldest disappeared on a Saturday, into a lake where largemouth bass were plentiful and the waters clean, until his friends saw him dive into the depths, not to be seen again before Tuesday, when his bloated body decided to surface for air and light—the same day she saw the cat skitter up the lone oak in the front yard.

The middle, her shyest, said goodbye from the bus depot, saluting them as he turned to the bus door a year to the day before he was shot through the throat on some horrid hunk of rock named "Iwo Jima." The cat was nowhere to be found that day, but she swore she heard him meowing all the night after they put her baby in the silent soil.

Her husband got the cancer and, on a Christmas eve, drifted off to some pasture she saw in the snowy sky. When they put him in the ground, the cat made no sound, though she saw him faintly, moving in some faraway fallow field, following his own soundless dreams.

To the Flatland, Beyond the Barn

The old woman stopped crying. She knew the tears would return like the prairie winds, without warning, from some place she could not see.

Soon they would come for him, place him on the gurney, cover him in white shroud, and wheel him through the door: a horizontal journey, like the vertical one he had made myriad times before, on two strong legs, to and from the pastures and pens where he did sweat honest work.

She leaned over to kiss him a last time in evening's fading light. The old wife had honored his final request and turned him, so he could face the open window—his old eyes toward the red barn, the gray fences, the ground his livestock grazed, past all this, to the flatland that seemed to go on forever.

6:00 AM

I see his pick-up in the yard. The grass is dead from the heat anyway.

He is nowhere to be found, except passed out on the seat. One of his feet touching the turf, the other still in the truck, afraid if it joins its partner on solid soil, it won't be a happy marriage.

He is my child—all quarter century of him and he won't bring in the paper. I am sure he rolled his truck on top of it...to protect me from the news of an awful world.

Dusk, 1959

The fireflies soon to make their appearance, accompanied by a chorus of cicadas. The men were lighting after dinner fags, and Moms were clanging dishes and scraping food into the trash—a noisy resentment.

I was on the street, with brothers named Harry and Johnny, playing baseball, mostly missing our catches. It had not registered in our grade school heads dusk was not good light for hardball, nor had we learned what it was like to see anything die (save the bees we suffocated in jars—forgive us our sins, Father). Though that night, the last day of school, the stars were all aligned *if* the creator wanted us to see mangled mortality.

The guy came around the corner of Vandenburg and Vine in his graduation gift, a hot new Chrysler, all chrome and crank. The telephone pole he hit didn't see him or complain. It remained straight, upright, when the driver went through the windshield and his skull introduced itself to dead wood and pitch.

My dad, a medic on Omaha Beach, was the first to come through the door, though other fathers followed. I recall colors, though muted by the fading light. Red, pink, red, even white and gray and blond—his hair, a flattop still in place. Well, it was on the half head I saw from across the street where Harry, Johnny and I were conscripted to stand.

My mother brought a yellow towel—to stop bleeding I thought I heard. My father never used it, telling her instead to bring the green army blanket, which he draped over the boy's body the very second before we saw the ambulance lights.

By then, the fireflies were beginning their dance. We were told to go inside, to hide our eyes from the body on a stretcher. Soon came the slamming of the ambulance doors, which I watched through our window, while my father used Lava soap to wash his hands. Then my mother pulled the drapes, blocking from view the pole, the crushed car, and the glow of fireflies sublimely drifting above it all.

No Old Soul

He poured the remaining Cheerios into the bowl, then covered them with milk he need not sniff to know was old, stale, curdling. Still, he ate, for he knew without this sour meal, he would tire on his mile journey to the bus stop and not be able to concentrate in school.

School, his red brick haven, where there was always running water, porcelain toilets, and adults who didn't reek of moonshine, piss and smoke. There he could read under electric lights, watch movies about the moon and strange rockets that would one day blast a man all the way there.

That is where he wanted to be, hidden from earth's billions of eyes, on the dark side of the moon, where grave gravity loosens its reins a bit. Another cleaner world he imagined: a sterile, silent white orb, pocked by boulders bigger than mountains, craters with names like Mare Serenitatis, a sea of serenity.

When he dared reveal this wish in the ears of his elders, they would whisper among themselves, saying he was an old soul. But barely double digits, he knew this could not be so; for his body was only tired from toil, and as far as his soul, he knew it had no age, not in years. Not here on this wretched third stone from the sun, nor in a crater as old as time waiting for him to escape the bounds of earth and the bitter milk of morning.

Bell County, Kentucky, 1964

Snap Franklin, Buffalo Soldier

Among the Few Things

Among the few sounds Snap Franklin could still hear were the coyotes yipping in the night. Even sixty years before, when his hearing was crisp enough to catch the cocking of a hammer from across a wide gully, he could never tell how many coyotes were singing to him.

His niece, Cecilia, his only kin, told him she would buy him some of those new hearing aids, but Snap figured his ears had caught about all the sounds of human voices he needed. Eighty years on this third rock from the Sun—Snap figured he heard enough. Nigger this, and nigger that.

One nigger too many one night outside Childress, Texas, right after the Great War when a cowpoke rode up to Snap in his bed roll and said, Hell, what's a coon doin' campin' on my uncle's spread?

Snap didn't answer at first, but the man dismounted and said, Hey, nigger, didn't you hear me ask what the hell you was doin' on this place?

Trying to sleep, Snap said.

The man kicked Snap in the ribs and told him to get up. Snap stared at him. The man then kicked him in the face at which point Snap pulled a pistol from his bed roll and shot the man in the throat. The man fell backwards onto Snap's fire and almost snuffed it out.

Snap rose and pulled the man from the flames. Snap heard coyotes howling in the distance—he made sure he dug the hole deep in the soft sand when he buried the man by the Prairie Dog Fork of the Red River. Snap rode the horse a good half mile from where he planted the man, then tied the stallion to a mesquite. Much as he hated to do it, another quarter mile down, he threw his pistol into the Red. The revolver was a gift a white officer had given him when Snap was a Buffalo Soldier.

In ten years as a solider, Snap never killed a man. He shot and wounded a Kiowa, but the young Indian survived, only to be fixed up by a doc and put in chains.

Another war had passed. Snap's soldiering was done more than a half century before. His cowhand days were over, too. He didn't want to live in the city with Cecilia and was thankful the rancher McNulty had let him stay in the bunk house and help cook for the boys. And they were boys—too young to have gone off to the war, but old enough to cowboy.

They were good boys, mostly Mex, and not a one of them ever called him a coon. Many nights, the boys would stay up playing poker for pennies under two eighty-watt bulbs dangling from the bunk house ceiling. Snap couldn't hear them much, but the lights kept him awake. Those were the times he would take his ancient bed roll and sleep on the prairie. He had found a good spot with thick Timothy grass atop a bluff. Wasn't as soft as the store-bought mattress McNulty had gotten for him, but it would do.

On those nights, among the few things Snap took with him in his bedroll was a pocket watch that long ago became a talisman to him. The same white officer who gave him the pistol had found the watch on a dead brave and had given it to Snap. The hands on the gold watch had never moved, but Snap kept in his coat. One stormy day on the trail, another Buffalo Soldier accidentally discharged his carbine. The round hit the watch at an angle and then grazed Snap's ribs. Without the pocket watch there, Snap was convinced he would have been killed.

Old man, old bed roll, and old gold watch often spent the night on the bluff. Sometimes, when the coyotes were serenading Snap, he would find his hand reaching for the spot where the gun had been all those years before. Sometimes, Snap would wake from a dream with his arm pointing towards the starry sky. For an instant, he would wonder where the man went. Then Snap would settle back into his cloth cocoon, and ponder why, among the few things he had done he thought was best, was to kill a man he did not know. Faintly, across the shallow canyons, the coyotes would yip some more, speaking to him in a code he could not decipher.

Snap in Town

Snap stayed at the McNulty place until he was nearly eighty-five. For years, he couldn't cowboy much, but old man McNulty let him stay on to cook for the boys—gave him cowboy wages and a bunk.

McNulty's son took over the operation when the elder McNulty died. Within six months, younger McNulty sold the stock, fired the cow hands, and had contracts to drill for oil.

Snap moved in with his only kin, his niece, Cecilia. Cecilia's daddy had been white, and he bolted and was never heard from again when her momma, Sally, got pregnant. Sally, Snap's younger sister, had raised Cecilia and stayed with her until cancer got her when she was fifty. Now Cecilia herself was fifty, never married and a teacher at one of the colored schools in Wichita Falls.

Cecilia had a modest new home in Wichita Falls. She also had a 1949 Ford she used to make the three-hour drive to pick up Snap after the younger McNulty had called and informed her Snap needed a place.

Snap did not like the idea of living in town—half the time, he had slept on the prairie in an old bedroll. But he had no choice. The week before his eighty-fifth birthday, Cecilia pulled up to the gate of the ranch and carried her only uncle back to Wichita Falls. That was the day before Thanksgiving, 1950.

Cecilia had bought her home in a white neighborhood. Her neighbors, Dub and Wilma Abbott, were friendly but most neighborhood folks ignored her. The Abbotts were from Childress and had moved to town when Dub got work for an oil drilling operation. Childless, they had lived in an apartment for thirty years but decided to buy their own place.

They had no kin left and Dub was close to retirement. He would have a pension, but he also had land along the Red River he inherited after his younger brother, Billy, disappeared in 1919. The land had belonged to his uncle and was supposed to go to Billy who had been working the place. One night, Billy, drunk, went looking for a calf and never returned. His horse was found tied to a tree near the Prairie Dog fork of the Red. Dub's uncle changed his will after Billy vanished, leaving the land to Dub.

In town, Snap spent most evenings on the back porch, staying there after the sun sank into the prairies. Snap was hard of hearing, but he often heard coyotes west of their neighborhood. Cecilia heard them also but thought nothing of them. Snap had always listened for them. When Snap was a Buffalo Soldier, an old Comanche had told him the coyotes sing not only to each other but also to special people who were chosen to listen to them. Snap thought he may have been one of the chosen since he had always heard their sour song, even when others didn't.

The Abbotts took an instant liking to Snap. They had made some colored acquaintances in the city, though schools were still segregated, and water fountains were still labeled "White" and "Colored." The pastor at their Methodist Church had invited colored pastors to preach now and again. Times were changing. And now they had a colored woman buy a house nearly identical to theirs. Wilma told Dub Cecilia was as fine a lady—colored or white—as she had ever met.

Cecilia mentioned to Dub and Wilma Snap was having a hard time adjusting to town life. Dub had figured as much since many mornings, Dub had gone outside and found Snap wrapped in an old bedroll, sleeping in the cold yard.

Dub had his land leased to a rancher who ran cattle there, but now and then Dub went out to check on the place or hunt dove and quail by the river. After a cold spell, there was a sunny, 70-degree Saturday. Dub invited Snap to drive out to his land. Snap was eager to come. Dub had quickly learned to speak loudly and face Snap, so Snap could hear him.

When they drove off in Dub's truck Saturday morning, Snap only knew the ranch was about two hours west of Wichita Falls. They drove through Childress shortly before noon. Dub said his land was by the river and they could stop and have lunch as soon as they turned onto the county road. From there, Dub said, one could see most of the ranch spread along the Red River.

The Prairie Dog Fork of the Red? Snap asked. Snap did not know why he had asked or how he knew this was the Prairie Dog Fork.

Yep, Dub said. Has a little water in it after fall rains but was almost a dry gulch last year.

They ate ham sandwiches and drank coffee on a bluff off the county road. From there, they took the ranch road down to the gate that marked the entrance to the half section. They drove by a stand of mesquite, a solitary copse on a stretch of land that had been mostly cleared. Snap felt something deep in his gut when they passed the thorny mesquites.

They came to place near the river where ranch road ended. Dub told Snap he generally hunted by the tall stands of grass near the river's edge. He asked if Snap was up to a walk. Snap agreed and when he was leaving the truck, he saw a coyote climbing the hill on the other side of the river. The feeling returned to his gut.

Dub also saw the animal and said, Probably gettin' him a drink in the river.

They ambled along the river, during which time Dub told the story of the night his brother Billy had disappeared. Dub and Billy had been drinking Mescal and they were soused. Billy wasn't too drunk to remember he needed to look for a young steer he couldn't find in the pastures where the other stock grazed. Occasionally, the calves wandered off to the river—some got stuck in the quicksand. Billy saddled up and went looking for the steer two hours after sundown. He was never seen again.

Snap looked back at the stand of Mesquite and asked Dub if that was where they had found Billy's horse.

Dub said, Yes, it was.

Snap then remembered. The Prairie Dog Fork of the Red. The young cowpoke who kicked him, the taste of blood in his mouth after the cowboy kicked Snap in the face, Snap shooting and the man falling into the flames of Snap's campfire. This memory hit him like a steel rod going from behind his eyes all the way to his old bowels.

Mr. Dub, Mr. Dub, Snap said. I am sorry. I am sorry. Then Snap fell to his knees and started digging in the sand with his bony hands.

Lord almighty Snap, what the hell are you doin'? Dub asked.

I think I planted him right here. I did. Right here, Snap said. He kept digging.

Dub put his hands on Snap's thin arms and tried to pull him up.

No Sir, I got to find him, Snap said.

Find who? Dub asked.

Dub tried again and pulled Snap to his feet. He steadied Snap with his hands on Snap's shoulders. Now both men stood beside the timeless river, not two feet from each other, staring into each other's eyes.

I done killed your brother, Mr. Dub—shot him right here when he called me a nigger and kicked me. I used to think it was a good thing I done. But it wasn't no good thing. I didn't have to kill your brother.

They stood facing each other for some time.

Dub said, Lets us walk on back to the truck. Both men were silent for a time.

In the truck, as they were driving away from the property, Snap told him exactly what he recalled about the night. Over and over, he said he was sorry.

Before they reached the highway, Dub pulled into a pasture and turned the truck off. Dub looked over at Snap and said, I ain't gonna say you killin' my brother was a good thing. I'm not sure what I would have done if I was you. But hear this, Snap. Hear this. Right here in this pasture, not a mile from where you said you killed Billy, there was a big old Hackberry. Billy and three of his friends hung a negro from that tree. He was just a colored man walkin' along the road who back talked them when they stopped and asked where he was going. They hung that negro and buried him down by the river.

The Sheriff never knew what happened. Billy told me about it, and I didn't think to go to the law. Billy and his friends killed a man and I didn't think of going to the law. That was not long before Billy disappeared. Then Wilma and I moved to Wichita. I ain't thought much about it, but when I do, I get a sick feeling in my gut. Let's let the dead stay buried Snap. Don't you fret no more about Billy.

That night was balmy, and Cecilia thought Snap would take to the yard with his bedroll. Instead, Snap lay in his comfortable new bed. He cracked the window just a bit. He listened for the sound of coyotes. As he was falling asleep, he heard the faint yipping. They were there, singing to him, but as always, Snap didn't know what the lyrics of their songs said.

Snap and the Gold Watch

Christmas Day, 1954, Snap tripped on the back-porch step and broke his wrist. He'd turned 89 a month before and had never broken a bone. He still had all his teeth and wore glasses only to read small print. His niece, Cecilia, had bought him transistorized hearing aids for his birthday. He could hear better with them, he said, but voices sounded strange. Snap didn't like them, but most days he wore them.

A week before Snap's mishap, Wilma had come home from the hospital after a mastectomy. Cecilia's mother had died of breast cancer thirty years before. Cecilia and Wilma had grown close in their decade as neighbors. Cecilia retired from teaching at the colored school the previous June and was helping the Abbotts during Wilma's recuperation.

When Snap fell, he walked over to the Abbott place and said, Cecilia, I know you're helpin' out over here, but I am pretty sure I done broke my arm.

Dub helped Cecilia splint Snap's wrist and said they would run him to the colored doctor on the east side of town the next day. In the meantime, Dub said, lets you and I drink some of that good Bourbon I got for a retirement gift last month. Drink enough and you won't be worried about your wrist. I also got a gift for you I picked up when Wilma and I was in Houston last summer.

That sounds fine with me, Mr. Dub. Snap said. Dub had told him for years to call him Dub and not Mr. Dub, but Snap could not break the habit. Ten years as a Buffalo Soldier and a half century working as a colored man for white ranchers and all non-negroes had a Mister before their name.

As the sun went down, snow began to fall. Neither Dub nor Snap could recall the last time it snowed on Christmas in their small north Texas city. Dub and Snap sat at the kitchen table in Dub's house and watched the yard turn from the color of oatmeal to white.

The men drank the Bourbon until the bottle was half gone. Snap's wrist still hurt like the dickens and since Wilma's diagnosis, Dub had been imbibing more than before. Dub was scared for Wilma—other women he had known to have the same surgery had died within a year or two.

Snap rose to go to the bathroom and his world began to spin. Only grabbing the icebox handle kept him from falling.

Whoa, said Dub, you had one too many—you want some help?

Snap said, What you gonna do, hold it for me, Mr. Dub?

When Snap returned, Dub handed him a wrapped package.

Where did this come from Mr. Dub?

Under the tree, only you weren't here this morning to open it.

I ain't gonna do much good openin' it with one hand, Snap said, holding up his splinted wrist.

Dub opened the package for Snap. In it was a framed picture of Buffalo Soldiers.

Thank you Dub, Mr. Dub. Snap put his reading glasses on his nose and took a good look at the old photo. Lord, I know two of these men. That there is Ezekiel Peckham, a sprout done accidentally shot me during a storm, and that white man is Colonel Carpenter.

I didn't know you had been shot Snap. You get hurt bad? Dub asked.

Nah, just grazed my ribs. I was lucky, and something saved me.

What was it Snap?

I'll show you—be right back. Snap got up slowly, steadied himself and went home long enough to retrieve his "good luck charm." The snow was piling up in the yard.

Snap handed Dub a gold pocket watch.

Where is the chain and what happened to the back of it? Dub asked as he examined the old timepiece.

Ain't never had no chain and that dent you see was where Ezekiel's bullet grazed it.

Well I'll be damned, said Dub.

I was lucky, Snap said.

You were, said Dub, but you see the name inscribed on the back of it? Well, you see what's left of the name? Dub asked.

Yes, the name was Harmon, but the "on" done got ruined when Ezekiel's bullet hit it.

Snap, we live in small world. You shot my brother in 1919 and moved in next door to me in 1950. As Dub said this his eyes never left the watch. Now, Dub continued, you show me a watch with Harmon on the back.

Yes Sir, all that is true, but what about it? Snap asked.

Dub placed the watch on the table and poured them both another Bourbon. Dub took a swallow and said, Wilma's uncle was killed by Comanche when he was deliverin' mail to Fort Richardson when he was only twenty. He had a gold watch that bore the name Harmon. It had belonged to Wilma's granddaddy.

You right, Mr. Dub, it's a small world. That watch come from Colonel Carpenter—he give me that after he took it off a dead Comanche. The very same week, he give me the pistol. The one that is done rusted to dust in the Red River. The one I used to shoot your brother that night.

I got to show this to Wilma before she falls asleep, Dub said.

While Dub went to the bedroom where Wilma and Cecilia were listening to the radio, Snap looked through the window at the deepening snow. The light from the kitchen window made a long rectangle in the yard.

Snap's eyes grew misty as he thought of that night on the Red thirty five years before: the blood in his mouth after Dub's brother, Billy, kicked him; Snap pulling the easy trigger and Dub's brother falling into the flames; the burial of the dead, and years later discovering he lived next door to the brother of the man he killed; Snap's confession to Dub and Dub's revelation Billy had lynched a negro for talking back to him. Billy and the nameless Negro, both part of the same earth again.

Dub and Cecilia helped Wilma to the kitchen. Wilma sat by Snap who was only snatched from his reverie when Wilma touched his arm. Thank you for showing Dub the timepiece, Snap.

Snap saw the joy in her expression. That is yours Miss Wilma, Snap said. It was your granddaddy's. It just took a long way around to get here.

Epilogue

Wilma died that spring. Her cancer spread like wildfire. Dub was alone now.

On the first day of summer, Snap told Cecilia he was feeling poorly. After dinner with Cecilia and Dub, who was coming around often after Wilma passed, Snap said he was going to turn in early. Cecilia checked on him throughout the evening. Each time she came to his room, Snap was in his bed looking through his window to the west. When the new summer sun finally sank into the prairie, Cecilia swore she heard coyotes yipping. She turned to ask Snap if he heard them. His eyes were closed. What ghost sounds he now heard would remain a mystery to her.

1952 Nickel

You were born in Denver during a white out blizzard. Like all round babes, you had no clue what was in store for you.

You couldn't have known...you would be the last nickel to chink through a five-cent coin phone box in El Paso, Texas, or that you would sleep for a year in the piggy bank, of a boy named Felipe, who would die of white blood cancer, before he could spend you.

And who would have thought you would be in the linty pocket of a serial murderer named Ray, when he was captured in Santa Fe, a sunny day on the ancient square, stalking his next victim.

A jailer used you that very night with a twin of yours he found in another picked pocket, of a drunk drifter, to buy a Hershey's bar, from a machine that would have taken a dime as well.

Your face began to show the fingered signs of age by the time the choppers found sky above the Saigon Embassy, where you had spent an aching April night in the Ambassador's pants.

When you turned a half century, you were tossed into a gallon jug, e pluribus Unum, no more special than others a third your vintage. I finally met you today, only because chance landed you on the top of the heap, waiting to be saved from further folly.

On the Golden Bridge

On the rail, not far from where a young woman jumped to a lonely death in the cold bay, I found you in the fog. A wedding ring. Perhaps once cherished, intended to seal an eternal bond, but now this band lay alone, silent and still on dumb steel.

Who left you there? Not the doomed woman, for she took her final leap two Christmases before, and her ring was found on her withered hand.

Soft rain began to fall, like a million tears for forlorn lovers. Yet I stayed on the bridge, frozen in time and place. Shivering, not from the shower, but by the sight of one round, gold trinket, left for fickle fate after another circle had been broken, forever, for my eyes to see, at the edge of another promised eternity.

The Ring

Shanghai

My maternal grandparents married in 1924. From the expression on my grandmother's face in the wedding photos, one would not get the impression she was happy with the union. Perhaps this was because she was pregnant with my mother and she knew my grandfather, nearly twenty years her senior, was given to excessive drink. After ten years of what my grandmother described as a miserable marriage, my grandparents separated. My grandmother did keep the beautiful and valuable wedding ring my grandfather had purchased at the time of their betrothal.

In 1936, my grandfather was poisoned. The Coroner's Inquest called the circumstances of his death highly irregular. He was cremated within hours after he died; therefore, no autopsy was performed. Given he was poisoned, the Coroner said the absence of autopsy made his death very suspicious, though he could not determine the cause of death to be murder. (Motive for murder? We don't know, but his younger brother was a very successful arms dealer, and, to quote the Shanghai Herald, a "known political operative." Both my grandfather and great uncle were reputedly involved in Shanghai's hot bed of espionage in that era.)

In 1946, when my father and mother were married, my grandmother gave the ring to my mother. My father could not afford such a fine piece of jewelry and I never had the impression the ring had sentimental value to my grandmother.

Columbus

We lived in Columbus, Ohio, from the day after my birthday in March 1959, until the summer of 1961 when my father, an Army medical service officer, was promoted and assigned to Walter Reed. I recall being told the cost of living in Washington D C was much higher. I also recall hearing the phrase, "Dammit, we can't afford it!" coming from my father's mouth dozens of times while we lived in Columbus. That was one of my most salient memories from childhood. My older sister's variant of that memory was from D H Lawrence's story, The Rocking Horse Winner, in which the child is haunted by chants from the walls,

"There must be more money, there must be more money." My sister was always more literary than I.

Even with his promotion, the pressure of moving to a place where the cost of living was much greater had to weigh on my father. He had come from the hills of West Virginia, trudging through the "five miles of snow" to his school when he was five years old. (Actually, I have seen the trek and it was not much more than a mile, though over rugged, steep terrain.) By the time he was seven, he had a job coming to school early to place the coal in the stove to warm the one room school house for the other students. In contrast, my mother had a houseboy, an Amah (nanny), dined with royalty as a toddler, and took vacations from their Shanghai home to Malaysia where her family had a getaway bungalow.

When we moved from Columbus to DC, a major moving company handled our relocation. During the move, my mother's wedding ring, stored in a jewelry box in a drawer, disappeared. I don't recall my mother being overly disturbed by the loss of the ring. Her recollections of her parents' marriage were not fond, and there was ample rancor between my mother and father.

My father reported the loss to the moving company and they said they hired day laborers who had not come back to work after our move. I wasn't old enough to know this sounded suspicious, and I also wasn't old enough to know my father was fallible.

Perhaps this alternative version of events flies better. My father had a coworker, Roger, whose car had been totaled. He had cash from his insurance company, but he was being assigned to Japan where he did not feel he would need a car. Roger was engaged and wanted to buy his fiancée, Sherry, a nice ring. Without consulting my mother, my father offered to sell him a beautiful ring for a very good price: $500. I suspect the ring was worth at least three times that much. In 1961, $500 was six months' rent in Ohio or three months' rent in D.C. The temptation was too great for my father.

San Francisco

The marriage between Roger and his young bride did not last. Sherry missed her family in Ohio and hated Japan. After a year, they divorced. Roger gave his soon to be ex-wife enough cash to purchase a bus ticket from San Francisco to Columbus. The military flew Sherry

56

from Japan to Travis Air Force Base in California the Tuesday before Thanksgiving, 1962. She was then transported to San Francisco via shuttle. Her ex-husband and the U.S Army were done with her.

With little money in her pocket, and a healthy dose of resentment for her ex, Sherry decided to sell the ring. She hadn't intended to sell it in Frisco, but there was a pawn shop next door to the bus station. The lettering on the window said, "Sagan's Pawn Broker. We Buy Gold."

Sherry approached an old man in the cage at the back of the shop. Sherry discovered he was the owner, Mr. Sagan, who immediately told her he could not give her what the ring was worth. Sherry said she didn't care and, without negotiating, accepted $375 for the ring.

Sagan placed the ring in a hidden box where he stored jewelry he did not display but would often sell to jewelers or collectors. Sherry's ring, he guessed, would easily bring a thousand.

Sagan, well into seventies, had a massive stroke and died in his pawn shop only six weeks after Sherry had sold him the ring. Sagan's will bequeathed the shop to his daughter who sold it by Easter of 1963. The new owner, "Fats" Powers, had done a cursory inventory but it wasn't until a year later he found the box in which some very special items were housed. The box had been hidden in the metal works of an antique piano.

Fats sold all the contents except my grandmother's ring to a jeweler. The ring he gave to his live-in lady friend, Marcie. When Marcie dumped Fats for her ex-husband during the summer of love, Fats got the ring back and took it to the shop. Before he had a chance to contact the jeweler to whom he usually sold rings of this quality, someone limped through the door asking if he had a nice wedding ring.

El Paso

In the spring of 1967, my parents divorced. My mother soon met and married a man who had spent much of his life behind bars. By the time my mother met him, however, "Harold" was a new man. To prove it, he had an article from the San Francisco Chronicle detailing his life of crime, including being shot and lamed by a cop during a robbery, and Harold's path to rehabilitation. In all, 11 of his 41 years were in California prisons. He had been a free man 6 years when he met and married my mother in the summer of 1967.

Harold had come to El Paso for a sales job which fell through. He convinced my mother his chances for employment were better in his hometown of San Francisco. My mother left with Harold in 1967, and except for a visit I made to California in 1976, she never saw any of her five children again.

San Francisco

Harold found a job in telephone sales. Hardly promising, but some good fortune came their way the week after he and my mother moved to San Francisco. An uncle he barely knew died and Harold was his only heir. My mother wanted to use the $5000 insurance money for a down payment on a house, but Harold bought a new Ford Fairlane and drove to Sagan's, where Harold had fenced many things during his life of crime.

Harold hobbled in and asked the new owner, Fats, if he had any nice wedding rings. Fats saw Harold's conspicuous limp. Rather than evoking sympathy from the pawnbroker, Fats saw the limp as weakness and an opportunity to clean up. Fats concocted story about having a ring which was once given from Clark Gable to Carole Lombard. (Years later, my mother and Harold would live in an apartment that had the furniture Clark and Carole once owned.) Harold believed the story and was sucked right in—the value was not just in the diamonds and gold, but in the history, Fats claimed. Harold handed Fats ten crisp one hundred-dollar bills and walked out with the ring.

It was raining when Harold drove home from the Pawn Shop. From the parking lot of their apartment to their door, Harold got drenched. He walked in, wet but smiling. Harold sat at their Formica table in their kitchen and asked my mother if she wanted a surprise. Harold told my mother close her eyes and put her left hand on the table. He placed the ring on her finger. When she opened her eyes, she wasn't shocked or conspicuously surprised. Over the years, my mother had grown more superstitious and was fully willing to believe it was divine providence that returned the ring to her. She told Harold the story of the ring being purloined by movers in Ohio. He too was willing to believe the ring was meant to be returned to her. See, Harold said, I told you I needed to spend that money on something other than a down payment on a house. I can make money for a down payment later.

Long Beach

Harold never made the money for a down payment and when San Francisco became too expensive for them, they heard of an opportunity to be apartment managers in Long Beach. (The furniture in their Long Beach apartment had belonged to Gable and Lombard.) In 1976, when the Fairlane threw a rod, my mother sold the ring for $900 which they used to buy a 1973 Pinto. Harold was happy with the Pinto which guzzled less gas than the Fairlane. My mother never knew the ring had left Columbus for Japan or the circumstances which brought the diamond studded circle of gold back to her second husband's home town. She never knew the father of her children had sold it. It seems it did not matter—she too was happy with the Pinto.

The Cat in Central Park

My window to the world has a view of Central Park. The window, the view, courtesy of Aunt Antonia, whose millions came from the slaughter of lungs in Pennsylvania mines she never saw. The lover she took leaving it all to her, for his penitence, and her tolerant presence in his penthouse for forty years and a day. The day she spent at his deathbed not even holding his hand.

No one contested the will, not even his drunkard son who squandered his fortune on five wives and landed in a trailer in Tenafly, some said.

When Antonia made her own last laps, I was not there, but in my old place by the river with my useless legs—the sticks of flesh and bone that never took one step. The same legs that earned Antonia's silent sympathy and divinely divested dollars.

A cousin watched her passing, pillaging her jewelry once she was gone, snarling to her nurses the cripple would get all else, and the cat, as part of the bargain.

And I did, and each morning, when I look onto the park through the maid's invisibly clean glass, the feline is pestiferously perched in mid frame, in park's green summer, or wicked white winter, reminding me of the mines, the insolent indifference, the passing of millions, the dead legs that were my first inheritance, my curled curse, that brought me a cat and a view of a park where I would never walk.

The Hawk and Matilda

I took rest on the river road by the big Platmann place. Two stout stories, white pillared and regal on this prairie. Envy ate my gut most days when I passed: a fine car, servants and the like.

Today though, it was curiosity stirred in me, since what I happened to see was a giant red-tailed hawk, splayed and stuck to an outbuilding, entrails dripping. An avian crucifixion, I was told, after the raptor snatched up the Platmann's tabby.

The pet was not saved, by prayer or the screams of the young lass who called the kitten Matilda, though a handy shotgun brought down the bird before it reached the stand of trees (where the hawk would have had its furry repast). Only winged and not shot fatal, the giant hawk was dragged back to the shed where a knife slit its gut, and a fire forged hammer and three penny nails did the rest.

The skies did not darken, nor did the sacrificed call out to an invisible father. This is not the way of hunters, nor their prey. I did tarry a while and wonder if a child's eyes saw this rapacious red reaping or knew of the dumb desperate need for a blood cleansing.

Passionate peach, the cream acrylic on their wall, filling the textured grooves the trowels had left. Almost pink in morning light, taking on the color of the fruit at eventide, when incandescence reigned. When fireplace flames flickered, the wall became a fickle facade: gray in shadow one moment, pale peach the next.

His favorite chair sat there, where she thought it looked best, a worn rocking guest in a room filled with modernity; that is where she found him, slumped over, eyes agape, blue metal gun in his lap, where it had landed, after the dead journey from his mouth, after he had squeezed the trigger but once, painting the flat wall behind him with hues of crimson, cherry, and bits of white.

What queer shape this scattering had made, she thought. Surely not a visage, though it appeared so, as she watched in paralytic silence while strangers washed the gore from the wall, leaving but a black hole where his rich red legacy had left its beguiling design.

Child of a Frightened Jewess

I didn't choose to be son of a scared Jew and angry Irishman, who never laid a hand on her, even when she turned the butcher knife on him, when he tried to stop her from slashing her red wrung wrists. This spectacle in plain view of five children for whom "woe is the world" was daily refrain.

I recall Father's blood trail on the concrete between our house and the neighbor's, a surgeon not expecting a bleeding Sunday guest, but my mother's madness didn't rest—on the Christian Sabbath, nor on her own.

After that, the shrinks did their magic: Mom did the Mellaril march, the Haldol hop, the Stellazine stomp, and the less alliterative Thorazine shuffle. None of those chemically induced dances did a thing to increase the chances for my mother's salvation. Soon she was behind the locked doors of "Ward 30," where I visited, and Mom told me she had found Jesus, a befuddled revelation since I didn't know she was looking for him. Her kin had hung him from a cross and taken the heat ever since.

The doctors released her to the street, where she made misty retreat to the hills of Saint Francisco's bay. Though she found faint solace in Pacific waters, she would never again see her sons or daughters. Half a lifetime later, I found a long-lost cousin my mother agreed to see, though not with me, for I was too much a reminder of scars which never heal.

She sat with Mother near the end of days, sharing silence, the scent of nursing home Salisbury steak, and a view of the distant shore. As my patient cousin rose to leave, my mother finally spoke of a sea she watched turn from cerulean to indigo dusk. Childhood beaches my mother did recall: the castles she crafted, the crawling crabs she followed, the sun-bathed sand where she made her bed, far from the one where she now lay, the one in which she would go smoothly into the night, perchance returning to blue waters, where hot blood trails could not follow.

When I was ten, I had dreams of being on the hillside above the Little Big Horn. I knew I was Custer in a previous life. I told my father. He said nonsense, this coming from the man who answered my question about whether I would live longer than Methuselah with, "It's possible."

At eighteen, I told a lover. She proclaimed transmigration of souls was crap. And god was dead. I mentioned it to a Buddhist. He said we never really know who we were, though he was convinced his dorm mate would return as a cockroach.

Still, I had those dreams. I saw the river. I saw the hordes of screaming men.

A year later, in a bunker on guard duty in Vietnam, Bob V. from St. Louis said he believed me. Not because of my dreams, or my obsession with the boy general, but because he had gotten a Dear John letter that morning. And Bob wanted to believe in something that night. Bob wanted to believe we had a forever past. And a forever future.

When I had told my mother I thought I had been Custer, she said she didn't know who I was, but we're all stuck in a chain of lives. She then related a story from her time in the camps in WWII when a girl named Victoria, my mother's age, walked through the gate with the Japanese guards screaming at her to stop. One guard, Inamoto, who looked as young as they, was begging Victoria to stop. Inamoto had been kind to my mother and the other prisoners, giving them rice cakes from his rations. He smiled and spoke softly, in a voice that had not yet changed, unlike the other guards who scowled and barked out orders in pidgin English or their native guttural tongue. Inamoto called for her to stop, even using her name, Victoria san, stop, halt. Victoria kept walking, as if she were crossing a dance floor to meet her partner and glide through a waltz in a Shubert induced trance.

Inamoto was crying when he fired a warning shot. By then, dozens of the inmates were at the fence, calling for her to stop, their voices a lugubrious chorus, one Victoria did not hear, their cries drowned out by her own mystic music.

Other guards were shouting at Inamoto, ordering him to shoot again—not imploring Victoria to stop her death march. Inamoto fired again over her head, his hands trembling so badly my mother thought his rifle would fall, but it did not drop. Victoria did when he fired a third time, the bullet striking her between her bony shoulder blades and exiting through her heart.

The guards directed prisoners to get the girl from where she lay. The men grabbed her arms and legs, leaving her facing the ground as they carried her. My mother remembered the steady flow of blood making a dotted trail on the hard dirt road, turning from crying crimson to bleak black as the day passed.

The prisoners were ordered to take Victoria to the compound cemetery. There she was buried unceremoniously while the camp population watched, some crying, others praying, some doing both.

Mother also intimated she had dreams that began the night of the event. She did not call them nightmares, though it was she who taught me what nightmares were. Mother simply said the event replayed itself in her dreams, but Inamoto hadn't shot Victoria. Inamoto was there with his rifle, but there was no cracking report of gunshots—only Victoria dancing.

In the light of day, Inamoto was never seen again. Some prisoners assumed he was transferred for his safety, though nobody blamed Inamoto. Rumors surfaced suggesting he had committed seppuku. My mother's sensibilities inclined her to believe Inamoto did take his life, ending his and Victoria's tale with some degree of moral symmetry.

In her liquid world of dreams, however, Inamoto reappeared many times. My mother was convinced he died that day, by his own hand, and came back as a child. Born to a family far from the war that surrounded her and kept her in captivity. A beautiful boy, building his own mazy memories with no sense of Inamoto's anguish. It was the dream she had: Inamoto dropping his rifle, walking into thick fog and emerging on the other side as the boy.

I had no more dreams of the Little Big Horn. I did dream of Custer walking through his own miasma, coming out the other side— whether an insect or a beautiful boy, I don't know. Whatever creature he became, that vessel too is gone, replaced yet by another, untroubled by Custer's folly or Victoria and Inamoto's waltz. When I see a cockroach now, I do wonder if the Buddhist was right.

I kissed Vivien Leigh

Well not really, though I told every grinning green Catholic soul at my school I did that and more. I did smell the wine on her breath and watch her trip into her trailer, gown hitting the floor before she closed the door. Her body as white as the fake snow spitting onto the set, and as cold perhaps.

I was sixteen and she was fifty-one. This was my one and only, her last, flick, not fling, though I would have cut off an arm for it to have been so. Not the arm she touched in our one immortal scene together-- her electric hand, all the blond hairs on my forearm standing at attention, me wondering if the camera caught their helpless vertical veer. It mattered not, since most of the scene landed not on the screen, but the cutting room floor, my two lines slashed to one, my forty-eight seconds with her shaved to twenty-two.

I did not cry when I heard she died, twenty months later, but my lie seemed soiled once she was in the ground. I confessed to Father Ryan. He was silent when I asked what to tell the fools who believed the dying star lay with me simply because she said, "Call me Vivien, not Ms Leigh."

Baguettes in Beirut*

Fridays, my cousin liked to have breakfast at an open-air café with his fiancée. The owner knew she loved French breads, she having been schooled at the Sorbonne. The bakery made them at his behest; he would tell his staff to keep one for her and to bring a bag when served. She always saved half for later.

Rush hour was madder than usual that night, until the bombs blasted and brought the synovial silence that comes in the wake of wondering, what has happened? The sirens screamed soon enough, and my cousin smelled the smoke. Cordite, yes, but burnt baklava, Maamoul as well.

His fiancée came to him that night, watched and waited to hear if anyone they knew was lost, their hands clasped tight, breaths shallow in the languid hush after the city slowed to its mournful rest. The sun rose, the skies clear, crisp, to their surprise, and they went to the café, where the owner apologized for the wicked, wicked world, and for not having baguettes after the bakery died in the explosions.

*Horrific events in Paris overshadowed the loss of 43 the night before in Beirut.

Death at the Diner

I can still see the lights flashing off the walls of the Crossroads Café. The red and blue turrets spinning gyroscopically as they loaded the old guy in the ambulance, sliding the gurney in like a tray of bread into the oven.

But that old guy ain't getting cooked and coming out smelling fresh. The EMTs worked on him ten minutes on that dirty diner linoleum, while our food got cold. Three of us, at least, punched in 911 on our cells, all being told by the dispatch the paramedics were already on their way, like maybe someone had a crystal ball and knew the ancient diner was going to fall flat on the floor when he got up to pay his check (for $4.88 I think).

I could see three quarters on the Formica. His silver goodbye to the world. His gift to some faceless waitress who would not sleep that night without an extra couple of beers because his face, contorted and staring into the florescent haze above him, would still be in her head when she closed her eyes.

After the cops and paramedics disappeared into the night, I ate what was left of my cold eggs and hash. When I got up to pay, my chest felt tight, only for a second, under that same buzzing light, when I crossed the spot where the old guy had lain.

A fat roach made its way across the floor through the last somber slobber the man would ever drip. I crushed him casually, remembering I had forgotten the tip.

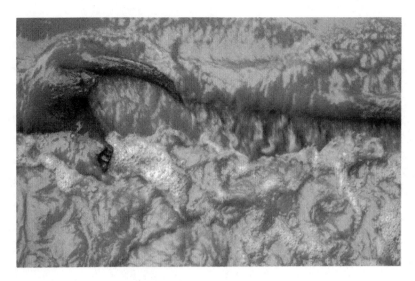

In the Freshet

His victim was stronger than Rex thought. A skinny runt a head shorter than Rex. Rex had knocked him down easy enough, and got his wallet without a fight, but now that Rex had him in the river, the runt was fighting like a cougar—swiping at Rex's face with his free hand, scratching his cheek and drawing good blood before Rex ground his knees into the man's chest to brace him down and got hold of the man's free arm and shoved it into the silt.

Rex was hungry, drunk and mad that afternoon. He was pimpled by mosquito bites from sleeping under the bridge after the homeless shelter had booted him out for messing with a black woman Rex said was "asking for it." He hadn't eaten since lunch the previous day but managed to swipe a pint of bourbon from another man who slept under the bridge. Rex finished off the bottle by noon and went looking for someone to rob.

The runt was alone at the bus stop. Rex looked down the street and across at the warehouse and saw not a soul. Rex knew this was his chance. He had mugged many a man before (and a woman once), and he could tell by looking at a face whether to demand money or just pounce.

With the runt, Rex had asked, and even nicely. Hey bud, you got a couple of bucks so I can grab a burger? His victim just stared at him and didn't answer. Rex repeated himself. Still, the runt was silent. Rex hit him hard in the forehead, knocking the man to the ground. Rex then straddled his prostrate victim and pulled a wallet from the man's back pocket. The runt had been dazed by the blow but as soon as Rex had the wallet, the runt got an arm free and hit Rex square in the nose. Rex had taken a hundred punches before, but it always enraged him when he was jabbed in the nose.

Rex hit the runt in the mouth with a right and in the nose with a left. Rex then dragged the man into the rain bloated river, straddling him again and holding the man's head under the water. When the runt freed an arm and lashed out at him, Rex cursed himself for not shoving the man in face down. Rex had killed before: once by strangling, and once with a baseball bat, but he had never drowned a man. Afterwards, Rex thought, if he ever had to drown a man again, he would stick him face down in the mud—quicker, he thought. Killing this runt had worn him out.

It didn't help that the river, normally slow trailing and only a foot or two deep at the place of the drowning was pumping ten times its usual volume and more than twice as deep after a gully buster the day before. Rex and runt had almost been swept down river during the struggle.

Rex pulled the limp body from the water and placed it in thick brush by the river. John law won't find this scrawny pecker here, he thought. Rex opened the wallet and found the man's social security card, a picture of a woman Rex found unappealing, and six one-dollar bills. Enough for lunch and a six pack of beer, Rex thought. Rex read the name on the social security card. Clarence Schmidt. Thanks for the bread, Clarence, you scrawny ass runt.

Rex washed some of the muck from his hands and went to the Day and Night convenience store. There he bought a six-pack of Lone Star, a loaf of white bread, and three cans of potted meat. He received twelve cents in change from the clerk who asked how Rex got so muddy.

Been swimmin' in that river? he asked.

Nah, Rex said, fell in while I was fishin'.

Rex guzzled down a beer before he got back to the overpass under which he would have his lunch. Rex sat down on some cardboard and drank another beer while he was spreading potted meat on the bread with his finger. He licked his finger and had a third beer before he took a bite of the sandwich.

Rex threw one of his empties into the current. The can bobbed on the river for a few yards and then came to rest in the crook of a branch that was stretched out into the water. Before the fierce rain, the branch would have been hanging a foot above the water. Rex gobbled down his sandwich, made another one and had another beer. When he threw the can into the current, it nearly hit something moving there. What the hell, Rex said. There was a dog being zipped down river. A pit bull it looked like. I love pits, Rex thought. He recalled a time when he made a clean twenty betting on the right mutt in a dogfight.

The dog's legs were useless in the force of the river. The pit came to a stop against the same branch the beer can had found. The animal began spinning in slow circles in the "L" made by the thick branch. Rex ran over to where the tree tilted into the current. He felt dizzy from the beer but steadied himself by placing one hand on the trunk of the tree.

I'll get ya, Rex said. A cousin of yours made me good money.

Rex leaned over and grabbed the dog by the scruff and tossed it onto the bank. As soon as the dog landed, Rex fell into the current. He was swept downstream, but he wasn't worried. Rex had swum in rivers and lakes his whole life. His boots made it difficult to kick and he tried to float on his back. Rex thought he could take his boots off and then swim to shore. He was able to get on his back, but when Rex tried to bend to take off a boot, his lunch came up into his mouth. Beer and potted meat sandwich cud. Rex began to choke. He tried to spit out the bile in his mouth but more came.

The river rolled him over onto his belly. The vomit cleared but Rex reflexively took a deep breath. He tried to breathe again but could not. He swallowed water and felt himself sinking towards the bottom. His head felt heavy. The river spun him, and he was facing skyward again, his eyes opening and closing in the murky water. The sun was directly above, but Rex saw no light coming through the current. There were no visible shafts and Rex would not have seen them if there were; his eyes were closed now. They would not open again.

On the shore, the pit bull shook itself off and followed the scent of the man who had plucked it from the freshet. Its nose took it to the bridge where two beer cans lay beside an uneaten potted meat sandwich. The animal ate the sandwich in two chomps. The pit then sniffed around the makeshift camp. The dog shat and sniffed its dung. It sniffed again for scent of Rex, fainter now, but still there. The pit trotted upriver, dry already and no longer sniffing for signs of Rex.

Texas 1979

Bobby's Dream Furniture

Bobby's couch has a biography: cigarette burns, food stains, and cushion wear, all there, though he doesn't know who wrote it. For $5 at the AmVets store, he bought a place to sit, and sleep on nights when he was too wasted to it make to the bedroom. There he has a mattress on the floor. Bobby knows its life story, because he filched it from a loading dock at Sleep World.

In five months, the mattress had three women sleep on it—all hookers who gave Bobby a freebie after they did copious lines of coke on the glass topped coffee table Bobby inherited from his brother, along with a recliner Bobby sold for meth.

Bro's doing hard time at Huntsville; he wanted Bobby to have a nice place. Bro gave his '73 Ford to their half-sister, since Bobby's license was suspended.

When Bobby gets that oil field gig, he's going to buy another Lazy Boy, and a refrigerator to stock with beer. Maybe later a color TV.

Sherman, Texas, 1978

Gutter Time

He sits on the curb, all twelve years of him, waiting to be a teen, when he'll have to pay adult price for a movie ticket or bus pass. Usually, he has no cash for either but wishing and waiting are art forms to him.

He's learned to move the brush of time slowly on life's palette, while he watches others whizzing by on store-bought skateboards and Huffy ten-speed bikes. He has only one gear for two feet, which now are clad in Keds from the thrift store and planted firmly on the cement. By the drain gutter. Where he last saw his favorite possession, a Super Ball, get sucked into the sewer.

After the storm ended, he yanked off the manhole cover and crawled into the dark, but the ball was gone forever. He returned to his spot on the curb yet lamenting his round loss. More boys on bikes buzzed by, their circles safely spinning on asphalt, far from the gutter and curb where he once again sat--wishing, waiting.

Baltimore, 1965

The Church and the Boy

The boy enters when he knows others will not be there in prayer—their silent entreaties to a god he is not sure listens or cares. Morning after mass is best, when the bouquets are fresh. He can smell them once the scents of the early worshipers fade: the pipe smoke from the old man's coat, the widow's perfume which lingers longer than the ammonia stench of the holy homeless who is there every day.

Christ watches over this—a white marble figure bolted to a cross, witnessing this spectacle for millennia. Long before this cold statue was placed in this cathedral, he was there, the slaughtered lamb, cursed to die again and again.

That is how the boy sees it. Not a promised life eternal, but the same death anon, anon. The pounding of the stakes, the blood offering: the old man, the woman, the mendicant, all crucifying Christ again with each plaintive prayer.

Once their odors fade, the funeral sprays, the bouquets remain. Cut, dying flowers, a fragrant impermanence with no expectation for life beyond their time in the vase. No imploring a godhead for forgiveness. No demand for blood and perpetual death. Only a little water for their brief journey in fragile glass.

1945, Brooklyn

Aaron Singer's nuclear family perished in a gas explosion that demolished their Brooklyn home in 1945. Aaron was at the roller rink. His ten-year-old twin brothers and parents were at the kitchen table playing cards when the fireball killed them.

When Aaron's family died, he had a choice of living with his Aunt Ethel in Boston or his Uncle Ray Tate. Ray was his mom's brother and had a ranch in west Texas. Aaron had never met him, but he had met Aunt Ethel and knew he didn't want to live with a spinster who would make him go to synagogue every day. The books he had read and the movies he saw about the west romanticized it. His choice was easy.

Aaron stayed with his science teacher, Mr. Connors, for two weeks before he took a train to Midland and a bus to Banner, Texas. Aaron had never been farther west than the Jersey shore. He remembered small mountains from a trip to Boston, but he had seen nothing like the Appalachians, which the train chugged over on a clear, crisp morning. Aaron had one photo of the ranch he placed against the window while the train was descending the west side of the chain. A million Blue Ridge trees framed the tiny picture of the ranch corral and stretch of flat desert behind it.

Riding the train, Aaron had done fine. On the bus, he couldn't hold back tears which came in waves. When Aaron arrived in Banner and walked down the steps from the bus at 6:15 AM, he was wiping a fresh batch from his face. He did not want Uncle Ray's first impression to be Aaron crying.

Ray was the only man at the Stockton Café which served as the bus depot. Ray's thick warm hand shook Aaron's firmly.

Ray's first words were, Sure sorry about your family son. Glad to have you here with us. You sure grew up tall.

Aaron was tall. Six feet when he was sixteen. Three inches taller than Ray who was stocky, muscular and the first man Aaron ever saw in person wearing a cowboy hat. A frigid blast of wind hit them while he was shaking Uncle Ray's hand. Aaron did not know it got that cold in Texas.

Norther came in overnight, Ray said. Let's get you to the truck.

The ride to the ranch was in a 1939 Ford truck on mostly dirt county roads. In Brooklyn, Aaron had seen few of either—trucks or unpaved roads. The ranch house was on a slight rise on an otherwise flat desert plain. Behind the house, Aaron could see tall mountains, sharp in form—nothing like the Appalachians he had seen on his journey.

You have mountains here, Aaron said after a long but not uncomfortable silence in the truck.

Sure do, Aaron, Ray said. Those to the south are the Tierra del Lobos. Land of the Wolf, though I don't think there are wolves there. A little past them, to the southwest, you can see the Holt Mountains, named after a rancher who settled there in the 1880s.

How long have you been here? Aaron asked.

Twenty-five years, Ray answered. When I came back from the War, I was stationed at Fort Bliss over in El Paso. That's where I met your Aunt Ruth. Since 1900, her family had these five sections that make up our ranch. I had worked cattle some in Arkansas where your momma and I were reared. But it sure was different. In Arkansas, we had a hundred acres and usually half that many head of cattle. Herd here isn't but 350, and it takes me buying feed to keep them fat on more than 3,000 acres. You can see the grass is a bit stingy.

And my mom went to New York because she met my father at the University of Arkansas? Aaron asked.

Yep. When they met, your daddy was a senior and the only Jew there. He went there because your grandfather owned that clothing store in Little Rock. You know about that didn't you, Aaron?

Yes Sir. My father told me he worked until college and he didn't have to go into the army because he had one leg shorter than another. And he told me he went to New York because he had a degree in business. He said he thought he would make a fortune, but he landed in a clothing store again.

Aaron, your daddy was manager of a large clothing store, and he did a fine job making a living, may he rest in peace.

I know, Uncle Ray, but I think he always wanted to be a stockbroker. Guess it was lucky he didn't become one since I was born on what they call Black Tuesday.

Aaron again teared up when he said this. He imagined his family sitting at the table in the kitchen. Playing cards.

That's right, I had forgotten that. You were born October 1929. Happy birthday a few weeks late, son.

Aaron's tears were coming fast now. Hearing this man call him son—the term his father used most often when speaking with him—pulled something deep in Aaron's gut. Will I ever see this man as my father, Aaron wondered? Aaron turned his face away from Ray. Arron felt Uncle Ray touch his shoulder. He looked and saw a handkerchief in Ray's hand.

I've seen plenty of grown men cry, Ray said.

When Aaron got out of the truck Ray said he would get his suitcases. Ray told him to go on in where it was warm.

Aaron could tell from the road the adobe house was big. He had never seen adobe except in pictures. Inside, the living, dining and kitchen were one enormous room—wood stove in the kitchen and stone fireplace in the living room. His cousin, Aggie, who refused to be called Agatha, was feeding the fire sticks of wood the diameter of the business end of a bat.

Ray came in behind Aaron carrying two huge suitcases effortlessly and said, Aggie, introduce yourself to your cousin.

Aggie strode across the large room, stuck her hand out the way a man would, and shook Aaron's hand as firmly as any man. Don't worry, Aaron, Aggie said, we have running water and a toilet. And even electricity.

Nice to meet you Aggie, Aaron said, still having his hand shaken by a girl his age but ten inches shorter than he. You must have read my mind. I was going to ask where the bathroom was.

The end of that long hall. Dad told me you chose here over Boston. I figured you might want to go cowboy style, Aggie said.

Cowboy style, Aaron asked?

Men just pee off the back porch in Texas. Didn't you know that, Aaron? And Dad left the old outhouse standing after we got the toilet. And this time of year, you don't have to worry about snakes or spiders in the privy. Aggie winked.

You're making him feel real welcome I see. The voice was Ruth, who came from a hall that led to the bedrooms and bath. Like Aggie, she was short, wearing dungarees and a plaid shirt.

I would have had breakfast ready for you, Aaron, but I came home only a few minutes ago. I was helping with a birth all last night. Ruth hugged Aaron and again his eyes filled with tears.

My mom went to the Hotel Dieu School of Nursing and was a nurse in El Paso two years, Aggie added. Then she gave it all up to come out here. Now she is pretty much the midwife and doctor for half the county.

Aaron could not tell if Aggie was saying this with pride or mockery—a little of both he guessed. He would learn Aggie was the most peculiar girl he'd ever met.

You eat bacon, Aaron? Ruth asked.

Yes Ma'am.

Good, have a seat and I will fix everybody some bacon and eggs. Sound good, Aaron?

Sure does, Aaron said.

Aaron wasn't hungry and hadn't been since his family died, but he thought It would be rude to say no. When they all sat down to the platter of fried eggs, thick cut bacon, and golden biscuits, Aaron became hungry and ate more than he had in weeks. Little conversation occurred while they ate. Aaron would discover the family did mostly eating at this huge wooden table.

While they were eating, a black cat hopped onto one of the outside window ledges. That's Edgar, Aggie said.

Like Edgar Alan Poe? Aaron asked.

Yep. Aggie winked again. Aaron couldn't help but notice Ruth roll her eyes when Aggie told him.

After breakfast, Ray and Aggie put on coats and went out to do chores. Ray said something about some hay from the Valley they needed to spread in a pasture to supplement feed. Aggie put her blond hair under her hat. A cowgirl, Aaron thought.

Ruth showed Aaron his room and told him to "Rest up a bit." Aaron didn't think he could sleep, though he hadn't slept much on the train or bus and his sleep had been fitful since the fire.

Aaron did not wake up until he felt Aggie tapping him on the shoulder. It was dark outside, and Aggie held a candle.

Hey, want to go someplace? Aggie asked.

What time is it? Go where? What time is it? Aaron realized he was still fully dressed. He had fallen asleep without undressing and had dreams—lots of them, but he couldn't remember the content.

It's a little after ten. You slept over twelve hours. You wanna go someplace or not?

What about your parents? And where are we going?

My parents are always asleep by eight-thirty and where we are going is a surprise. Just don't talk or slam the door—my dad is a light sleeper. Aggie handed him his coat.

Outside there was a gibbous moon. The wind had slowed, but it was still cold. Aaron stopped a few feet from the house and stared at the stars like a man seeing the ocean for the first time.

Geez, are they always that bright?

They don't have stars in New York? Aggie asked.

Of course, but they don't look like this.

When they got into the truck, Aaron asked, you drive this??

Mostly I drive my mom's '41 Ford, but we need the truck tonight. You don't drive?

I catch the subway and the bus, Aaron said.

Not here, city boy.

I figured we would be in a wagon pulled by a mule team.

Smart ass.

Brooklyn girls used their share of profanity but this surprised Aaron coming from his cousin.

You know I am adopted, right? Aggie said.

Yes, my mom told me I had only one cousin and she'd been adopted.

So, I am not really your cousin. I just happen to be someone the family snatched from some girl who didn't want a baby.

Is that how you got adopted?

I don't know. My folks don't like talking about it. I just know they went to Santa Fe to get me when I was about a week old.

Where are we going?

To see ghosts, Aggie answered.

The rutted ranch road they traveled went straight to the wolf mountains Aaron had asked Ray about. Aggie stopped the truck near the foot of the mountains.

Time to go to church, she said.

Aaron saw the ruins of an old stone structure. Behind it, he saw crosses and one headstone.

We supposed to be here? Aaron asked.

Who's gonna care? Come on.

Aggie took his hand and they walked through the cemetery. Aaron saw crosses strewn on the ground. The few left standing were leaning. Nobody had tended to the place in years. The one headstone read, *Hector Morales Fuentes 1840-1895*. Aggie said that was the man who built their house in 1890. The gringo ranchers killed him after he had a dispute with A.B Holt.

The one those other mountains are named after? Your dad said he wasn't here until the 1880s. Was Hector here first? Aaron asked.

Darn right he was. Not long after Holt came here, he started quarreling with Hector over water and grazing rights. As soon as there were enough white ranchers in the area, they shot Hector off his horse on the road between here and the ranch. Holt's son moved into the house and somehow got deed to the six sections. He was a bad gambler and a drunk and he sold the place to Ruth's father when he needed money to pay his gambling debts. Didn't do him much good—someone shot Holt Junior dead during a card game in El Paso.

Ruth's father meaning your granddad?

Nope, he is no kin to me—remember, the stork dropped me in Santa Fe.

Aggie took Aaron past the graveyard to what she called an arroyo. Looked like a little canyon to Aaron. He could see half a moon reflected off a small pool of water in the bottom. Aggie told him it was only a trickle now, but when it rained, it was like a river coming down the six thousand-foot peaks.

Listen, Aggie said. It's better if it's windier but listen.

It was faint, but Aaron heard it. A howl coming from the mountain.

It's wind coming down that canyon up there, Aggie said, pointing to the dark peaks above them.

Maybe that is why they are called Tierra del Lobos.

Of course, Aggie said. That's what I wanted you to hear. The ghosts.

The ghosts in the graveyard?

No, the ghosts of the wolves. The ranchers wiped them out too.

The entire time, Aggie had been holding his hand. Aaron had held girls' hands before, but only on the few dates he had.

When they got up to leave, Aggie kissed him on his cheek and said, We'll come back when there's more wind.

Aaron was about to say, you're my cousin, but Aggie beat him to it.

Yes, I know we're cousins, but I am adopted. We aren't blood. Besides, you are more handsome than any boy in the county, and you passed the test. You knew Edgar was named after Poe.

That was a test?

Yes, a test to prove you weren't like the half dozen inbred philistines in my class.

Aaron was handsome. He looked very much like his father who many said looked like a Jewish Errol Flynn. Aaron knew who the actor was but couldn't figure out why they had to add the Jewish to the comparison. Regardless, Aaron knew he looked like Flynn. And his father had.

When they got back to the ranch, Aaron was awake most of the night, thinking about Aggie. The next morning, Aggie acted as if nothing had happened. Aaron was just her cousin she only met the day before and knew little about. That was still true, but things were different now. Now, Aaron couldn't keep his eyes off Aggie.

Ruth said she had talked to the school principal and he'd said for Aaron to wait until after the Christmas break to start school. The break was a week away—that meant all week with Aggie at school and him at the ranch. Ray took Aaron with him to do chores, most of which entailed checking on the cattle that were scattered wherever Ray had dropped hay. Ray had Aaron help put some bails in the truck and take them to the pastures. Aaron felt great pitchforking hay onto the prairie, watching some of the steers trail the truck for the feed.

Ray had given him a hat and said, Here, son—keep your head warm.

It was already warm. The norther had passed, and it was probably sixty degrees and a white sun was shining in an azure sky. In Brooklyn, it would be twenty degrees colder and the sky would be overcast and filled with the smoke of the city.

The first day of school in January 1946, despite Aggie's protests, Aaron wore the hat Ray had given him.

You wear one on the ranch, Aaron said.

I do, but only when it's cold out, and I don't want you looking like all these cowhands at school.

Aggie drove them and said as soon as Ford started getting some new cars to Texas, she would be stuck with the car. Her mom would have a new one.

Stuck with the Ford? It's a nice car, Aaron said.

I want the truck, but my mom said a young lady should drive a car.

All the boys in the small school wore hats. And they all shook Aaron's hand when they met him. And they all sounded funny with their rural Texas accents. Aaron knew he must have sounded funny to them. Some asked him about the Dodgers since they had been told he was from Brooklyn. There were thirty boys in the entire high school. Thirty-three girls. His previous school had been fourteen hundred.

The school work was easy. Aaron wondered if he would be able to get into a good university—or any college—after a year and a half at Banner High School. He had straight A's in Brooklyn. He was thinking Columbia or Princeton. Ray had taken him aside and told him to not worry about "his schooling." Ray said with the insurance money, the money from his parents' savings and bonds, Aaron had the money to go to any college he wanted. Ray said they would make sure he had a solid car to take with him. Ray had already begun teaching Aaron to drive the truck. Aggie had volunteered but Ray said something about a man teaching a man and gave her a look that meant, "you usually get your way Agatha, but this time, no."

The nocturnal sojourns to the desert continued, usually on Friday nights. Aggie continued to hold his hand and kiss him on the cheek. Then she began pecking him on his lips until one night just before school let out for the summer, sitting on a boulder above the arroyo, she asked Aaron to kiss her. Aaron kissed her casually on the cheek. She repeated her request and Aaron kissed her on the lips. A peck, like he had been getting from her. Then Aggie put her hands on Aaron's cheeks and

French kissed him, exploring his mouth with her tongue. Aaron reciprocated. They kissed a while on what they decided was "their boulder."

After chores one Saturday afternoon, Aggie asked Ray if she could give Aaron his driving lesson that day. Aaron was supposed to get his driver's license the next week.

Ray said that would be fine but to be careful since it looked like a storm was headed in. Thank the Lord, Ray said. Since November, the county had been in the worst drought anybody could recall. A few teasing sprinkles now and then and two good snows, but if rain didn't come soon and perk up the grasses, Ray would have to sell some of his herd.

While Aggie and Aaron sat on their boulder that afternoon, clouds rolled over the peaks. Cool rain fell on them. Aaron began to rise to run back to the truck, but Aggie held him there.

You think you're gonna melt? Aggie asked.

The downpour lasted a good half hour. Aaron and Aggie were drenched. The sun came out and they rose and walked down towards the arroyo which was now a freshet.

Unless it rains more, Aggie said, it will be puddles and mud in a few hours.

Aaron pulled Aggie towards him and kissed her. He realized it was the first time he had initiated a kiss. Though he enjoyed the affection between them, he still felt the taboo of being with his "cousin," despite Aggie's repeated assertions they were not truly related. Aaron knew the logic of this was sound, but he yet had the lingering reservations.

Well, Aggie said, that was nice.

I agree.

You smell that, Aaron?

What?

That smell after the rain? I bet it's nothing like New York.

You're right, it's not. In Brooklyn, it's muggy after a rain like this and it smells worse. This smells…nice.

Petrichor.

What? Aaron asked.

It's the word for the smell right after a rain. You never heard the word?

Nope.

You were top of your class and you don't know petrichor.

Aaron shrugged, and they walked back to the truck. Aggie initiated another kiss before they got in and drove back to the ranch.

At dinner that night, Ray and Ruth were quieter than usual, which is to say they spoke not one word beyond Ruth's please pass the rolls.

Ruth and Aggie cleared the table and Ray remained seated. Still taciturn. After the dishes were piled by the big sink, Ruth told Aggie to sit at the table.

What for Mom?

Just do as you are told, please.

Aaron was pushing his chair back to get up when Ruth said, This concerns you too, Aaron. Please stay.

Aaron's heart began thumping. He had wondered if or when this was coming. Ruth looked directly at him for some time before saying, I think you two know why we want to talk to you.

Aaron said nothing and looked at the grain of the table, not wanting to make eye contact.

Aggie said, I don't have any idea.

Ray, who had been looking at Aaron, fixed his stare on Aggie.

Ruth said, Don't play naïve. And it disappoints me you aren't owning up to this. We taught you to be honest. I am talking about you and Aaron—you think we are always asleep when you slip off in the truck on Friday nights? You think we don't see the way the two of you look at each other?

Ray spoke. It's just not right. And don't tell us it doesn't matter because you are not blood kin. It does matter. Aaron, please look at me, son. You are not a guest in this house. You are family. If you were only a guest, we would have sent you off to Boston when we first had our suspicions confirmed.

Aaron teared up. I am sorry Uncle Ray. Sorry Aunt Ruth.

So, you agree what you are doing is wrong? Ruth asked.

Yes Ma'am.

I don't agree it is wrong! shouted Aggie. We are NOT related, and we are not even having sex!

Well, I am glad to hear that, but your father and I don't share your opinion about whether this is proper. Ruth turned to Aaron again. Can you give us your word this will stop?

Yes Ma'am.

Aggie got up so fast her heavy wood chair fell backwards on the floor. She stood akimbo and said, Aaron, you can't even be on my side! You are the only boy I ever loved, and you are quitting on us. Just because you are afraid of my parents. With that Aggie marched from the room into the yard.

Aaron, Ruth said, I pretty much expected the responses I would get from you and Aggie. I swear we didn't rear her to be so stubborn and strong willed, but she is. Guess it's in her blood.

Ray added, I think she will do as we ask, but she'll be riled up about it for a while. I did hear you promise to put a stop to this didn't I, son?

Yes Sir. But I don't know how easy it will be. I like Aggie a lot and she sure doesn't sound like she will obey you.

Ruth said, Aggie will, or she will spend her last year in high school with my Uncle Del in El Paso.

Aaron was shocked and blurted out, You mean you will kick her out instead of me? That's not fair. She's your daughter. I am only here because, because... Then Aaron began crying. Ray placed his hand on Aaron's shoulder.

Ruth said, I can understand how that would seem unfair Aaron, but what you don't know is until you came to live with us, Aggie had been asking to move in with my uncle. In fact, for years she expected to be able to go to high school in El Paso. We would have allowed her to go, but my Uncle Del's wife, Priscilla, got cancer the summer before Aggie's freshman year. Aunt Priscilla died a week before your birthday. School had already started, and we told Aggie we would consider letting her go at semester. All talk of that stopped when you came. Now Del would be happy to have her around to help. His only son, my brother, died in the Great War and Del is alone.

Aaron's tears had stopped but now he was trying to digest all he had just heard. Aggie had talked about what hicks she went to school with and how she couldn't wait to go off to college at Texas Western in El Paso, but she'd never said a word about finishing high school there.

She did say her great uncle had a "mansion" not more than a mile from Austin High School in El Paso, but nothing beyond that.

May I go talk to Aggie? Aaron asked.

Of course, but don't be surprised if she isn't too agreeable right now Aaron. But we have an agreement, right? Ruth asked.

Yes.

As Aaron left the table, Ray said, Aaron, we want you here. Don't you worry about us sending you off. If you want to go east to your aunt's place after all this, we won't stop you, but that's not what we want.

Aaron saw Aggie pacing in big circles around the old well in the yard, like a predator would its prey. Behind her was the most spectacular sunset Aaron had ever seen. An orange orb, with clouds that looked like they were on fire burning beauty across the entire horizon.

Aaron expected rebuke from his cousin, but he saw tears streaming down her face. She grabbed both his hands in hers and said, Aaron, I can't stay. I can't stay away from you if you're here. I have to go live in El Paso.

With your great uncle? Were you listening when they talked to me?

No, but I knew they would give me that ultimatum. Will you hate me forever if I go?

No, I will likely love you forever.

They turned towards the sinking sun, Aggie's right hand clinging to his left. She took a deep breath. Aaron thought, petrichor.

2015, Taos New Mexico

Aaron was tired. He had flown from Washington to Albuquerque, spent a short night there, and drove his rental to Taos. The "Celebration" of her life was to begin at 1:30. He arrived before noon and sat on the square, waiting to meet the man at La Fonda. The man was Jorge Villareal, the son of Aggie's caretaker. Jorge arrived on time at 1:00 and drove Aaron to a hacienda style house where Aggie's memorial was to take place.

No clergy were in attendance. Several people near Aggie's age spoke of her, saying what a fine artist she had been, and what a fine human being. The last person to speak was a younger woman, perhaps nearing forty, named Zoey. She had blonde hair that reminded Aaron of the Aggie he knew. Aggie adopted Zoey when she was three. Adopted in Santa Fe, just as Aggie had been. Zoey spoke of the spark of spirit she could yet see in Aggie's eyes even in her final days, even though Aggie had been ravaged by Alzheimer's for a decade.

After the service, Zoey sat with Aaron. She told him "Ag" (not Mom, but Ag, by Aggie's choice) had spoken of him often. When Zoey read Aggie's will, she discovered her adopted mother's final wishes. Aaron did not know Zoey existed until she called him the week before to inform him of her mother's passing. Aaron had not heard from Aggie in fifteen years, but the last few years, her caretaker had written him and kept him abreast of her decline.

They had lived separate lives, not seeing each other since 1951 when Aggie drove from Boulder, Colorado to Houston where Aaron was attending Rice. He had majored in biology and after his two years in the army in Korea he got a job for the government, ultimately working as an administrator for the NIH. Aggie had majored in art at the University of Colorado, had never married and spent her life in Santa Fe and Taos. Aaron had married and divorced after a thirty-year union from which no children came.

The night Aggie visited him in 1951 was a surprise. She had driven non-stop from Boulder to Houston, only cat napping on the way. When she arrived at his apartment, he had just returned from a date with Norma who was to become his wife. Aggie had just broken up with a young man she had been dating and decided she had to see Aaron. They had corresponded only infrequently by mail since the summer of 1946, though the connection between them still existed. They made love that night and again the following night before she began the long journey back to Colorado. The last thing she said to Aaron in person was, some would think what we did was a sin, but I think it would have been a sin if we never had consummated. Aaron was ambivalent about what had happened, but even in his eighties, he could recall every detail of their hours of nakedness. His sex life with Norma had been satisfactory, but nothing like what he had with Aggie. The first kiss on their boulder was more memorable than Norma's climaxing in his arms.

Aggie's final wishes, scribed in her will fifteen years before she died, were simple. Zoey and her friends could have any service they chose to have in Taos, but she requested her ashes be strewn in the arroyo behind the old Mexican church in Texas. If Aaron is able, Aggie wrote, I would like for him to be a part of that.

At eighty-five, Aaron was in good health, though the thought of a journey to the wilds of west Texas tired him. He wanted to do it, not simply because Aggie had asked. Zoey said she would drive the whole way. Aaron had Mapquested the route—499 miles.

On the trip, Zoey told Aaron her mother had many lovers, but she traded them for newer models as often as most people traded cars. Aggie treated all her men well, Zoey added, but Aggie never wanted permanency. She told her lovers this up front. Zoey also said her adopted mother often reflected that her "true love" may have been her first—her cousin. The boy from New York who looked like a famous playboy actor.

Aggie's serial monogamy did not surprise Aaron. He had imagined that would be her life. And he was not surprised she adopted a little blond girl from Santa Fe.

Errol Flynn, Aaron said. The actor was Errol Flynn.

Zoey and Aaron spent the night in Artesia, New Mexico and arrived at the ranch before noon the next day. The adobe dwelling was still there, 135 years old, with many cracks repaired, creating the impression of veins and capillaries snaking their way across its surface. A living thing, Aaron thought. The family who now occupied the house was named Fuentes. Though they claimed they were unaware of any relation to the original owner who had been shot dead, Aaron felt they had to be connected in some way.

Zoey had a new AWD Subaru which barely made the trip down the ancient ranch road. The ruts were deeper, and it had rained that morning, making the road far slicker than it had been when he and Aggie drove it in the old Ford truck. When they arrived at the site, only a few stones of the church remained. Aaron could see the Fuentes headstone, but little evidence the old wood crosses had been there. Time, chemistry. Both magical in the speed of their passing, he thought.

This was our stone, Aaron said. We first kissed here. Aaron felt the old familiar pain. The lump in his throat. He could not recall the last time he had cried, but tears streamed down his cheeks. I don't know why I told you that, Zoey.

I am glad you did. Ag told me about the boulder—your boulder and the arroyo. And how much she missed you, even in her last years.

The arroyo had a steady stream from the morning rain. Aaron and Zoey took turns pouring Aggie's ashes into the current, watching as the cremains were carried downstream, likely to sink into the silt until the next gift from the heavens. When the earthenware urn was empty, they did as the will directed and placed it on the boulder. Aaron looked back at the arroyo and inhaled deeply. He looked at Zoey and said softly, Petrichor.

Uncle Parrot

She had an uncle who spent twenty years in the ring, landing solid blows until he landed in a downtown Oakland hotel, older than he. The wrecking ball got it in the dawn of the cyber age, but for ten droning years, it was his cage.

He never had a title shot, but he kept his belly full and had cash for the women, the drink. He never drove a car; cabbies knew him and knew the smell of gin meant, "keep the change."

When his legs got weak, and his left eye went to blur, the money stopped rolling in. But he still thirsted for the gym, the gin. He got himself a gig at Big G's. Just enough hours to clean out the showers and to keep the johns from smelling of piss, and a few greenbacks comin' his way.

He would end each day alone in his room, inhaling the gloom that seeped over the transom like smoke from a smoldering fire. But there was no fire left in the ancient hotel or Parrot's burned up belly. Only fading memories of a wounded warrior who taunted his opponents by mimicking every word they said in the ring, where he earned a bird's name but never its sweet song, before time took its tattered toll.

The Clothes He Chose

The only jeans with holes. The polo shirt with "passionate peach" paint from the kitchen remodel his wife ordered. The yardwork shoes. These were the garments he chose for his final drive, the one in "Park," in the garage, with the engine idling, its humming a monotonous lullaby sung by compliant pistons.

He wandered through the house like a sated forager, looking at everything, for nothing. Old pictures on the walls: children, parents, one of himself, the Yale mortar board tilting on a face who could have been a stranger, and was, that last afternoon. Books on shelves, mostly read, their stories now forgotten. Even Moby Dick, his favorite. Eight silent vertical letters replacing a white whale he relentlessly pursued with Ahab. A sink with one small plate and the disposal's shining ring—the burial ground for his last, uneaten meal.

Those were the visions he chose before writing his notorious note (BYE, ALL MY PAPERS ARE IN THE ROLL TOP), taking the keys from the peg, and taking his final steps into the cluttered gray garage, to his 2011 Volvo, where some hand turned the key, igniting a welcoming flame. A few intrusive notes of a Beatles song came through the six speaking speakers, yanking something in his gut, pulling his hand to the handle to open the door, to return to the house, the pictures, the stories on the walls; but the other, the right hand, ejected the CD, rejecting the beguiling voices that would have him stay for another desperate, deaf day.

He folded his hands in his lap, allowed his chin to rest on his chest where his eyes could see the holes in his threadbare denim, taking solace in the fact that he had chosen the right clothes so those still in the house, yet in the blur called life, would have only whole and clean reminders of him to fold neatly and leave on the porch for the Salvation Army.

Trailing the Wild Dog

Erin Perkins was fascinated by coyotes, though she would confess she knew little about them. Wild dogs had never captured her interest until a dead December morning when one ran in front of her Explorer on a county road. Erin trailed along behind the mongrel at its loping speed and followed it when it turned onto a ranch road.

The mutt looked to be a large pit bull. Its chocolate brown color reminded her of the lab her neighbors recently put down with distemper. "Charlie" was an unruly but lovable pet that never failed to jump on her when she visited.

I dub thee Charlie Two, Erin said aloud. Why am I following you, Charlie Two?

Erin did not know why she followed a dog across the prairies. She did not know why she was on this ranch road, thirty miles from town. It was late morning and she had been driving farm to market and unpaved county roads since dawn. Dawn, an hour after she awoke and stared at the ceiling where Erin saw his face in the darkness. She could see his green eyes and smile, an expression she had never learned to trust in her moody ex-lover, Brandon, who left her for his dental hygienist the day after Thanksgiving.

Since then, Erin had been waking early and skipping her two-mile jog she'd made religiously each morning since she was twenty. Erin felt like her despondency would lift, but Erin knew avoiding her jog and taking leave from work had not helped.

Erin was a police homicide detective—the only woman to ever hold that position in her Texas city. She had been assigned to that job after only six years on the force. Now, after an equal number of years in that job, she and her partner, Tim Hoffman, had handled twenty-nine cases. One had made national news. A woman, Tammy Tomlinson, had shot and killed her intoxicated husband Ray when he attacked her with a knife. As Ray lay dying on their kitchen floor, his brother, Sammy, also inebriated, managed to get the gun from the woman and fatally shoot her. When the police arrived after neighbors reported hearing gunshots, Sammy fired upon them, critically injuring a rookie cop.

Sammy escaped before backup arrived. He hid in his uncle's abandoned ranch house a week before a sheriff's deputy discovered him.

There was another shootout and both the deputy and Sammy were mortally wounded. The deputy, Reuben Rodriguez, a state senator's son, died in the yard immediately after he and his assailant exchanged gunfire. Sammy walked two hundred yards into thick mesquite before he expired from loss of blood.

On that cold morning, Erin realized she was not far from the old ranch house where the shootout occurred. Erin had no sense she had come in this direction purposefully. All morning she had been making larger circles around the city. She would have described these as random in nature.

The ranch was the next section to the north, the direction the cur was trotting. Erin had been to the scene with the Sheriff and Department of Public Safety officers. Inside where Sammy had hidden, they found only empty tins and beer cans, ammo for the 357 magnum Sammy and his sister in law used for the killings, and a sleeping bag. She recalled blood stains on the sagging wooden stoop. This was the spot Sammy was standing when he and Deputy Rodriquez shot each other.

Erin had been following Charlie Two at least a quarter mile and he did not appear to be tiring. Snow had begun to fall. At one point, near the barbed wire which bordered Sammy's late uncle's ranch, the dog stopped. Charlie Two sniffed and then hiked his rear leg and marked one of the wooden fence posts. He then turned around and stood facing Erin's Explorer.

You are better looking than Brandon, Erin said, and a better runner for sure. Charlie Two's head turned to the side when Erin said this. How could he hear me, Erin wondered? I am twenty yards from him and my windows are up.

Charlie continued his run on the ranch road. In another quarter mile, he would be at what had been the Tomlinson section. Erin followed and was not surprised when the dog left the road, slipped through the sagging wire and went towards the location where Sammy's body was found. Everything happens for a reason Erin thought. Despite her thinking of the common adage, Erin did not believe this.

The stand of mesquite where Sammy died was downhill from the ranch house but elevated from Erin on the road. Erin watched as Charlie Two trotted towards the spinney. The snow continued to fall, and the wind came from the north, Erin's wipers clearing it from her windshield.

Erin pulled to the side of the road, put on gloves, zipped her coat and exited her vehicle. She followed Charlie Two who had just moved out of sight in a ravine by the mesquite. Erin saw him skitter up the other side. Charlie Two stopped and looked back at Erin. I'm coming, she said to herself.

The dog disappeared again behind a clump of the mesquite. Erin followed and traversed the ravine cautiously. The ground was becoming slick with the snow. Only a few paces after she cleared the ravine, she saw Charlie Two, tearing the flesh from a small doe. Fresh kill, Erin thought. The mongrel's snout was covered in blood. Scarlet. Bright, even this overcast snowy morning.

Erin took one step too far. The wild dog looked up from his feast, growled and began coming towards Erin. Erin instinctively walked backward, reaching for her service revolver, which sat on the seat of her Explorer a hundred yards away.

She again took one step too far, this time falling into the ravine, landing on her back. She felt little pain but had used one hand to block her fall and had dislocated her middle finger on her right hand. Erin popped the digit back into place. The dog was then upon her, his teeth tearing into her left wrist which she had placed in front of herself defensively. Fortunately, the thick coat and gloves offered some protection. Only one spot on her wrist was directly exposed to the cur's teeth. That pain she felt.

Again, her training came into play. Rather than pulling her hand away, as most would, she moved into the bite with her left hand and smacked the beast in the nose as hard as she could with the palm of the other. As a 125-pound patrol cop, Erin had used the exact same blow to disable a man twice her size when she was unable to get to her night stick or mace. The dog, dazed, released Erin, stood and growled a few seconds, then returned to the doe.

Erin jogged back to her SUV, looking back often. No Charlie Two. She retrieved her service revolver from the seat and trotted back to where the mongrel was devouring the deer. The snow was now blowing sideways in a stout north wind. Erin stopped ten paces from the predator and its prey. There was a blood mass in front of her in the white snow. The jugular of the fawn ripped and throbbing with precious blood until it had no more to give. Erin raised her revolver to the firing position, noticing the drying blood on her tan coat and fair skin, wondering if part of that blood was the doe's.

Erin was an expert shot, better than all but one man on the force, so she knew it was intentional when she first shot the dog near its hindquarter, aiming for the groin. The beast dropped. It turned towards Erin and pulled itself up, only to fall again in the snow. Now the pristine white was being fouled by the blood of the cur. Erin then aimed and shot the animal in the head.

She digested the scene of carnage in front of her. The winds slowed. Erin felt her eyes swell with tears. She thought of a pit bull puppy she and her partner had saved from a storm drain the first month she was on the job. She thought of her father telling the story of shooting a child armed with a grenade in Vietnam. She thought of Brandon, walking out the door with the Thanksgiving bottle of wine. As she turned to go back to her car, Erin saw a strand of yellow police tape draped from one of the mesquite branches. How far from here did Sammy die she wondered? How far am I from home she wondered? Across the white prairie, Erin jogged, her lungs loving the thrust of freezing air. Her tears continued, but all was quiet, the snow now falling softly.

Alone on the Mountain

Your Colorado village was freezing, even the eve of May. The bus dropped me there. You weren't waiting. I toted my duffel bag, now turned sixty, to your place. You didn't answer for an hour; when you did, it was not sleep in your eyes.

We didn't fight—it was too cold in your apartment for heated arguments. You didn't bother to say you were busy or forgot. Your father's only son had agreed to this visit. You had only stale bread, stingy swirls of peanut butter in a cold jar. You left with a promise to get food, and my last seven dollars.

I waited for you until dusk, then dragged my bag to a locked church. I put an extra ancient sweater under my coat and leaned against the chapel's small west wall. I watched the sky turn from mauve to black, and then fell asleep and dreamed of a time I carried you on my shoulders under a warm sun.

After the Light is Switched Off

Each night, the father would enter his boy's room—Bobby's tomb, he had come to call it—and turn the TV off. Before remotes, 24/7 programming and the infomercial, plump with desperate promises, the tube gave a final hail, the stars 'n stripes whipping, the national anthem screaming, and an anonymous promise to return tomorrow in a perfect world.

The world would not be perfect for Bobby, no matter how much thoughtless Thorazine, hazy Haldol, or mesmerizing Mellaril they shoved down his throat. Bobby would still be Bobby.

Now and then before flipping the knob to off he would sit with his sleeping son and stare into the screen, listening to its hissing. He would swear he saw something in the gray ocean of static. Not trillions of senseless photons busily bouncing, but a lone sailor, rowing away in a foaming sea, riding raging swells, bound for an abysmal black horizon, one his tormented son had reached long ago.

Easter on the Edge

Etched in my memory is a chair in the Rexall Drug, Easter eve. Me sitting on the edge of it, waiting, and the despairing look on my father's face while he too waited for some pill or potion to heal my big brother.

Sitting across from me, asleep, was a woman. I believe the oldest person in the world. Together we were half this lonely planet, my father and the apothecary the rest of its survivors. Every other soul was gone, perhaps snatched early by some unexpected rapture. Resurrection was nigh, but I was expecting only an egg hunt, and perchance a chocolate bunny.

Across the street, a church sat in silence, its steeple cross barely visible through the Rexall's glass door. Thunder echoed through the night, and for a flickering moment, it was daylight outside.

The druggist handed my father a small white paper bag, for which my father gave thanks. Dad said, "Let's go, David." Not "Bud" or "Podner," his normal appellations for me. And he didn't wait for me to get up. Even though it had begun to rain, Dad moved slowly through the lot to our parked car.

Every time I think of that night, I wonder who was born the next day to take my brother's place. Death I discovered, is not on a schedule. The doctors had said he had a year, maybe more. Gods don't explain themselves to men or monkeys, at least not to the mortals I know. Easter was a good day to die I guess, but if my brother thought so, he didn't say.

The Old Man by the Cove

The gale blew Bernardo a kilometer down shore from where he wanted to land. He was not concerned. This cove was fine. The rains and winds had stopped when he pulled his raft onto the sand. The full moon was now rising so it would be easy to reconnoiter the area and make his way back to where he needed to be.

The light would also make it easier for him to be seen. That did not concern Bernardo either. He had completed missions on moonlit nights before. Tonight, only one man, and an old one at that. Easy assignment.

Bernardo stashed his raft in thick brush and didn't bother to cover it. He would not be gone that long, he thought.

He walked through the jungle within sight of the beach. Bernardo knew the man would be in his hut by the cove where Bernardo had intended to land. In his hut, very likely asleep two hours before dawn.

Bernardo took only twelve minutes to make it to the other cove and the hut was exactly where he was told it would be—on the opposite side overlooking the gulf. From the hut, much of the cove was obscured from view, but the old man had a perfect vantage point from which to watch the sea and the waves break against the spine of rocks on the shore.

Bernardo swam across the cove. When he reached the other side, he was but twenty meters below the hut. The man must feel safe, Bernardo thought. Secure in this isolated house of mud and straw. Secure in his belief only his loyal, loving daughter knew where he was. Bernardo thought this man must feel safe most nights, alone and his belly full of fish.

But the old man's daughter was flesh, blood and bone, and Bernardo knew all creatures made of such could experience pain and death. And the old man's daughter had. Bernardo's associates had tortured her until she revealed her father's location, then led her believe they would grant her reprieve once they determined she was telling the truth. This was a common practice, as was the continued infliction of pain after the confession. So, the daughter was tortured again until her captors were convinced of the veracity of her revelation. Then they slit her throat.

Bernardo emerged from the water as slowly as the minute hand on a clock. He had been trained to move that way—silent, slithering from one spot to another. It took him longer to crawl the twenty meters up the acclivity than it had to swim across the cove. Bernardo snaked through the few feet of tall grass beside the hut and then stood by the bamboo door. He unsheathed his long knife, one he had used many times before. He pulled open the door and took one step in, cautious but confident the old man would be asleep on his cot.

Bernardo saw a flash of light and felt the agony of the pain where the bullet had gone through his kneecap. A light then shone on his face. Bernardo raised his knife to strike the figure he saw standing in the hut— the old man, as tall as Bernardo with a thick mane of white hair. A revolver in his right hand, a flashlight in his left. The old man fired again, the round hitting Bernardo in his hand. The knife dropped to the dirt floor. Another crack of the revolver and Bernardo fell to the ground, hot bullets now in both his knees.

The old man came to Bernardo, picked up the knife and threw it into the grass. Mi hija. Tú la mataste, the old man said.

No, Bernardo said. We didn't kill your daughter.

Mentiroso, liar, the old man said.

How do you know? Bernardo cried, How do you know?

I was one of you! the old man shouted. I was one of you.

The old man shot Bernardo dead center in each thigh, the rounds breaking his femurs. Then the old man said, Die slowly, asesino. Die slowly in this lonely place.

The old man fired the last cartridge into his own temple and fell on top of Bernardo. Bernardo tried to use his left hand to move the old man, but his strength waned. The old man's bleeding head was resting on Bernardo's sternum. With each labored breath, Bernardo saw the white mane, scarlet stained now, rise and fall, the dead old man's blood warm on Bernardo's heaving chest.

The Archer County pastures are dotted with trailers where meth is cooked, but "Killer" stuck to growing green weed from seed and let the roughneck rejects push the peppy powder.

Rumors blew across the prairies like tumbleweeds. One held he slit the throat of the youngest Baker boy, with a steak knife, for filching a half-grown plant, but Bobby Baker's body was never found, and a long hauler swore he saw Bobby in Midland, changin' oil and washin' rigs at a truck stop.

Then came another about an old man from Throckmorton County, who they said Killer shot through both knees for an insult, but nobody who went there for cattle auction ever could ID the man. Maybe crippled he had no steers. Maybe he was an oil man. Or gone.

Still, many men said he had done those deeds and more, not counting what he did in the war, though my own daddy said he got those medals for saving lives, not taking them. And a noisy night at the VFW dance, I heard a drunk driller call him "Doc," not "Killer."

I don't suppose we'll ever know the truth, for nobody has seen Killer in two dozen days; the old ranch house where he grew his crop is dark, and the plants chopped down or wilted dead.

I am sure another prickly rumor will blow in, filled with reckoning for some other imagined sin. Soon I bet we'll have a fine story about how Killer met his demise, a buzz of words to save the cabs of our pick-ups from dreadful silence, until another mortal man is made a legend. Most times, those tumbleweeds cross the road and skitter through the brush fast.

The Yellow Haze of the Sun

After dinner on the porch was the best time. He and grandpa would watch and wait for the storms. A thunderclap, the sweetest note to both.

Sheets of rain rolled across the big pasture. Downdrafts made the boy shiver, even cradled in the old man's arms. Neither spoke. Grandpa's good arm pointed and waved, these movements a code between generations. Theirs at least.

Finally, a twister appeared in the west, growing plumper as it spun across the fields, spitting gray dirt from its base, a zigzagging dancer without a care in the world. Grandma and Aunt Helen fled to the cellar, imploring the pair to follow.

They would not, for all their hours gazing at the heaving heavens would have been profligate had they hidden in the ground, missing creation's greatest crescendo. The angry funnel ate a section of fence wide as a football field and felled a tree not a quarter mile from the house—its roots too shallow, grandpa surmised.

When the tempest passed, the sun made an appearance, slipping between the cloud bank that birthed the tornado and the silent soil in the writhing devil's wake. In its final moments, the orb glared at the interlopers on the porch, perchance admonishing them the promise of its golden rays was no sacred contract, but only a fickle gift.

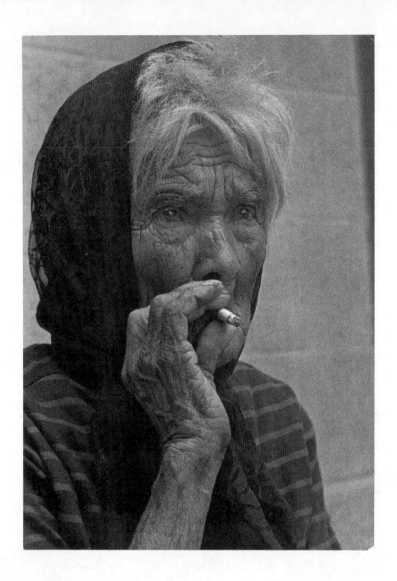

What Dolores Saw

She said her name was Dolores, and she demanded a cigarette and a dollar for me to photograph her. I had quit smoking and had to go to the Rexall Drug to buy a pack of Marlboros. I wondered if she would be there when I returned. She was, sitting on the same bench. I opened the Marlboro flip top to give her one and Dolores took the whole pack and said, "Dame el dinero tambien." I gave her the dollar.

Dolores said she was from Chihuahua where she had lived in Barranca del Cobre with the Tarahumara—the Indians indigenous to that region. Dolores was not Tarahumara but had married a Tarahumara man. Dolores told me her daughter, Alma, had moved to Juarez in 1963, a dozen years before I met her. Dolores had come with Alma because Dolores said she was too old to live in the canyon, the Barranca. The trails were too steep. Once, Dolores claimed, she had run fifty kilometers in the canyon. She was twenty then, married with a daughter and Dolores followed her husband and the other men on a run. Dolores said the men did not want her to come, but she followed anyway. Her husband forbade her to ever run with the men again, but he died a year later, falling drunk from a wall in the canyon.

That was during the Great War, Dolores said, and she was pregnant with her second daughter. The same year, her first daughter died of the influenza as did many people in her village. None of the surrounding villages had death visited upon them at the time. Dolores claimed it was because a brujo had placed a curse on her village, a spell that caused the maize to fail and the sickness to fall upon them, decimating them. She also claimed the jefe of the village was made to go blind by the curse—the brujo had told them all this would happen. The jefe lost his sight the same night the curse was placed upon them.

The brujo also said the men from the village would fall from the walls of the canyon. Dolores's husband and three others did. Only Dolores's husband had been drunk. The others fell because of the curse, Dolores believed. When I asked why the brujo had placed the curse on them, Dolores said she could never reveal this.

Dolores said she was seventy-seven, but the curse had made her age very quickly, causing her hair to become white before she was forty. I had no reason to doubt the veracity of her statement; she did look much older than her stated age.

Dolores was also convinced the curse made her daughter barren. Alma had been married to a man many years, but no children came from the union. The man left her and married another woman and had many children with his new wife.

Alma never remarried and was now working as a maid for rich gringos in El Paso. Alma stayed with them during the week and came back to Juarez each Saturday, often meeting Dolores at San Jacinto Plaza, where the bus dropped Alma. There, Dolores would sit for hours, an accomplished mendicant. When I first approached her to ask if I might photograph her, she showed me a hand full of silver coins she had obtained by begging. It was then we made the bargain for the cigarettes and the dollar.

I saw Dolores again a week after I photographed her. I offered her money to take her picture again. I had not yet developed the first one I had taken, but she refused. Dolores told me she had become ill the afternoon I had taken her picture and, in her dreams, that night, she had visions of me, my camera, and large ferocious cats. The afternoon after I photographed her, I had gone on assignment to the zoo to photograph lions the zoo had just received. Those shots were on the same undeveloped roll of film on which Dolores's image was stored.

During our second encounter, Dolores told me she awoke that morning knowing she would see me again. She said I carried a curse of my own, but she didn't know who had placed it upon me. Dolores revealed her waking vision of me that morning was one in which I had no legs.

I visibly gasped when she told me. When she saw me do this, she covered her face with her hands and said something unintelligible. I asked her what she said, and Dolores told me she had spoken the name of the brujo for the first time since the curse. The brujo had forbidden them from ever saying his name. Dolores had not until she saw my response when she said her vision was of me without legs. That morning, I had visited a friend, Bill Anderson, with whom I had served in Vietnam. On a patrol I missed because I had food poisoning, Bill took my place on point and had his legs shredded by a land mine. Both Bill's legs were amputated at the knee.

I asked Dolores if she was sure I was the one in the vision. Yes, she said, except Usted tiene barba. (You had a beard.) I was clean shaven, but Bill had a thick beard.

When I asked her if she saw anything else, Dolores covered her face with her ancient hands again and said death followed me closely. I asked her to explain what she meant, but she said she did not know. That afternoon, when I was driving home, I witnessed an accident in my rearview mirror. A black truck t-boned a VW bug at the intersection a block behind me. The driver of the VW was killed in the accident.

I never spoke with Dolores again. Months later, I did see her in the Plaza. She appeared to see me at the very same time. We turned and walked away from each other.

Locked in my safe, I do have the picture I took of her. I haven't shown it to anyone but Bill, and that was last year, the week before he died. I only then told him the story of what she said, forty years after the conversations with her.

I have never understood why, when I was in the dark room developing Dolores's picture a few days after my last conversation with her, not one of the photos of the lions turned out. Except the time I showed the photo to Bill, I have never looked at the photo of Dolores.

Talking on the Cell Phone and Wishing I Was Amish

I had one of the first—a clunky chunk of modernity in my 1984 Beamer. No speed dial, no contact book, and Bluetooth was as far away as the moon. But boy I was cool yapping while cruising down the PA Turnpike, my Lab on the seat beside me, eavesdropping and slobbering in equal measure.

The dog got to witness the end, the news delivered over the airways. She was dumping me because I was too needy: too many flowers, too many calls and unannounced visits, affection morphed into the smothering mother it could be.

I exited the pike with the news lumped in my throat, looking for a place to hide. A roadside stop with a view of farmed fields. The sun too bright. I dialed her number at least thrice, but never completed the call. The connection would have been dead or dying anyway.

In the distance, I saw their carriage: a procession with the clopping hooves of obedient beasts, the laughter of children, and monogamous men and women who didn't know the meaning of "co-dependency," "neediness," or "smothering," and eyes that would have stared in disbelief if they saw the damned cell phone.

Dirty Thief I Was

On the puke and blood painted walk in front of a Juarez whorehouse sat a blind mendicant, his cup half full of pesos, pennies and a grand FDR dime or two. Beside him a cur loused in lassitude, perhaps the personal, impotent Cerberus for this den of five-dollar iniquity.

Sixteen I was, an acute expatriate from a drunken El Paso house home, free to roam the streets of old Mexico, so long as I didn't wake any Policia or piss on the wrong curb.

An empty belly and nascent love of drink swung my moral compass from wobbly to dead down, and I filched the eyeless beggar's blue tin. He couldn't see, but the jingle jangle of his coins sliding into my pocket filled his old ears.

Ladron, ladron, cabron, he screamed. Thief, thief, dumbass.

The blind man's words trailed me down the alley into an avenue of neon noise, until I slipped into a bar, nouveau riche. My booty was better than a buck, so I ordered two beers and a double tequila, feeling fine until I smelled the dung of the dog, scribed penance in the grooves of my Keds, olfactory justice for stealing from the blind—a small price to pay for the riches of drunkenness, the sweet taste of oblivion.

Juarez, Mexico, 1965

Gentler Climes

In Ohio, Mother hung our laundry humming, clothespins in her mouth. In Texas, she made my father buy a dryer after angry wet sheets whopped her face more than one blustery afternoon.

Scarcely a score before, Panhandle winds were often roiling clouds, black as charcoal, laying waste to everything that grew and breathed. Old men at the feed store talked about the dusters from back then, and about every drop of rain, every white flake that fell.

I missed going barefoot and fast learned to hate goat heads and all thorny things that thrived in that flat land. Mother despised the hot winds almost as much as the cool stares she got from the church women whenever she opened her mouth, revealing she wasn't one of them. Mother ended her words with "ing," the extra consonant considered superfluous at best, blasphemous to some. In the Texas panhandle, men and women both sounded to me like they had grist from the silos in their mouths.

My father had lived there as a boy and swore he would never return, the dreaded dust still clinging to his clothes when he left for the war. Oil money brought him back but only long enough for his skull to be cracked dead by hard pipe.

His insurance settlement bought us a place in the Buckeye State as quick as the lid flapped shut on our mailbox. Mother wept little until our first night back in Ohio, when a blizzard knocked out the lights, and our two candles burned flat in the cold. My uncle brought bread, butter and warm soup, which we ate in the gloom while Mother told my father's favorite brother how much we loved the Texas sun.

Columbus, 1958

Terry Cotton had never imagined himself a tracker. A horseman, which he wasn't. A soldier, which he was for only four months before being booted out, but not a tracker, until that Tuesday on the hiking trail when he followed the blood. Fresh. Drops a few feet apart, evenly separated as if whatever beast was leaving its mark there was pumping the crimson cream out in cadence with its heart.

The sun was hanging low when Terry spotted the blood, yet there was enough light for anyone to see the blood was fresh. Terry followed it for at least a hundred meters on the trail and when he no longer saw it on the main trail, it was easy to see on a narrower path that led to the river. From his vantage point, the path was visible until it reached the thick stands of trees by the river.

Terry followed the dirt trail down, still tracking the blood. All the way until he reached the river, he saw the spots. Terry eased himself down the bank to the river's edge. Then he saw her about twenty paces from him. The petite woman. Fair skinned with a thick shock of blonde hair, wearing jean shorts and a baby blue tee shirt. One side of the shirt, her shorts, and one of her legs painted red with her blood. She must be weak Terry, thought. How is she even alive with all that blood?

On the narrow strip between the river and the brush, Terry walked towards the woman. Her eyes were closed; she was holding her side and breathing heavily. Terry thought he saw movement in the brush across the river. He paused long enough to reconnoiter the area. Nothing. Terry took a few more steps towards the woman, watching the other side of the river. Then he saw movement again—a deer coming down through the brush to the water. Terry and the deer were motionless, the two looking at one another. The doe dropped its head and lapped water from the river.

Terry then took the last few steps and stood in front of the woman. Her eyes opened, then fluttered shut. Her breathing was steady but shallower. Terry knelt and leaned close enough to her smell her. Alcohol. Sweat. Blood. The smell of the tequila and the sweat were stronger than the iron scent of the blood, Terry thought.

Terry glanced back at the doe. It was still on the bank. Not drinking but looking straight at Terry and the young woman. Terry picked up a small branch and threw it in the direction of the animal. As it hit the water a few feet from the deer, the doe startled, turned and went back up the bank to the thick brush from which she had come. Good, Terry thought, I don't like it watching.

Terry gently took hold of the woman's hair with his left hand and pulled her head back. With his glove covered right hand, he tapped the side of her face, now even fairer as the blood drained from her. He didn't say a word. He hadn't said a word since she had jumped from the big log on which they had been sitting and drinking Cuervo Tequila. Only the best for her, Terry recalled her saying. He tapped her face again, harder. He thought he saw her eyes open again, but the light of dusk was fast fading and so was the woman. Terry grew tired of kneeling and her body was becoming harder to see. He placed his hand over her mouth and nose and held it there. Her legs, which had been bent at the knees, stretched out straight and moved as if she were walking, but only a few seconds. She was too weak. Soon, she was still and not breathing.

Terry pulled off her shorts and tee shirt, being careful not to get blood on his own clothes. Her panties were covered in blood as well, though the bra had only a little on the cup of the right breast, just above where Terry had stabbed her. He knew to stab on that side. The left side was too close to the heart and would kill too fast. Terry always wanted time with them after. After he did what he was supposed to do.

He looked around in the gray dusk. All alone. The doe nowhere to be seen. He pulled off her drenched panties. Then he slipped the straps of her bra down around her slender arms, pausing before pulling the bra down and exposing her breasts. When he took the garment completely off, he could barely see her small pink nipples. Terry kissed each several times before he began the suckling.

Always the same, but she had been easy, Terry thought. From the time he picked her up hitchhiking, she had been easy. She had stayed in his van when he bought the Cuervo she asked for. She walked with him off the trail to the log where they sat and drank until she was drunk. She sat close and rubbed his leg while they downed the tequila and laughed. It was easy when they were closer, Terry had learned. Terry was surprised how hard she had hit his face when he stabbed her, but he had been hit harder.

Terry knew he shouldn't have taken time to bury the knife after he stabbed her. It gave her a good head start, but he knew she would not get far. Not to the highway. She had headed for the river. Just running and not knowing where she was going, Terry figured.

Easy. All he had to do now was toss the clothes and the young woman into the river. With some of the others, he had to dig deep holes, or drag them a great distance. After the clothes floated downstream, Terry stared at the woman for a while. Even in the gathering gloom, she still looked so young. He rolled her into the river, its flow swift enough to pull her from his sight in a less than a minute.

He removed his gloves and tossed them into the water. He counted on his bare fingers now, saying their names if he knew them. One, Mary, two, the black chick, three, Estrella, until he got to eight. Sadie. Eight women. Eight pairs of gloves. Goodbye Sadie, Terry said aloud as he turned to hike up to the bluff.

As he made his way on the trail, it was too dark to see the blood, though he tried. A tracker he was now. A good one, he thought. But this had been easy.

California, 1970

His ancestor, a coolie, laid the rails many long years but returned to Peking to fight white devils. This was the tale passed through the generations with the jade necklace which never left his mother's neck.

First born son and spawn of two doctors; expectations were high he would practice honorable healing arts. Early in his years he fueled their fears, and ire, coming through their sterile door with bloodied knuckles, black eyes, fat lips.

They tried various exorcisms: confinement in the temple, lashings and hushed cabals with head healers, but none could shrink his will. Much to their dismay Stanford rejected him. He landed at a community college, where he spent an indolent year before vanishing.

A thousand tears and fears later the PI revealed what a hundred billable hours had reaped. Their son was so far west he was east, in a village on the Yangtze, stooped over paddies, his feet firm in the mire the generations had yearned to escape.

Jack and the Banyan Tree

A refugee from wealth, he and his Dartmouth degree found the spot farthest from his New England roots, and the first roots he saw there were those of a banyan tree, giant gray tentacles clinging to the Asian earth, imploring the black soil for atonement, he thought.

The natives said the tree was older than God immortal but cursed with some blight that bedeviled them and prudent pruning of ailing arms would be wise. The young man had only a Swiss Army knife with its minuscule saw, but soon he set about the task of trimming the behemoth, one mad millimeter at a time, and mad was all the natives saw.

This white wingless creature, high in the canopy, often from dawn until the sun sank in the jungle behind him, sawing away, a half branch a day, treating the gargantuan arboreal like a prize bonsai.

Villagers would come, hunker, watch in the shade of the tree. Once in a great while, they would see a branch crash on the ground, at which time they cheered the pitifully patient woodsman. Even during monsoon rains, the man's labors did not desist, though his audience waned.

Many offered to help, some leaving bow saws, axes at the banyans' base, but he would have none of that. Over and over he received new red knives with their tiny saws—these parcels the only mail he got.

Appearing to defy physics' enigmatic laws, the tree was nearly felled, but the man disappeared before his colossal task was done, the locals claiming he climbed into the thinned canopy one day and never came down. Not even a well-worn blade was found, allowing the witnesses to aver he was yet high in the heavens resting after love's labor had wearied his hands and perchance healed his heart.

The Short Life of Walter Smallshadow

Walter Smallshadow eschewed the label, "Native American," for he was Injun, and he wasn't ashamed he liked his spirits. Dollar wine worked as well.

Cirrhosis was a family trait, though he didn't learn the word until an army doc admonished him, saying he would earn the curse by forty-five, if he kept it up. And Walter did, even more after that crazy Asian war, where he killed a dozen men they called yellow. Though to Walter, they looked to be his emaciated brown cousins.

Walter could stand tall and straight with a pint of rot gut in him, burning his belly, but not causing his head to spin, though it helped him block them out: those he did not know; those he slaughtered like lambs with the gun they issued him; those who inhabited a space just behind his eyes whenever they closed, night or day.

Someone found him, in his pickup bed, dead from exposure, from too many years on the bottle, too many dreams he tried to drown. And too many ghosts to haunt his nights.

Gallup, New Mexico, 1999

The Buffalo Cafe

No bison on the menu at the Buffalo. This diner never served it. Big Mike, long gone, named it for the high shelf on the prairie behind it, where Lakota learned to stampede bison over the edge, massacring hordes of the beasts without bow or sweat.

The gully below, their forgotten bone yard, left little trace of them, save half a skull Mike exhumed. This he hung on the wall in the time of polio, before the wide whizzing interstates, when truckers still landed on his dusty lot, their rolling behemoths content in pasture.

In a new millennium, the state highway cafe is but an accidental detour. The shack now guarded by thistles. Long departed the Detroit steel. The truckers now in the ground also, their bones free from pillage, but the Buffalo Cyclops on the wall remains, eyeing the vacant prairie they all once roamed.

Torches in the Woods*

I kept quiet as a mouse. Soppy did too. We stayed snake close to the ground in the tall grass.

We didn't hear no hounds, but that didn't mean them dogs weren't there. Soppy and I had done what old lady Lucinda said—waded in the deep creek a good hour to leave them curs nothin' to sniff

With my one clear eye I could see them flames bobbin' up and down, like gold ghosts in the willows. The air smelled like rain. I prayed real hard it would come down and drown out them fires. That would be one mighty sign the good Lord heard my prayers and took pity on us. Soppy, me and whatever other souls hid in the devil's dark, watchin' the flames, fearin' they meant eternal damnation.

*The phrase "torches in the woods" comes from a quote by Harriet Tubman.

Betty's Steps

Betty was 79 in 2008 when she walked the 1.3 miles to the church where she had voted in every election since 1966. When Betty arrived at the Church at 4:39 PM, over two hours before polls closed, she discovered the Church was no longer a voting location. A youth pastor was there, and Betty asked why they didn't have voting machines. He said the location was one of three closed in the previous year.

Betty asked the pastor where she could vote. The pastor said he did not know and asked if she had a cell phone. He told Betty she could look up her location on the internet. Betty explained she had a cell phone her granddaughter gave her, but she sure didn't know how you could get in the internet with it. Betty only knew how to get on the internet at the free computers at the library. The pastor pulled his iPhone from his pocket and asked Betty's address. Within a minute the young man had the information. He told Betty she voted at Shelton Elementary school. Her grandson, Terence, had attended that school.

Terence had been gone a year. Killed in that Iraqi war. His daddy, Eddy, Betty's oldest, had been luckier. Eddy came back from Vietnam only missing two fingers on his right hand. And something else. Something else Betty couldn't define. Something deep inside lost, Betty thought.

Betty said that school is a long way and the bus doesn't go from here to there. The pastor said he would be glad to take her, but his car was in the shop and he was going to spend the night at the church.

Betty thought about calling a cab, but she had given most of her cash to Eddy. She made him promise to not buy beer and to buy the cheapest dog food for his pit bull. Betty thought he might follow her advice about the generic dog food, but she guessed he would spend plenty on tobacco and Budweiser. The VA gave him a small check each month but that went for rent and who knows what. His ex-wife and Terence's widow got some money when Terence died, but Eddy got nothing.

Betty began the two-mile trek to the school where she had gone to PTA performances fifteen years earlier. When Terence was there, young and full of hope.

The rain started again as soon as Betty began walking. Her umbrella protected her face and upper torso, but the angled downpour was drenching her from the waist down. The farther Betty walked, the deeper the water got on the sidewalks; when she would cross a street, there were places she was trudging in water almost to her ankles. Betty was glad she had worn a warm coat, but her legs were very cold and becoming stiff.

Betty's mother had never voted. Betty remembered her mother telling her when they moved back to Georgia from Tennessee in 1956, she had tried to vote for President Eisenhower in 1952, but after she walked through a freak snow storm to the polling station, she was told she didn't have the proper identification. Her mother had told her a white person walked into to the same place, exchanged greetings with the polling officials and filled out a ballot without showing anybody anything. Betty determined then she would always have the proper identification. Always.

Now, it was even more important. A black man running for President. And the papers said he might win. Praise Jesus, Betty thought. If a black man could do that. Praise the Lord.

Worn out from the walk, Betty took a break. Ever conscious of the time, she knew her respite would be brief. Sitting on a park bench, looking through the gray torrents of rain, she rubbed her cold stiff legs. A large oak gave Betty scant protection from the storm. Her great Uncle Ely had been lynched from just such an oak. Why her granny told her the variety of the tree when she told the terrible story was a mystery to Betty. An oak. A Red Oak.

Onward, Betty said to herself. Her legs and feet ached with every step, but she kept going. Only another two blocks. She looked at her watch—6:35.

The rain let up and only a cold drizzle fell when Betty arrived at the school. 6:56 according to her watch she had synchronized with the time on the TV. The double doors at the entrance were locked. Betty looked through glass plates on the doors and saw a school clock that said 6:57. She began pounding on the door first with her fist and then with the curled wooden end of her umbrella handle. Betty could see three voting booths and two women sitting at a table in front of them. The women were drinking coffee and talking. Betty rapped harder on the door with her umbrella. At 6:59, one of the women walked over and opened the door. By the time Betty was inside, the woman said they had just closed, pointing to the clock on the wall which now read straight up 7:00. We haven't had a soul in the last half hour—the storm.

Betty said, I have always been a civil woman, but I come through Noah's flood to get here. I will vote or be carried out of here by the police.

We turned off the machines, the woman said.

Then turn them back on. I was here at 6:56. Betty said as she pointed to the clock and then to a security camera at the entrance. You want me to get proof you closed early? Betty asked.

The other woman, who had remained seated, said, Please show us your voter registration card and we'll take care of you.

Betty, shivering, mad, and exhausted said, I don't need to be taken care of. I been doin' that my whole life. All I need from you is a ballot, so I can help elect the first black man President.

The women were silent. Betty handed her state ID and her voter registration card to the seated woman who did not make eye contact but found Betty's name on a list, had her sign and handed her a ballot.

Betty strode as upright as she could to the booth. She cast her vote and walked toward the exit. The woman who had let Betty in said, Ma'am, your umbrella. Betty had left it leaning against the table leg where the voting officials sat.

The other woman said she had forgotten hers that morning and this was not a good day to be without one, especially as far away as she had parked.

Betty said thank you and picked up her umbrella. As she was opening the door to leave, she saw the rain had picked up again. She returned to the table and handed the woman the umbrella. For that walk to your car, Betty said.

Betty turned and walked out the door without looking at the women. She stood under the small overhang at the school entrance and called a cab. Ten minutes later, Betty was in the cab with a driver who may have been as old as she. The driver said he had been taking folks to and from voting stations all day. Said he didn't usually work Tuesdays but volunteered as soon as the forecast predicted rain.

Good Lord, he said, we are going to have a black President. Time was I couldn't vote in this town or carry white people in my cab.

Betty said only one thing. It took a lotta steps to get here, didn't it?

When Betty tried to hand the man the fare, he refused. Been taking folks for free all day. A good day to help other folks, he said. Betty and the driver clasped each other's hands.

Betty smiled and pulled her weary body from the taxi. She made herself black coffee and turned on the TV. She could not recall feeling more exhausted, but Betty remained awake until Barack Obama and his family walked off the stage after his speech.

The rains stopped. In her warm bed, Betty looked through her window at a few stars shining in a gap in an otherwise cloud shrouded night.

Half Light

In the hall, I listen as she calls out his name, not aware I am there, nor would she care. If I open the door without making a sound, I purloin a few seconds to watch her before she sees me. When her eyes catch mine, she looks away.

The morning sun makes a sympathetic effort to light our room. "Our" room which from which I have been excommunicated. The drapes she sewed only last summer are never open.

That is her world, staring through baby blue curtains which mute the half-light of morning, though not enough. Not enough to blind her to the spot where our son's crib waited, until I committed the unpardonable sin of taking it to the cold cellar, only a fortnight after our stillborn child was placed in the ground.

The Seine does not run red. Eiffel still stands, though both the river and the tower a million miles farther from our hotel than they were at our last meal.

Had we not had a cancelled cruise, we would be listening to blue waves' soft song in Nice. Not now. Instead, we hear the sirens' cacophony—premature dirges for the dead, wails of the maimed, yet unnamed.

Tomorrow, their biographies will be in print, their families numb in disbelief, longing for relief and wishing numbers could be reversed: 11-13-15, 9-11-01, 12-07-41, or perhaps AD plus one. When will this end, and how much farther from Eve's curious breach must we fall?

Nighthawks and the Youngest Man at Iwo Jima

Inspired by Edward Hopper's Nighthawks

Aunt Gracie took me for a Philly and nickel cigar. I spun my stool like I was on a carnival ride (had one beer with Uncle Lon—the first is the best). Gracie looked at me like I was still the kid who broke her window with a bad pitch when I was ten.

Big, round, Gracie looked like she was gonna cry. She signed those papers, making me old enough to be a killer.

The couple eating omelets asked if I was shipping out.

Six AM. Yessir.

The man nodded. Kill a Jap for me

Yes Sir. I saluted.

Killing one of those Japs wouldn't be any different from playin' God with birds, which I had done a time or two with my Daisy.

The cook put my Philly on the counter. He was in that diner, forever, feeding me and other nighthawks who came there.

That's free, he said, but the man eatin' eggs said it's on me.

The cook limped to his sink. I asked how he got hurt. He kept his eyes on his pans.

Was a long time before this night.

Were you born that way?

Nobody born this way.

Seventeen and a day, full of one beer, I kept askin.'

How...?

Was a long time ago. Guess you'll know soon enough. We were crawling from a trench filled with gas and gasps of boys with your face when those gunners cut loose. I got some good luck and one of those rounds in my knee.

Gracie put her hand on mine.

You got shot in the Great War?

He didn't say anymore. I didn't eat.

Gracie wrote but we didn't always get mail on those big ships. Many men would leave their suppers on the floor in a sea of seasick. They taught me poker, told me jokes, gave me Lucky Strikes.

We were going to some place, Ee-wa Gee-ma. At night, I would close my eyes and see someplace green, Ee-wa, sunny, Gee-ma. With trees and birds for my Daisy to shoot. Sometimes, in that stale stink of puke, I would see the light of the diner and would think how Gracie begged me to confess my sins to the recruiter. To stay home.

After that, I heard only voices of men, some barking commands, others whispering in the dark of the hull. Then I saw grey rocks and flak-filled sky, heard the swoosh of surf, the thunder of our ships' guns and rat-tat-tat from invisible holes.

Happy, we called him, was dead. Nineteen years of him on that shithole beach. Guts strewn across the sand making peace with crabs and the black blood of other boys who played cards and flipped open Zippos to light my smokes and laced their boots with me that very morning.

The ramp dropped. We fell into the Pacific and ran to the dunes to hide, but only long enough to breathe, smell cordite, fear-sweat, and burned flesh. Twenty of us headed for a boulder no bigger than Lon's '36 coupe. By the time we crouched behind it, only eight were left. The others were where? I didn't care. I had my piece of rock, rounds poppin' off it from those invisible holes filled with slant-eyed demons.

I heard the corporal say put fire on that hole.

What hole? The words were stuck somewhere, inside, not in my throat, but they were there trying to ask him. What hole?

The corporal again said put fire on that hole. When he got up to shoot his M-1, something made his helmet fly off and most of him went to the ground—the part that didn't go out the back of his head.

Tommy, Tommy who taught me a full house beats a straight, grabbed my arm and said, OVER THERE.

I saw them, one with a tan helmet, the other with a shiny black hair. Tommy was pointing his M-1 at those Japs who were firing their 92-machine gun at boys on the beach. I pointed my M-1 at them too. My hands were shakin' too bad to aim. Tommy and I both kept shootin' at those Japs who finally looked like they went to sleep, but they never woke up. Neither did the other boys who were hiding behind that rock, because as soon as Tommy and I started shootin' at those Japs, they turned that 92 on us. Those boys were in front of us, pressed so tight against that stingy rock they couldn't move enough to turn their M-1s. So, when those Japs aimed that 92 at us Tommy and I were in the right place behind five poor boys who got their bodies peppered with every round that came from that hot barrel.

Once those Jap boys were asleep, I felt something warm on my arm. Blood from Hector's face, but Hector didn't have a face. But I didn't look. Hector wore a Saint Christopher to keep him safe. Hector didn't lose all his head like Saint Christopher, but that pendant and all his mama's prayers didn't save him.

I don't remember when I could sleep through a night without wakin' up, shivering, seeing Hector and those boys behind the rock. There were other rocks where boys went to sleep and didn't wake up feeling Hector's warm blood before it got cold, dry, and black.

Gracie told me the diner closed. Now, when I can't sleep and walk the pavement in the night, I go to that café looking for the light. I want my cigar. I want to hear words the limping man spoke. I don't have any more questions he won't want to answer. If I did, they might be stuck inside, deep, where things churn but don't ever get heard.

I wonder if those other boys at all those rocks are taking night walks, or if they talked with a man who fed them for free, who thought he was lucky, and spoke words no young eager bird killers could yet understand.

He lay in a bed at the Salvation Army, in a last row of bunks he knew well. Through the window, he heard birdsong. Not the lugubrious refrain of mourning dove, but a song he did not recognize. Sad nonetheless.

The Captain brought him ice chips and let him stay, for he knew this was the closest thing to home the old man had. This and a spot under the bridge he shared with bats, most springs, summers and autumns until the first frost.

Never again would he be outside. Never again would he see the bridge. Never again would he leave this bed.

How nice to have music in your final hours, he thought. How nice to have a bed and pillow to rest his head. Outside the window, sitting cross legged on winter's dead grasses, a girl played her flute, unaware of the audience she entertained. She was young enough to be his granddaughter, but was not, for his only child had died of white blood cancer when she was nine.

In all his years he'd heard myriad birds' song, chanting chirps wedded to the winds, winsome, but not like today's trilling. What he now heard faintly, as if through warm water, soothed him, lulled him closer to a deep sleep, one he knew would come soon enough.

He did not fight it. Take a nap he thought. When he woke, the lullaby would still be there, white winged creatures would yet make song, though now in great flight, far from this bed.

BCD-2468

The plate, BCD-2468, was pressed into service by men chasing their own vanishing souls. Back then, the hollow men at Folsom made 30,000 a day.

BCD-2468 was put on a 1979 Ford Pinto, a graduation gift from parents to Manuel, a son they expected to attend UCLA that fall. The twin plates BCD-2468 were on the new car only a month before Manuel, filled to the brim with hope and promise the day he got the car, took his life. Manuel used the same gun with which he killed his best friend, Steve, twenty hours before he put it to his own temple, in his shiny new white Pinto he had driven into a ditch in the desert north of El Paso, 750 miles from his Fullerton home.

Steve's death was an accident. Everyone would swear to that, but everyone at the graduation party where it happened was drunk. And Manuel knew someone dying at your hand when you were drunk had to have consequences. His own cousin was on probation for negligent homicide because she drove her VW into the rear of an idling truck, killing her passenger and disfiguring herself. Had it not been for the fire that ravaged her beautiful face, the judge would have made her do hard time.

Manuel imagined the worst possible outcome, especially since he fled the scene after he killed Steve. He drove east into the night and stopped for gas in Blythe. There, Manuel called his former girlfriend, Teresa. She had been at the party and saw what happened. On the phone, Teresa did not ask where he was; she said the police had arrived a few minutes after Manuel left. Teresa said the people at the party who were there when the police arrived—about half had fled she claimed—were confused when they talked to the police. She said she wasn't sure the cops understood the shooting was an accident. When she told Manuel this, he hung up.

Manuel drove into the mountains of southeastern Arizona. He found a roadside park and lay on a picnic table while the sun came up. He stayed in the park, hungover and thirsty, until mid-morning. Manuel had seen a phone booth at the truck stop where he filled up. He wanted to call his parents but did not. Too much fear, too much shame, too much guilt.

While Manuel was driving the dead stretch of desert between Indio and Desert Center, Steve's Uncle Bob was working his shift at Folsom. He would not know until the afternoon, when Manuel was breaking the New Mexico border, that his nephew had died. Manuel knew Bob was tough and mean spirited and Manuel had wondered what Bob's response would be when he heard about Steve.

Bob had worked at Folsom ten years and he had learned he could supplement his corrections officer salary by bringing inmates drugs. His shift supervisor was also involved and that cut into Bob's profit. Still, Bob's "shitty job bonus" made his truck payment each month. The day Steve was shot was a good day for supplemental income—Bob had smuggled some meth in and sold it to Fabian, inmate 667893, who had, earlier that spring, been the one to stamp out plates BCD 2468.

From the early morning hours after the party until dark, Manuel's parents had been talking to the police, two lawyers, and a judge who was a first cousin to Manuel's father's boss. They were hopeful—it looked as if the worst that Manuel would be charged with was unlawful possession of a firearm. Steve had actually sold Manuel the gun when Steve needed money for tires on his '67 Mustang. The fact that the weapon came from Steve was a mitigating factor the courts would consider. Steve had also asked Manuel to bring the gun to the party. Why he did was unclear— what was clear was the gun went off when Manuel was handing it to Steve, the bullet going directly into Steve's heart.

This occurred in front of two witnesses by the pool in the backyard of the home where the party was held. The owner of the home was in Phoenix, not expected back until early in the morning. The owner filled his tank at the station in Blythe where Manuel had called Teresa— he turned into the station as Manuel pulled out. The man knew Manuel. His daughter had gone to school with Manuel since sixth grade. He thought it was Manuel he saw pulling out but decided it must have been someone who looked like Manuel. Why would Manuel be in Blythe at 2:00 AM?

Manuel wound through the Gila Wilderness before heading south towards El Paso. There he might look for a lawyer. He might turn himself in. Manuel never made it to the city limits. He swerved to avoid a coyote crossing the highway and drove into an arroyo. There, he took the gun from under the seat and pressed it against his temple. The decision to pull the trigger took an eternity—at least 30 seconds, during which time he saw four faces: his mother's, his father's, Steve's and his own in the rearview mirror. The car was still running when Manuel died, front plate BCD-2468 embedded in the Permian stone on the side of the ravine where he crashed.

The Watch and the Shell

Orlando wanted to leave his pocket watch to his grandson, Jimmy. Little time was left. Orlando was in and out. When awake, he reminded his daughter, Patty, Jimmy must have the watch.

The watch had been given to Orlando by his uncle Fernando on Orlando's sixteenth birthday in 1942. Fernando was his father's younger brother and had been like a father to Orlando. Orlando's father drowned drunk when Orlando was ten. Fernando joined the Navy the week he gave Orlando the watch. Fernando made it through the war without a scratch, though he wasn't as lucky when he returned to New York, dying of pneumonia before he was 30.

Patty would never tell her father the pocket watch, which Fernando won in a poker game, had been pawned by her brother, Paco. Like his grandfather, Paco was a drunk. Paco didn't remember where he pawned the watch. And Paco was three weeks in to a six-month stint in County. Patty knew the watch was gone for good.

Fernando didn't recall the name of the man who wagered the watch, but on the back was engraved, "Good Luck Jimmy." Even without the inscription, Orlando would have wanted the watch to go to his grandson. Jimmy knew of his grandpa's pocket watch, but never did Orlando tell him it was his intention to give it to him.

Orlando worked for the transit authority from 1947 until he was forced to retire in 1996. He wanted to make the half century mark, but his eyes had become too bad for him to continue. Now, five years later, his diabetes driven glaucoma had blinded him completely.

Each day for 49 years, Orlando carried the watch to work. It was important to know the time when you worked for the subway, Orlando said. When Orlando retired, he placed the watch in his bedroom chest of drawers. Patty was determined he would never know Paco later purloined and pawned the watch.

Jimmy's father never married his mother, and Patty had been with Jimmy's father only a few weeks a dozen years before. Patty and Jimmy lived with Orlando in Brooklyn. Orlando was father and grandfather to Jimmy.

Even though it was a school day, Patty allowed Jimmy to come with her to Hospice that morning. Patty knew the end was near and wanted Jimmy to be with his grandfather.

When they arrived just before 8:00 AM, Orlando was awake. I have been waiting for you, Orlando said. The watch, Orlando said.

Patty said it was safe in his chest of drawers. Orlando waved a hand in the air and said Jimmy, come here. Jimmy came to him and placed Orlando's hand on his face.

Do you remember your great Uncle Fernando's watch with your name on it? Orlando asked.

Yes, Jimmy said. I love that watch Grandpa.

I want you to have it. It will bring you good luck, Orlando said.

Jimmy kissed his grandfather on the forehead and said, thank you. I love you Grandpa.

Patty kissed Orlando on his cheek. She and Jimmy pulled chairs up to the bed and each held one of Orlando's hands. Orlando closed his blind eyes. His breaths became more labored. In an hour, Orlando was gone.

Patty told Jimmy to get the nurse. When the RN arrived, she checked Orlando, noted time of death, 8:44 AM, and told Jimmy and Patty she was sorry for their loss. The nurse looked through the window towards the Manhattan skyline and a strange expression came over her face. Then the nurse said, let me call for a doctor to come to make the official pronouncement.

Patty went to the side of the bed where Jimmy sat and hugged him. They both kissed Orlando on the cheek and told him they loved him. Patty went to the window and saw smoke coming from one of the World Trade Center towers.

Jimmy remained by his grandfather's side and asked, what are you looking at Mom?

Patty said, I see smoke from—

What Mom? From where? Patty had seen a second plane plow into the other tower. She kissed her grandfather a final time and led Jimmy from the room.

That evening, after watching the news for most of the day, Patty prepared a meal. When they sat at the table, Patty began sobbing. Jimmy got up and held her—it's alright Mom.

Both had tears in their eyes much of the day, but the attacks had distracted them. Neither had broken down—they were more in shock over the events of the day than they were over Orlando's passing, a loss for which they had time to prepare.

I am not crying because he is gone, Patty said. Well, I am, but there is something I need to tell you. The pocket watch, the watch your grandfather wanted you to have. It's gone. Paco sold it. I am sorry Jimmy. Patty held Jimmy tightly. I am so sorry.

Jimmy kissed his mother's hair and said, I will be right back.

Jimmy loved swimming and many sunny summer weekends, Patty had taken him to the beach. There, they collected shells. When they came upon larger shells, they would play a game, imagining the shells had stories to tell. When they found a good-sized conch, they would press it to their ear and the other would ask, what did the shell say? Often Patty would say, This shell says it's time to go home. Jimmy would always respond with This shell says it's time to swim some more. These exoskeletons became time keepers for mother and son—calcium carbonate hosts for the sound of the sea and the ghosts of the mollusks who once inhabited them.

Jimmy returned with a shell they both loved because it was nearly a perfect circle. Jimmy put the shell to his ear and asked his mother what she thought the shell was saying.

I don't know. Maybe it is saying I love you.

Well yes, that, Mom, but also it is telling me this will be our watch from Grandpa. If we have shells to keep the time, we don't need the watch. Maybe his silver watch is with another Jimmy now.

Like millions that night, Patty and Jimmy watched the news— their tears a mixture for the loss of Orlando and a thousand anonymous faces. When they went to bed, Jimmy placed the shell on his night stand, but not without putting his ear to it a final time, listening for the breath of the sea—believing somewhere in the phantom wind sounds he heard the voice of his grandfather saying goodnight.

Cedar Rapids

Flung in the back of the '55 Chevy like another suitcase, the child knew not where they were going, only that they had been there before, more than once, when Daddy's drink turned to anger, and anger turned to fists pounding a boss and another job was lost.

And the child would again see the lights of the town vanish, He, the car, his preternaturally silent momma, and his hungover father would become part of the night. Another flight, this time from Gallup New Mexico, where Daddy had tried to out drink every Navajo in every bar and almost did.

On these nocturnal hegiras, the child would lie and stare at the headliner—the round dome light a faint moon against a mysterious sky. Beams from passing cars would roll across his otherwise empty constellation, transforming dark matter into fleeting nebulae.

This, his wide world, while a slow clock spun, and tires hummed, eternally, until his father announced where they were going this time. Iowa, a place the child conflated with Ohio, vowel sounds similar, soft and more meaningful than marks on maps—Cedar something...

Cedar Rapids, and the child knew rapid and rapid meant fast and fast meant soon, only a few more saturnine stars around his dome light moon. Soon.

East of Gallup, New Mexico, 1960

Letting go of Harriet

He took the cliché sabbatical when his wife died, careening through the Rockies to the jagged Pacific coast, seeing old lovers along the way, ending in Iowa with his daughter's family. Flat lands, with no ups and downs, surprise turns, or fatal strokes.

There his grief was level. His daughter was of strong faith, and his granddaughter young enough to yet see heaven in blue sky. Mornings after Cheerios, his grandchild would lead him around the section, edifying him about the livestock, their purpose. She introduced him to Hazel, her pet pig.

He couldn't help but think of his Harriet, and if the consonant and vowel were coincidental or a contrivance of a child's supple mind. His granddaughter spoke of Grammy Harriet with sublime ease, absent the halting staccato utterances of adults when they mentioned his dead wife's name. After all, his grandchild saw his wife as a whiff of passing cloud in clear azure sky, or in the glint of moonlight on the pond.

Soon it came time to say goodbye to the hog, who had been with the child a sixth of her years. But the child knew this was the way of things—feeding and fondling new beings, watching them grow, becoming cautious when their mass exceeded your own, when the beasts began to look away.

It was then it was time all God's creatures would lose footing, even in this flat place, and go to sleep. Though the child would not forget Hazel or Harriet, for the former was on the table, sizzling and succulent, and the latter on the mantel, framed in gold, smiling with eyes open.

Blue to Black

Matt stopped in a ghost town in west Texas. Shells of three buildings remained. A post office closed since the 70s. A one room school house that hadn't heard a child's voice in a generation. One wall of a church burnt black by vandals some desert night.

Matt parked behind the church wall and lay in the bed of his pick up under a million stars he could not name. The full moon was snow white.

A world away, on his patio in El Paso, his wife, Ramona, watched the same sky. Only a third as many stars were in her sights, muted as they were by the light from the city.

Ramona drank a glass of wine, her fourth that night. On the road, Matt had drunk coffee. He wanted to stay awake. To avoid dreams. For in sleep the thoughts returned. Every night for a month. When Matt's eyes closed, he saw Colby's face.

In Matt's dreams Colby's face was more vivid—even more than the photo of him Matt kept in his wallet. All photos in the house had been buried in drawers.

Matt had downed a pint of vodka the night after the incident. Still he saw his face. Ramona had been drinking wine like water. She said it helped. The counselor suggested her doctor medicate her. Ramona scoffed at the idea.

Ramona claimed she hadn't dreamt at all. Though she slept all the time. Matt fought Morpheus' grip with all his will. He slept little. But the dreams. They came.

Dreams of water. Blue at first, then black. Recurring. Blue water becoming black. Impenetrable. Then Colby's face. Round. Pink. Alive.

Ramona poured another glass of wine. She called Matt's number for the twentieth time that night. Over and over, she texted him the same five words: where are you? come home.

But Matt could not go home. He left three nights ago. After. After Ramona tried to talk to him and he threw a patio table onto the tarp that covered the pool since a week after it happened. The pool service had made the tarp taut. The table did not sink when it landed near the edge of the cerulean canvass. Instead, each night, a little of the tarp would give way under the weight of the table. Like a growing thing, this slow dreadful sinking. A lifeless forged metal circle, legs pointing to the heavens. In the same spot Colby had been found. Drowned. The day before his fifth birthday.

Ramona fell asleep on the lawn chair after glass number seven. A dreamless sleep.

Matt climbed from his truck and walked to the ruins of the school. Among cool moon shafts, he saw part of a blackboard hanging askew on the wall. What was the last thing scratched there with ancient calcium carbonate, he wondered? Was it written by a young school teacher, full of life and dreams of leaving this hardscrabble half town for something grander, gentler? Or was the last word written with yellowed chalk in a bony blue-vein claw of a hand. An old schoolmarm who never tasted the fruit of this life. A womb unfilled by man or babe.

He imagined Colby in the front row of phantom desks. Leaning on elbows. Eager to learn. To live. But the teacher who appeared in front of him was not the young woman, propped up with promise. No. It was the old woman Matt saw in front of his son. Clad in black. Writing a riddle on the board. One his boy would never decipher.

A dead doe on the baked prairie grass, buzzards circling overhead. We're in lawn chairs, downing Buds, waiting for the feeding to begin. But Donny is impatient, expecting the birds to dine on his schedule. NOW, this very second, while they are riding the currents above, watching, waiting to see if we move closer to our kill.

Donny curses them: damn dumb birds, I shot that deer for them. He shoots at the kettle, but they continue long loops, unperturbed. Donny again cusses the buzzards and shoots the doe again, as if killing her twice will hasten the descent of the birds. Donny complains sweat is stinging his eyes. He pours the last of our water over his head and removes his shirt.

Near sundown we are out of beer, and Donny is asleep. One by one the birds land, until the wake is feasting before me. Talons, beaks at work, tugging, tearing. The eyes the appetizers it seems. I don't wake Donny, though I know he will be mad for missing this meal, hungry as he was for a blood mass. But I'll let my brother sleep. while the shadows of skillful sculptors grow longer on the plain, and the fawn becomes a crimson work of art Donny would never appreciate.

A Leash of Foxes

The skulk was mostly vixen. Hens were haunted by either gender. The farmer's wife feared them, though the foxes were small, and they ran from most two-legged beasts. The farmer shot the foxes for sport— guarding chickens not his concern with a thousand acres in corn. The farmer's son had trapped a red Reynard. The fox perished in captivity, starving itself.

The night of the caged fox's demise, the rooster crowed tirelessly. For good reason, since the leash gobbled a dozen hens under a gibbous moon. The creatures prosecuted a moral symmetry it seemed, while the farmer was febrile with the grippe, the son fast asleep, and the wife dared not make a peep, witnessing a scarlet carnage she likened to war.

In its aftermath, a naked sun rose on waves of white feathers and trails of blood. Perhaps 'tis not good to trap a wild thing, the farmer's wife thought. Then she made her way to the coops, fetching eggs enough for breakfast. All the while the skulk watched from the thick brush— watched and waited, without will as we know it, but with a red reckoning ready, should they again be victims of man's folly and sin.

Jackson and the Tenant

When Jackson Boyle was twelve, he wrote an essay on why hot dogs came in packages of six and buns in packs of eight. The essay had nothing to do with food. Jackson also penned a short story about a street vendor who would tell your fortune when he sold you a hot dog. Jackson was truly gifted, and his teachers recognized this, double promoting him from 7th to 9th grade that year.

Jackson, therefore, turned thirteen the month before he entered high school. Jackson was tall for his age but very thin. His widowed mother had tried to fatten him up, but food meant little to Jackson. His world was in the written word, the petri dish, the infinite stars. The promotion to high school was more curse than blessing. He enjoyed his honors classes, but despised physical education where his hirsute and bulky classmates would taunt him. Each day, Jackson would breathe a sigh of relief as he exited the double doors by the boys' locker room at the back of the gym.

After the short walk home, Jackson would read or work on his novel, a tale so disturbing he would hide it from his mother. A story about a diabolical medical doctor who gradually killed patients he was "ordained" to remove from the earth would likely be disturbing to any mother, or father. The doctor, or Jackson's imagination, had devised a remarkable way to commit the acts without being detected.

If their tenant, Mr. Hensley, was home in the converted garage apartment behind their two-story home, Jackson would play chess with him. Mr. Hensley had no visitors or friends unless Jackson counted as one. He worked in a slaughterhouse and would rarely bathe. Jackson thought this made sense. Why bathe if you're going to get dirty again the next day? Jackson figured one could make better use of one's time. If it were not for his mother's strict edict, Jackson would not bathe.

Mrs. Boyle was aware of Mr. Hensley's slovenly nature and required him to leave his rent check in an envelope in the mailbox. She felt like she needed to inspect the apartment in case Mr. Hensley's lack of concern for personal hygiene was also a reflection of how he maintained her dwelling. Jackson assured his mother the place was very clean but did have a very foul odor which Jackson attributed to the man himself. Jackson had used the bathroom there at times and had noted the tub was cleaner than their own bathtubs. Little surprise Mrs. Boyle said. Based on his smell, I would say he never uses it.

Though Mr. Hensley did stink, he played chess well. He and Jackson were evenly matched. The two spoke little during their games. Mr. Hensley always thanked Jackson for playing. Jackson would have probably pitied the man, but Jackson, though not selfish, had little empathy for others. He'd always felt awkward with his peers—being so much brighter and curious than they didn't help—and he always could converse more easily with adults. Jackson's mother sensed this about her son but felt compelled to make him attend parties and other social events. Invariably, he would find an isolated corner and seek refuge there until he was able to make his escape.

By Jackson's sophomore year, Mrs. Boyle had decided he was who he was, and she ceased her efforts to make her peculiar boy a social creature. Jackson finished high school in three years and received several scholarships. He missed one question on his PSAT and made a perfect score on his SAT. He had continued to write and was increasingly interested in science. He wanted to be a molecular biologist, but his mother convinced him to apply for med school his third year at the university. At nineteen, he was accepted into the two schools to which he applied. Upon graduation, Jackson decided to become a pathologist. He was particularly interested in forensic pathology and ultimately worked as a medical examiner in a city two hours' drive from his hometown.

Jackson visited home primarily on holidays. The day after his thirtieth birthday, his mother called and told him she had a malignant lump in her breast. Jackson returned home and very dispassionately reviewed the film and lab results and told her exactly what the local doctors had. She would be fine with a lumpectomy and a round of chemo.

While Jackson was home, he and Mr. Hensley played chess. Mr. Hensley still reeked from the killing floors, but there was something different about the odor now. Perhaps, Jackson thought, not the odor itself but the way Jackson perceived it.

Jackson's mother was fine post op and cancer free the remainder of her life. Mrs. Boyle died in her sleep twenty-five years later when she was eighty-nine. Jackson had not been home to see his mother in over three years. He had come home for her eighty-fifth birthday after missing number eighty for a conference. Jackson could never see the wisdom in attaching more significance to one year than another.

Mr. Hensley had moved to a nursing home a couple of years earlier. Mrs. Boyle felt she was too old to have a renter and she could never get the smell out of the apartment. Mr. Hensley's five decades in the tiny abode left an indelible olfactory stamp on the place.

The person Jackson retained to handle his mother's estate recommended a minimal updating of the home, but he said the apartment should be razed. Not only was there the foul smell, but the old place was in disrepair. The neighborhood was becoming gentrified and likely buyers would want a real a garage they could build in the space.

Jackson truly didn't want to be bothered by those details. He had little sentimental attachment to the place. In his way, he loved his mother but saw her so infrequently, he thought of her little in life or death.

His best memories of the place, he recalled, were watching the Twilight Zone, reading books after he was supposed to be asleep, and playing chess with Mr. Hensley, a man whose first name Jackson never knew until after the crew came to demolish the apartment. When the conversion was done sixty years earlier, the original garage had become the living room and bedroom of the apartment. That portion was on a concrete slab. The add-on kitchen and bath were pier and beam. When the floor was being torn up, the workers, who had been complaining about the stench the entire time they had been there, discovered its fetid origin.

First only a foot. A foot wrapped in heavy plastic. A foot connected to a body buried beneath the kitchen. A half foot of soil was on top of the body. In total, twelve bodies were found, stacked two deep and covered with the soft dank, rank earth. Apparently, Cyrus James Hensley had removed floor planks and replaced them each time.

In the first month after the ghoulish discovery, ten of the dozen were identified via DNA or dental records. A year later, the other pair had not been identified. All were male. The ten had been among missing persons in the same state. Two of those were local. Their age at time of death ranged from approximately twenty to forty. The newest body appeared to have been placed there a decade earlier, when Cyrus James Hensley was in his seventies.

One of the local victims had gone to high school with Jackson. Jackson remembered being teased by the boy who apparently went missing shortly after high school. The boy, Dean Whittaker, had some trouble with the law and it was assumed he absconded to avoid prosecution. Instead, he was decapitated like all the victims. Their skulls placed neatly above their necks when Mr. Hensley slid them into their burial bags.

Cyrus Hensley was suffering from Alzheimer's and was no longer verbal or ambulatory. The court went through the motions and convicted him of multiple murders, but he died in the nursing facility before the ink was dry on the court paperwork.

Jackson himself felt compelled to help with the identification. The local coroner found this odd—he could not fathom how Jackson could consider being part of this macabre endeavor. It was not in Jackson's jurisdiction, so Jackson could not mount much of an argument. Jackson really didn't know why he wanted to be part of the process.

Over time, Jackson recalled the foul odors. He found himself wondering about how Mr. Hensley transferred his skills from the slaughterhouse to the old apartment. Mostly, Jackson recalled the chess moves Mr. Hensley often made.

A Thumbtack, a Roll of Duct Tape

Through my microscope, I spend hours looking at the interstices of a plant cell wall; if the earth did not spin, I could endure the whole frigid night staring through my telescope at one violently still crater on the moon.

But I eat ONLY soggy cheerios for breakfast, ramen--chicken flavor--for lunch, EVERY day, and either Dinty Moore stew or cheese ravioli for my evening repast. My toothbrush must be blue, the paste pure white, and I could never tolerate the plight, of socks slipping down past my ankles.

I love Vivaldi, Brahms, and the sound of soft rain, but hail batters my brain like a billion ball bearings on a defenseless tin pot. My alarm must face due north and my bed sunset west, beyond those things I have no peculiar request. Except that things remain EXACTLY the way they are/were for eternity.

I can't play a savant symphony like some would expect, or do cataclysmic calculations in my head, though I can recall, two years and four months ago today, a gold thumbtack sitting alone on my dead granddad's wood work bench, and the gray smelly roll of duct tape I placed precisely three inches from it, to keep it company. And if I ever again travel 365.26 miles to visit Granny in Milwaukee, Wisconsin USA, it better be there, not having dared to move a nightmarish nanometer.

George told me, "Ain't how long you live, but how you live that counts." Strange he had clung to this rock for double eights, and that he swore he'd jump from a plane when he hit ninety, without a parachute if he chose.

Those long linoleum journeys when I wheeled him from his room to the dining hall were the best part of my day—a minimum wage slave, ending my graveyard shift watching one after another "resident" leave a thousand different ways.

He called me "brown sugar." I took no offense, for colored girls get deaf to such jabs before we get bras. I knew, from him, it was a term of endearment since his red blood had earned him nigger names like "Charlie Chief" and "Drunk Injun Joe" long ago.

He told me grabbing melons along the Pecos beat cotton picking on the prison farm, and I never asked how he came to know either. He said his squaw was dead some forty years, his own trail of tears since would never dry. No children had lived to become great warriors or proud princesses, though he never said why.

When I would leave George at his table, the end of our daily stroll, he would bless his eggs with words I did not know. Those who shared the table sat mute and chewed their cud. As I walked away, I would never fail to wonder, if I could find a plane and pilot.

Anna Hawkins was trapped in the storm cellar for six days after the twister. Six days, Anna struggled to open the door. And on the seventh day, she managed to push the hatch high enough to squeeze her thin frame through. The dead oak which had fallen and blocked her exit should have been cut down and used in the fireplace last year. Her father, William, hadn't gotten around to it. William hadn't gotten around to much since pneumonia took Anna's mother, Abigail, the year before.

Anna's eyes, in the dank dark for nearly a week, squinted in the assault of light even though it was a gray overcast day. The house was still there, the second story painted pale green. The bottom, the raw russet color of the boards. Abigail died when the job was half done.

From the county highway a quarter mile south, the house did not appear odd. From the storm cellar door, it was the first thing Anna saw when she made her escape. A freakish reminder. A house half green. A dead mother. An inconsolable father. Anna, eighteen years old. One leg shorter than the other. Anna, alone while her father worked in a mill in Sherman for the spring.

Other than stealing a few shingles from the roof, the storm had spared the house. Anna walked past it toward the road. William's truck was not parked on the dirt drive. Anna may not have stopped if it were there. She had no idea where her peregrinations were taking her.

In the pasture in front of the house, the stock tank was full. No cattle grazed there. Two strange, bloated shapes lay beyond the tank near the road. As she got closer, she recognized them. Steers, black as night, on their stiff spines, hooves pointed towards the bleak heavens. Victims of the tornado.

East of the beasts, on the side of what passed for a hill on these prairies, debris was strewn—pieces of rusted tin, boards, a sign that had hung on a business two miles west, Deems General Store: Feed and Farm Implements.

Anna walked by one of the dead cattle, wondering what this apocalyptic scene meant. A week and nothing had molested the flesh. Not a buzzard to be found. Not a bird anywhere, and not a sound save her soft footsteps on the grass.

She came to the county highway. A long straight whip of a road to the horizon, the Oklahoma border. Usually, a car would pass at least twice an hour during daylight. Anna stood staring at the pavement in front of her. She searched for beetles or grasshoppers. Nothing.

Anna continued on the farm road south of the highway. An abandoned house had been there before the storm. The house where her father was born. Gone now. In the mesquites to the east, Anna thought she saw the ghost planks from the house. Sixty years ago, Grandpa Hawkins held those boards in his hands. Eighteen years ago, the week before Anna was born in the new house, Grandpa died of blood poisoning under the roof that was now scattered to the winds.

Anna looked for rabbits she had often seen in the pasture by the old house. Nothing. Nothing but gray pasture that had been plowed and planted for years but now lay fallow.

Anna walked further south, towards tracks where trains passed at five AM, two and nine PM. When she came upon the tracks, Anna looked at the watch which had once been her mother's. 1:58 PM. Anna looked both directions. Nothing. Two silver rails stretching through fields, shrubs and dwarf trees to eternity.

Beyond the tracks was the river, swollen from spring rains. Anna felt drawn to the water, though she did not know why. She took one small step towards the river but turned back towards her house. She saw something move in the mesquite; she walked to the stand of small twisted trees as quickly as her uneven legs would take her. When Anna came to the spot where she thought she had seen movement, Anna found a strand of ribbon, white, tattered and flapping in the gentle breeze. Anna imagined she saw dried blood on one corner of the ribbon. Anna reached for the strip. When she did a stiff breeze snatched it and sent it to another thorny branch of mesquite.

Anna walked again past one of the bloated steers. Not one fly on its carcass. The end of the world, Anna thought. The world ended when I was in the ground. Why am I still here when everything else is gone?

When she climbed the porch stairs to her house, she was startled by her own dim reflection in the panes of a window. Anna swung her arms to and fro. The person in the window is alive, Anna said aloud. Half expecting to find her doppelganger behind the window, Anna went into the house—empty, and silent, except for her footfalls.

Anna walked upstairs to her parents' room. There she sat in a rocker where her mother often sewed in the fine southern light that poured through the windows. Pale green paint had dripped down one of the panes. She did not move from the chair until dark.

She went back downstairs. There was no electricity. Anna switched on every light in the house. Candles and matches were on the mantle, but she did not use them. She lay on the couch and fell fast asleep. Anna dreamt. She saw her mother's face. Then came the black cattle grazing, buzzards perched on their backs. Next Anna imagined herself in church, unclothed. This is a dream she told herself. A dream yet when she woke in the dark house, Anna saw her mother kneeling beside her, smiling.

Anna reached for her mother to embrace her, but the rude incandescent lights came back on, extinguishing her mother's visage. Alone again. The lights flickered and went off. Dark again.

Outside, a car drove across the moon drenched silver pastures. Anna was still on the sofa when the sheriff knocked on the door.

Anybody in there? he called out.

Anna did not move. The lights came on again. The sheriff saw Anna sitting, still as stone staring past him as if he were not there. He came into the house.

Anna, he said, You all right?

Anna did not answer or move. The sheriff crouched in front of her.

Anna, it's me, Sheriff Baker. Anna. The sheriff snapped his fingers not six inches from Anna's eyes. The catatonic creature in front of him did not stir.

Anna would never know the sheriff had come to check on her and to tell her William Hawkins had driven his truck into the swollen river and drowned only hours before the twister tore through the county.

Afterword

Anna Hawkins was not her real name. Her initials were A.H. I knew her when I worked at a state psychiatric hospital in 1978, thirty years after the storm. A.H was still catatonic. She was one of the most intractable cases we had ever seen. No speech and no movement except the waxy flexibility associated with that diagnosis.

I did not expect to see A. H. again. Last fall, when I was a volunteer coordinator at a local hospice, A.H was admitted. She looked familiar—very familiar though she was four decades older. A.H. was a transfer from a nursing home where she had been placed in the late 1990s. All our modern alchemy had done little to improve her condition. No psychotropic drug had made a dent in the stubborn wall of madness that engulfed her since she the day she emerged from the cellar.

I was in the facility the day A.H. passed. The nurse who discovered her said A.H. was sitting upright in her bed. Outside was a fierce storm. To the southwest, a funnel had been spotted.

Fragrant Ladies Rocked Slowly*

From the Diary of the Last Sane Woman on Earth

In that pale green room, one sat, rocking slowly. An improvement, the white coated ones said, but catatonic was not a word she knew. Another crouched in the corner, also swaying to and fro, her Haldol doubled the week before, so she stopped scratching her legs, but not before she had carved a Picasso on her thigh, a Dali on her calf. There were no "cutters" then. Those black clad children who need razors. We had our own claws.

My cell mate, in her sleeveless jacket, rocked too, by the window, where the mesh cut the afternoon sun into a hundred dappled diamonds on her frock. The oldest woman in the world was also there, crawling the linoleum highways, counting each square, spouting off formulas to prove the universe had order, though she did not have to say much to convince us. This was eons before "chaos theory," and we knew all the butterflies flapping in China and all the world would not make a sound, their vibrations scarcely noted, and no hurricanes would emerge from their winged tempests.

I rocked too, and pissed my pants like the others, because I could. If I did not, the white ones and the zombie zoo doctor god might decide to release me to the warped world, where I would be expected to never rock again, where there would be no queen counting squares, where the clock would try in vain to measure the sun, and the scent of ammonia would be replaced by nothingness.

Three years I worshipped in the red brick cathedrals by the ugliest lake on the planet, but I was cast out of the holy halls, with mounds of Mellaril, and other sacred potions in pill form. I was to see the "outreach caseworker," though I never knew what she was reaching for. My husband had divorced me. Both my sons were in Dallas, dealing cards at Wall Street casinos, holding the aces for themselves and a chosen few—like I really knew anything about what filled their days.

My sister took me in, fed me finger foods, and had her maid bathe me. She invited the ghosts from my past into her house. They all hugged me and told me how nice my hair looked—now that I was no longer yanking it out by the fistful and choking on it as it went down. They smelled of sycophantic scents from Macy's and Neiman Marcus, and I longed for the odor of my cellmate, who had to be submerged in a scalding sea once a week, after they had pumped enough of Morpheus' brew in her to mellow a mad mammoth.

I missed her and her truculent silence, and the way her arms writhed in her jacket, like so many snakes squirming to be free. Perhaps those were the last sin eating serpents in their death throes, but I would never know; for in a thousand days and a thousand nights, her jacket was never removed except when she was bathed, for the white ones feared a black storm waited inside, so they allowed it to hide someplace in her fetid carcass.

Now when I look across the charcoal stillness of my room, cluttered with dead distractions, I imagine her there, on her cot, producing anthems on mad marching afternoons, or singing lullabies in evenings' last gasps, all without making a sound. Then my eyes well with tears, for I know she would miss me too, and worry what I was doomed to hear and smell now that her mystic music and sacred stench were stolen from me.

*"Fragrant ladies rocked slowly" is a phrase from *To Kill a Mockingbird*.

Mad Martha

Martha was on the phone with AT&T tech support because her Internet service was down. The agent from AT&T asked if he could put her on hold briefly. When he returned, he said, I am sorry, we are experiencing an outage in your area. We are working to restore your service.

Martha said, Thank You. When things like this happen, I generally attribute them to interference from the alien force that has set up a colony on the head of a straight pin in a sewing box in a drawer in a house in Poughkeepsie, New York.

The AT&T agent laughed and said they were working to restore service. Martha assured him it was not AT&T's fault.

The pinhead in New York—it's to blame, Martha said and then she hung up. Martha was accustomed to people laughing at her.

Martha had never been to Poughkeepsie. In seventy-two years, the greatest distance she had traveled from her Andrews, Texas home was Broken Bow, Oklahoma. That trip was the week before 9/11, the fall after she had been asked to leave her job as a middle school math teacher. Fortunately, Martha had enough years to retire. If she hadn't been eligible, the Human Resources Department had assured her they could secure a disability retirement for her. This was one year after what Martha referred to as the "event."

Martha had never married, but she did have a long romance with an older man, Ronnie Abel. Ronnie taught math in the Iraan-Sheffield School District, 80 miles south of Midland. Ronnie and Martha met at conference in Dallas.

Ronnie died a month before the event. Martha was driving to his ranch to retrieve a few of her belongings when her new 2000 Hyundai Sonata died. It was the first week of school and Martha had been very busy; she didn't leave Andrews until dinnertime. By the time her car stopped in the desert, it was dark. She attempted to use her cell phone, also new, to call for roadside assistance promised by the warranty, but her cell would not work either. Martha knew there was little service in this remote area and thought nothing of it. Martha was less than a mile from Ronnie's ranch house and the home phone was still in service.

Martha invariably kept a good flashlight in her car. When the Sonata died, Martha took her flashlight and began the walk to Ronnie's place. Martha recalled walking up the first hill from where her car died and then feeling a sudden pressure inside her head. The feeling was accompanied by a boom. Martha immediately fell, feeling as if the asphalt was metal and her head a magnet. Later, a doctor told Martha she received a slight concussion from the fall.

Another doctor, one of many "specialists" she saw the first few months after the event would tell her she had an Otolithic Crisis of Tumarkin—in laymen's terms, a "drop attack," something which occurred when the tiny organs in the inner ear which sense gravity were askew. Martha did not believe this doctor or any of the doctors who posited traditional medical explanations for what happened to her.

Martha remembered nothing after the fall except lights approaching as she hit the pavement and a dream which occurred. She awoke several hours after the fall, on the same spot in the highway. When she did wake up, she was sitting upright with her legs crossed.

To the one journalist willing to listen, Martha would report what happened during her period of unconsciousness: I had what I thought was a vivid dream. I was prostrate on the highway. I heard a humming sound and saw a bright disk hovering above me. From this sphere emanated two colorful shapes—round rainbows if you will. Both these beings covered me like a blanket. I felt nothing but the sensation I was moving, moving at the speed of light. Suddenly, I stopped, and I was on the head of a pin. All around me were people I did not recognize. I thought I had to be dead. These were other souls in the afterlife, I assumed. More people kept arriving, all teetering on the edge of the needle. That is all I recall except being teleported back to the spot on the asphalt where the colorful entities left my body and returned to the sphere which disappeared.

Martha recounted this tale to many people before she spoke to a journalist from Midland. He never ran the story. He thought she was crazy. Everyone thought Martha was crazy. After she told the few friends she had and her school principal, they all suggested she see a doctor. She dutifully followed their advice and saw several, the last being the neurologist who said she had a "drop attack." The psychiatrist she saw before that could not decide if she was psychotic, but he did inform the school district he would write a letter to that effect if necessary.

When Martha retired, she located a person in the mountains of southeastern Oklahoma who was supposed to be an expert in such matters—thus the trip to Broken Bow Labor Day weekend, 2001. The man she met there was Sammy Turner and he had a small cabin in the hills just north of the town. Sammy assured Martha she was not crazy, but he also assured her only other abductees would believe her. Sammy was the one who explained she had been transported to an "alternate universe" that was located on the head of a pin in a sewing kit in a drawer in Poughkeepsie.

When Martha asked if the person who owned the kit knew what existed there, Sammy said, Of course, the owner was the first person abducted and had been instructed to leave the kit exactly where it was. The woman was a spinster and was related to Eleanor Roosevelt, Sammy claimed. When Martha asked if he had spoken with the woman, Sammy said, Only telepathically.

Martha had been on antipsychotic medication for ten of the seventeen years since the event. She never wavered in her belief about what happened on the highway that night. Martha did not know it, but the night of "the event," 47 UFO sightings were reported in west Texas.

Martha did know after her wound from the fall healed, she had not had one ailment. Not one cold or stomach virus in seventeen years. Martha also knew that Sammy Turner never answered his phone after their meeting, nor did he respond to her snail mail or email. When she inquired about him with the Broken Bow Police, Martha was told he no longer lived in the area. Martha saw him in dreams more than once, always on the head of the pin with her.

Martha still had the flashlight she carried the night of the event. Seventeen years later, the 4 triple D batteries worked perfectly. Martha told people about the flashlight, but nobody believed her. Nobody, including Martha, looked at the batteries to see their expiration date was October 2004, fourteen years ago.

The Cur at the Landfill

From a distance, I thought you might be a wolf straying from your pack in the high country, confused by the cacophony of scents. But no, 'twas my poor vision. You were only a mongrel, perched high on the mound.

The odors of suburban fast food ghosts and tuna tins were familiar to you. You stood atop the reeking remnants. Your right front paw resting on the shredded files of a grand embezzler, your left rear on the ear of a legless teddy bear. Another on an orange rind until you shifted your weight and found footing on a crinkled crushed water bottle (one of about…33,448,899 in the heap, or maybe 33,448,900) and the last on the ubiquitous cell phone.

The phone heard its final voice a fortnight before, when its master spoke his last light words before he tossed it into a dark dumpster and replaced it with another plastic confessor whose fate would ultimately be the same, after some sublime texting and sexting and a few vain words to other deaf dogs.

The Pay Phone for the Weary and Cell-less

EVERYBODY got 'em a cell phone. Pissant with not a nickel to pay his rent got him one. I ain't got one or the quarter to use this pay phone, sittin' there behind me waitin' for me to feed it and hear that jingle like some slot machine that always pays out. Temptin' me like some shiny new toy. I got but two pennies and I ain't even rubbin' them together.

Back then, back when nobody had no cell phone, I filed pennies down on the street to make them the size of dimes, when one of them dimes could by me a marshmallow pie from a vendin' machine at the bowlin' alley that ain't there no more. But some cell phone store is. That and one of them nail salons.

But that don't matter. I don't want no cell phone. I would like me one of them marshmallow pies and an extra quarter to give this hungry phone. Yesterday, some lady give me three quarters and I give two of them to Jose to call his mama and sister. He gave me two smiles. I kept that other quarter to make a call but couldn't think of no number or no soul want to hear my voice. So, I give that quarter to another little boy who was all alone and didn't have no cell phone.

(Image courtesy of Dana Newman McCartney)

The 1957 Brother Atlas

Darrel Wilson sat on the same bench most days. I would see him as I exited my car and went into my office. I knew Darrel's identity because he owned the office building my firm leased. Darrel also owned two strip malls, an apartment complex, a few convenience stores, and an oil company. And a 1957 Brother Atlas sewing machine. Darrel valued the machine more than any property. He would have gladly given up his wealth to rewind the clock to the summer afternoon he gave the sewing machine to his wife, Maxime.

If Maxime was worried they could not afford it, she did not show it that afternoon sixty years ago. All Darrel saw on her face was unadulterated joy.

By evening, she had stitched a pocket on a pair of Darrel's pants and finished a baby dress she had been making when her old machine petered out—one of many such dresses she would make for a baby they would never have. This was Maxime's way of filling the gaping hole she felt from being barren. Once, Darrel had seen Maxime hold a new cotton creation to her belly, as if the act of placing it there would imbue her with the power to conceive, to wed the seed so willingly given but profligate in her womb.

Maxime was blessed with pulchritude. Blessed now. Fifteen years earlier, her beauty had been a curse. A young Catholic girl in occupied France—perfect fodder for the wolves who scavenged and ravaged as they chose. Her small village had become favored by the German invaders. Over and over, she was their victim. Twice she had used a kitchen knife to cut her wrists, but God had not allowed her the solace of nothingness.

Instead, He kept her alive until the devils were defeated. He kept her alive until Darrel and the American liberators came rolling through her hamlet. Darrel's convoy bivouacked near Maxime's village for two weeks. Long enough for him to fall in love with her. Darrel knew she had been hurt and approached her cautiously. He too had been blessed with a comely face and a disarming smile. Darrel convinced a reticent Maxime to let him write her, which he did daily after returning to the states. His letters were short and to the point. Come to Texas and marry me, which Maxime did after his hundredth letter. She had counted and decided if this handsome young man was that persistent, he was worthy of her hand. In truth, after her ordeal with the SS officers, Maxime didn't feel any man would want her.

After years of marriage, the couple knew and accepted they would never have a child. Darrel was a volunteer baseball coach when he wasn't working as a roughneck. He satisfied his fatherly instincts with that endeavor. And Maxime had her sewing. Being with young children was too much for her to bear. Her sartorial creations were the sole substitute she possessed for motherhood. Perhaps the depth of her longing accounted for the beauty of her creations. Each dress, though pieced together with modest materials, looked as if it was made for a princess.

Maxime never kept a dress she sewed. Usually, she took them to the House of Charity and Hope where all the donated items were given to the needy. Many of the goods went to the families on the other side of the tracks—predominantly African American families who had not reaped the economic benefits of the post war boom.

The first dress Maxime made with the Brother Atlas was donated there. The Saturday Darrel drove her there to deliver the dress and some of his old overalls, Darrel recognized his boss's wife, Mrs. Hoffman, who was donating clothes there as well. She had met Darrel and Maxime on occasion but had never seen Maxime's fine work until the morning they met at the House of Charity. The same afternoon, Mrs. Hoffman called Maxime and asked if she ever made wedding dresses.

Maxime said, No. I had not even made my own.

Mrs. Hoffman explained her oldest daughter was getting married in a month and hadn't found a thing she liked in the wedding department at Neiman Marcus or any other Dallas store. Mrs. Hoffman was tiring of trips to Dallas and frankly was running out of time. She asked Maxine if she could meet with her daughter and tailor one to her daughter's liking. With some trepidation, Maxime agreed and sewed a magnificent wedding dress for the wealthy and particular bride to be. Both Mrs. Hoffman and her daughter were overjoyed.

Maxime had refused to take compensation for her labors. Mrs. Hoffman reluctantly agreed but the week after the wedding, Mr. Hoffman found Darrel on a rig and handed him a large envelope. Inside was a deed to two acres of land Mr. Hoffman had received in a swap for his wife's Cadillac Mr. Hoffman had recently replaced with a newer model.

Isn't much to look at Darrel, Mr. Hoffman said, but I thought if you and your missus ever wanted a place in the country, might be a decent place to build.

Darrel never built a house on the land, but he did make a loan and risk all his meager savings to drill there. The gamble paid off. By 1960, Darrel had a producing well on his initial plot of land and two more on other acreage he purchased with the proceeds. By Darrel and Maxime's twentieth anniversary, for which he took Maxime to France to see her aging mother, Darrel had thirty producing wells. He had begun to purchase properties with the cash from his black gold.

As his fortune grew, so did something wicked inside Maxime. First, the cancer was discovered in her womb. Then it ravaged her body, one organ at a time until 1971, the week after her forty-fifth birthday, Maxime succumbed to the metastatic monster.

Maxime had never stopped sewing, even making a valiant effort to create a final dress exactly like the one that given them such good fortune when Mrs. Hoffman admired it a quarter century before. Ten days before she drifted off into a sleep from which she would never wake, Maxime finished the dress.

Darrel hung it in a locked wardrobe. The 1957 Brother Atlas celebrated its sixtieth birthday in a huge safe Darrel bought to store only the treasured machine.

Without heirs, Darrel had bequeathed his estate to various eleemosynary endeavors and a few loyal employees. His will decreed the sewing machine and the final dress were to be entombed with him.

Stanza 99

Penning a poem in his Oakland flat, he was stuck at double nines. Each of the lines was fueled by a Winston; each stanza, cheap red wine and quiet desperation. Outside, the beat of bongos, the pop of zip guns and the wail of sirens. If the summer of love was hot at Haight, nobody told the Panthers who crashed in the pad below his.

He wanted to tell the world this, epic style: an odyssey on asphalt, a choreography of elbows breaking glass, and boys running fast, in 'hoods where every mother's son died too young. But he couldn't weave the right words to end a story that started with shit filled hulls of ships, the crack of whips, a war of bro against bro, and Jim Crow to keep the nightmare alive in the light of day. Slavery was history, but now the "Man" snatched them up with draft notices, turned boys into men and men into monkeys to be mowed down in jungles in a question mark on a map most had never seen.

Stanza 99, where were the words? Another fag, another swig of sweet red wine, though nothing came, until he heard it—a baby crying in the night, and he picked up his Bic and wrote:

Here you are, coal black child of a distant star
calling out in a language as old as time, "I am hungry!
Hungry for more! Fill my belly with mama's milk,
my lungs with God's free air, and let me grow strong,
straight and brave—brave enough to dream through
all this dreaded darkness."

Oakland, August 1967

13:01

Sixty-one minutes ago, a stormy midnight. I watched the clock hands join as lightning struck my high pastures. Only last month, a twister snatched a steer and dropped it in my neighbor's stock tank—not a scratch on its hide after a cyclonic half mile ride. Tonight, I had no fear funnels would find my fields, though the distant thunder claps taunted me, reminding me they have fierce fire but don't always bring rain.

I watched the clock, waiting for 13:02. Last month, while the steer was flying, my wife hid with me in our storm cellar, praying. I prayed with her, though I doubted a god was listening, or cared; my entreaties were not for refuge from the storm. Instead, I begged the black sky my woman would be saved from white bone cancer.

That was not to be—the almighty saw fit to perform a miracle for a dumb beast that very eve but not for my wife of fifty years. She lasted until 1:01 AM yesterday. 13:01 I strangely conceived. I had the lucky steer slaughtered at high noon today.

I'd let it rot in prairie grass, were it not for her. She would not want it to be carrion for buzzards, a profligate desecration. She would want its flesh to be a feast for a family she did not know—hands clasped, giving thanks to the same god that saved it but not her.

I can't rest. I'll watch the clock, waiting for 13:01, again and again.

In July 1968, I obtained a library card using the wrong address. I didn't intentionally use a bogus address. I was crashing on my sister's couch and she told me she was moving to the apartment building next door. I used that address when I checked out Robert Ardrey's *The Territorial Imperative*. We never moved to the other apartment. I did not return the book that summer and joined the army in 1969. I left the book on my sister's cinderblock and board bookshelf.

I didn't see my sister often the three years I was in the military or during the three years I was in school. I finished my undergrad degree in '75. I used the GI Bill and money I saved from my tour in 'nam to pay for my education, but the last two semesters, I received two fat scholarships. One went for an engine in my VW. The other for a plane ticket from El Paso, where I had gone to school, to Austin where my sis was finishing her doctoral degree.

The first thing I noticed in my sister's apartment was an antique roll top desk a professor had given her. Beside the desk was the ageless cinderblock bookshelf. On the bottom board of three, *The Territorial Imperative* sat, a reminder of the origins of my career in larceny. (I was a medic in the army and I also purloined a *PDR* and a *Merck Manual* from the Medical Center to which I was assigned my last year in the military. A biblio-thief, I was.)

I took the book with me when I returned home. At the time I was living with an Amerasian woman, Mariko, who intended to move to Japan, the homeland of her mother, when she finished her master's degree. We had met shortly before I was discharged, and Mariko chided me for stealing the books. I pointed to the conspicuous scar on my arm from shrapnel that hit me when I was putting a tourniquet on someone during a firefight in 'nam. I did get a purple heart and recuperated well enough to return to the bush for most of my tour, but I did not receive a penny for disability. Mariko said stealing was stealing, period. This didn't stop her from filching my copy of *The Territorial Imperative* when she moved to Japan.

For the first year after Mariko left, we exchanged letters. Our writing became less frequent and then nonexistent by the two-year mark. In 2011, we reconnected via Facebook. In PM, I jokingly asked if Mariko still had *The Territorial Imperative*. Mariko said she finally had begun to read it but left it at her cousin Natsumi's house in Natori. Mariko lived west of Tokyo in Sagamiono. She said she would grab the book when she went to Natsumi's again the following week. Mariko said the infamous stolen tome would be with her when she returned.

Mariko did return to Sagamiono from Natori with the book, but not until they had found Natsumi's body in her Mitsubishi. Natsumi was one of hundreds who drowned the day a 9.0 earthquake spawned a tsunami that wiped out Natori while Mariko was driving there to visit. Unlike many others, Natsumi's body was not swept out to sea. Her car and body were found upside down against a bridge.

Natsumi's home was on the outskirts of the city and only partially flooded. On a bedside stand in the guest room, inches above where the water had crested in the home, lay a dry *Territorial Imperative*.

Once Mariko was allowed into Natori, she helped Kyoko, Natsumi's roommate, clean up the partially flooded house. Mariko stayed a full week, until after Natsumi's service and Kyoko had relocated to a town inland.

A month after the tragedy, I found a package from Japan at my door. *The Territorial Imperative*, I assumed. Inside was a book and a note. The book was *Future Shock*, hardback, first edition, signed by the author, Alvin Toffler. The note in the package read, "Ricky, I told you I would send this back—only took 40 years. Best wishes, Mariko." Ricky was Mariko's beau before I.

I sent her a PM on Facebook but didn't hear back from her. A few days later, I discovered an entry on her page and several entries which followed, expressing condolences. The initial entry was from her longtime lover, an Aussie named Reginald who worked in Tokyo. It read: "Our beloved Mariko passed last week. The doctors believe she had an aneurysm. I will never stop missing her or loving her." Mariko was a week short of her 62nd birthday.

I wanted Ricky to have the signed book back—I'd never met him, but I knew she dumped him, and she said he had taken it hard. Finding a Ricky (Richard) Parker in Chicago, if he was still there, would be difficult. I did internet searches and narrowed it down to the two Richard Parkers who would be about the right age. Neither phone number was in service, so I sent both letters.

Three days later, on my cell, the number for which I had included in my correspondence, I heard back from the right Richard. He informed me he had The *Territorial Imperative* (with the El Paso Public Library label still clinging to its spine). Richard asked how far El Paso was from Las Cruces, New Mexico. He was to be there on business the following day. We both agreed it was freaky he was going to be in the area right after he had heard from me. We met for lunch at Sombrero's and reminisced about the woman we once knew.

As we were getting into our cars, Richard said, "Hey, you know she mailed the boxes the day she died." I did not know, but it did not surprise me.

I didn't read my note until I was sitting in my car. "Jim. I remember telling you stealing was stealing. I remember you pointing to the scar on your arm. I remember making love that night. Today, I remember lots of things. I really felt the need to send this to you. Don't know why. Love and thoughts, Mariko."

I returned the book to the library the next day. *The Territorial Imperative* was just shy of 43 years overdue. I confessed my sins to a young lady sitting at the return counter. She asked why I was returning it then. I didn't have an answer.

I Was an Oud

You found me in a second-hand store on Lincoln Avenue. You bought me for nine dollars and tax because you thought I was a mandolin. You told Tyrell, the clerk who would sell me into slavery, your wife always wanted one.

You took me home to your twelfth story apartment. I discovered your wife was gone many years, but her photo on the living room wall got to see me, and hear your lament: you wished you would have found me seasons sooner, though my strings were rusted even then—my last song played at a bar mitzvah before your hair turned white, before your wife's many colored regrets.

You played me but once and didn't like what I had to say. You tossed me from your balcony to the street. I made the same flight your wife did and landed in the same spot. I suspect she was more a disappointed music lover than you.

That afternoon, the boy fried an egg on the sidewalk, sunny side up. Mother said to waste food was sin, though she had no qualms about dumping Daddy's rot gut and gin. While Daddy was comatose with drink, down the sink she would pour it. The son knew the ritual well.

Tonight was the same, Daddy soused and couched, Mother cleaning his puke before the dinner dishes. Daddy wouldn't recall a thing tomorrow, another day which held mother's silence from fear, shame and Daddy's from ethanol's eager eraser.

Daddy would never know a transformer blew but a block from their house, leaving unsettled scores in the dark, or that for once Mother and son wouldn't have to look at Daddy's hangdog face, the incandescent haze which bathed it absent, thanks to a blessing from a blackout of another sort.

Cutting the Hand

She wrote an entire novel about a man who cut his hand on a can of sardines he found in a silent cupboard of a prairie house abandoned since the dust bowl, or perhaps since the eighth day of creation.

The can he opened with a rusty blade he found in yet another home of ghosts on a treeless lane in Topeka. There he spent four naked nights hiding from the cruelest January, his memories, and the devil who his mama said eschewed the cold. And he believed her but built a fire all the same, until a fat fisted sheriff came and sent him into the night, where a wailing wind waited and blew him south through the dark like just another tumbleweed.

When he finally landed, dry and thrashed in his new sagging palace, the snows had melted, and the winds had calmed. There he found fine fodder in a tin with sailor standing proud with a feast of fish at his feet. Seemed a shame to behead the mariner with such a dull tool only to find mush and ancient fetor anointed by three drops of his red blood the can demanded in exchange for its long dead bounty.

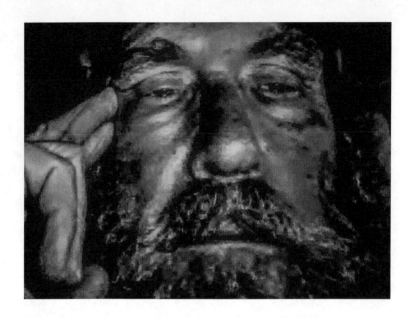

Dark Visage

I had no power. From my Mumbai hotel I could see the stream of people in the narrow street below. A cart carrying the dead listed and nearly toppled over. The ox pulling it did not stop dragging the askew carriage along.

Passersby steered clear of the primitive hearse, knowing it carried the curse, the fever felling the denizens of this muggy megapolis. A plague harvesting souls quicker than they could be burned. The Mithi was thick with their ashes, diluted only by tears of the mourners who harbored fears they would be next.

I was there, a helpless healer. A doctor turned detective, running a race to find a cause, a miracle cure. All my potions impotent, all my staring at slides a lesson in limitations, ignorance—a discovery of crawling creatures too miniscule to be dissected, too beguiling to be understood.

My eyes were tired of looking at the tiny death moguls and their victims; my ears weary of the entreaties for relief from suffering. Yet I stood and watched, one wagon after another, hauling carrion for the pyres.

I prayed the power would stay off, for light would have shone on me. Me, a curious survivor, unworthy of whatever grace kept me from the heaps of lifeless limbs bound for the fires of the night.

What it ate I do not know. If it ate, I do not know. The coldest winter in a century starved many a beast, yet it survived. I had never seen such a lean wolf, nor had I seen one so black. Its eyes were green as emeralds.

The wolf visited my frigid ranch thrice before I fed it. I asked my brother, who had the spread north of mine, if he had seen it. Nope, he said, hadn't spotted a wolf or coyote since the first hard snow. Dead deer, and a frozen steer or two, but not it, Lobo Negro, as my former hired hand Pedro would say. Black Wolf.

Pedro said when he was a boy in the mountains of Mexico, far from my Wyoming ranch, an old man told the villagers a tale of a Lobo Negro, a black wolf that would never die.

The old man was a brujo and much respected. He told the people of the village, if they saw this wolf, they should leave food for it. The wolf was there to protect them from the evil of men, the brujo claimed. An offering would be wise. For years, not a soul in the village saw the Lobo Negro. Yet the villagers did as the brujo said and left half a rabbit or a calf bone with meat for the wolf.

Pedro said shortly before the brujo died, he told the villagers the Lobo Negro would come to them with the first snow. Wicked men, the brujo said, would follow and ride through the village, but they would hear the haunting howls of the wolf and harm no one.

Pedro swore this came to pass, just as the brujo prophesied. A snow dusted the mountains around the village on New Year's Day, and that night, many of the villagers swore they saw the wolf amble by their hovels, while they huddled around their fires and claimed they heard the howls in the icy night as the wolf returned to the mountains. The following day, banditos on stolen stallions rode through their streets but did not stop and said not a word. In the distance, while the nefarious ones passed on the frozen dirt roads, the wolf could be heard howling, admonishing these men to leave the villagers in peace.

Pedro had told me other stories like this. Who was I to question them? My entire life, I had prayed to a God I never saw, and my prayers were not usually answered. I prayed plenty the year before and it didn't save my wife from cancer. Of late, I had been praying for another miracle. Times had been hard, and I owed back taxes on my place. I prayed for a way to keep my ranch.

I don't know if his story played into my decision to feed the wolf, but the third time it appeared, not fifty feet from my mud room, I threw it a raw rib eye. The wolf picked the meat up with his snout, stood motionless in the moonlight, fixed his green eyes on me, then turned and walked slowly into the stand of pine behind my barn.

I fed the black wolf every time it came around after that. I had never seen a wolf that close. Wolves avoided people. Maybe it was Pedro's story. Maybe it was the early stirrings of madness in me, maybe it was desperation, but I didn't find it odd this solitary figure came so close. Some nights, I would wonder, while drifting off to sleep, if the wolf was even real. I could have been throwing flesh to an apparition or a figment of my imagination.

Then one night after a stout blizzard, I was driving back from town and saw taillights blinking in a ditch off the highway—two red eyes in a sea of moon gray snow. I pulled over and walked through the deep drifts to the car. Inside what turned out to be a white Mercedes was a young man. He had seen me and rolled down the window as I approached.

Can't get a damn cell phone signal out here, he said. I swerved to avoid some damn dog and here I am.

You won't get a signal out here, I said, but I got a land line at my ranch not a mile up this road.

I cleared enough snow for the man to open his door, and he introduced himself as he slipped out of his vehicle.

I am Ben Redwine, he said.

We extended and shook glove covered hands and walked quickly to my truck.

At the ranch, I made coffee while the Ben made calls to find a tow. I asked what the heck he was doing up here in the Wyoming wilds at night. Ben had California plates on his Mercedes. He said he was scouting locations to film a movie after a deal to make one in Canada had fallen through. Ben had been in town with the only realtor, hoping to find a ranch for sale in repo, but, despite hard times, there were none. Ben asked if I knew of any ranchers who might be interested. I don't know why, but before I answered his question, I asked what color dog had caused him to drive into the ravine.

Black, he said. Looked like a wolf, but I figured it more likely a mongrel.

Ben, I would be glad to lease you this place to make all the movies you want. Depending on the money you are offering.

Ben said the producer's budget allowed for purchase of a small place or a lease; he offered me twice what I owed in back taxes to use the place for the three summer months. I would move in with my brother for that time and keep my ranch.

Ben spent the night, and, in the morning, I drove him to meet his tow. I stayed until after the truck hauled his Mercedes to town. I looked up at the tree line on the high ridge above the ravine. I swear I saw something black moving slow in the white bark pines.

A Casual Killing

I had been in country one week when I pulled guard duty. Bob V. from St. Louis was assigned the bunker with me. Bob had been in 'nam a week longer than I and already had received a Dear John letter from his fiancée, April.

Earlier that day, the Lieutenant in charge of the guards told a cautionary tale of a ROK Marine getting shot for falling asleep on guard duty. We didn't know if the story was apocryphal. We did know Koreans were punished far more severely than American GIs, but we were newbies, and the story (told by the Lieutenant to everyone we heard) stuck with us.

At ten, we were dropped off at our bunker at the north end of our compound. The bunker sat between two hills, one of which had a guard tower.

Bob was dead down about April. Our conversation for two hours alternated between how Bob intended to get April back and how this guard duty was the "real thing." Here we were, green as our new jungle fatigues, in a bunker staring at concertina wire and a small valley our bunker was positioned to guard. The guards in the tower could see most of what we were assigned to watch. Lighting was good too. Bob and I were still vigilant, and newbie serious, but not afraid at that point.

At midnight, the Lieutenant made his first check at our bunker and asked how things were going. When the Lieutenant left took off in his jeep, Bob again started talking about April. He said they began dating four years ago as high school juniors and were engaged at Thanksgiving when he was home on leave. Three weeks later—dumped via airmail.

I managed to get him talking about the Cardinals; we discovered we had been at the same game—the last home game of the 1958 season. St. Louis was Bob's home, but I lived there during first and second grade. I would always remember the game because my dad managed to get us in the locker room afterwards, at which time he introduced me to Stan the Man Musial. I reached out to shake the legendary player's hand and he dropped a ball into my glove (eight-year old boys always carried their baseball mitts to games, hoping to catch a homer). On the ball Stan had written, "To Dave, keep getting on base! Best wishes, Stan Musial." My father had fought the battle of Anzio with a man who worked for the

Cardinals' organization. We had free tickets to several games, but that night was the only time my father had taken me to the locker room to meet a player.

Bob predictably went on to tell me April and he had often gone to Cardinal games. When the Lieutenant pulled up at 2 AM, I was ready to tell Bob we had to change the subject, or I would lock and load my M16 and shoot either him or me.

Immediately after the Lieutenant drove off, Bob asked if I saw something move in shadows beyond the wire. I didn't have time to answer before two satchel charges went off in the wire and tracers from the tower began filling the valley. Whoever was there had been seen by the tower. We saw muzzle fire coming from the valley, first towards the tower and then rounds started whizzing by us.

My hands were shaking but I had pulled the bolt back and flipped off the safety and was ready to begin firing when I heard more explosions and small arms fire behind us in the compound. Though I didn't realize it at the time, the incursion we were attempting to repel was a diversion. I managed to block out what was behind me and focus on putting down fire towards the wire in front of us.

Bob was already firing bursts on automatic, the way we had been trained to do when in a firefight at night, but I could see his tracers going all over the place, even peppering the bottom of the hill where the tower was. (Later he would tell me that was intentional because he thought the sappers would head up the hill to the tower—his fire pattern was too random for me to believe it). I hated auto because I always worried I would run out of ammo. I began firing directly into the mangled wire on semi. Bob had gone through three magazines before I ejected my first empty one. On his fourth, his weapon jammed. He began swearing and a round from the VC grazed his steel pot. I pointed my weapon at the exact spot I saw the muzzle flash, fired five rounds on semi, and saw a body fall backwards. A few more tracers came from the tower, then everything was silent.

During the brief firefight we had at the wire, six sappers had hit the convalescent center behind us, killing 2 and wounding 15. We saw choppers from Nha Trang coming in to Medivac the wounded not twenty minutes after the attack.

In the melee behind us in the compound, only one of the six sappers was hit. As it turned out, a major who had served with my father in WW2 was mooching a bunk from the mess officer while he was visiting a recuperating buddy at the convalescent center. The major emptied the magazine from his 45 at the sappers as they made their escape after they had lobbed a dozen satchel charges and sprayed two to three hundred AK 47 rounds into the wards.

The rapid reaction force (on which I would later serve) had formed and was headed to reinforce us when the VC slipped in, undetected, from the opposite side of the compound.

At dawn, the Lieutenant, the CO, Bob, two other guards and I reconnoitered the perimeter wire where the firefight occurred. Of the three VC sappers who attacked our position, the tower guards had killed one, and I had killed another—the first and last person I would kill in eleven months in the 'nam. The VC killed by the tower's firing was flat in his stomach, his black pajamas covered with dried blood. The VC sapper I killed was leaning back into the concertina wire, a trail of blood from his mouth down to his groin. The back of his head had exposed brain. Apparently, I shot him in the mouth.

After an hour in HQ debriefing, Bob and I went to the mess hall. I remember eating powdered eggs and toast and having coffee with lots of sugar. Bob had the same chow but had his coffee black. We smoked the first cigarette since before guard duty—a Lucky Strike.

Bob began talking about April. I watched his mouth as he spoke. I tried to remember what the sapper's mouth looked like after my high velocity M16 round knocked out his teeth and spun wildly through his brain until it came out the back of his skull. Then I asked Bob if he thought April might take him back.

Proxima Centauri

Tonight, I lay on the ground looking at the stars. Something I haven't done since...never perhaps. A scant half century ago, Joni Mitchell told us "We are stardust, we are golden." Not sure we needed to know about the Big Bang to understand our kinship with these balls of fire. (And I was never certain we were golden.)

I don't know many of their names. The light from the closest takes over four years to get here. I am, therefore, staring at pinholes in that black tarp that may now have been filled in by the solder of time.

But I won't ever know, even if I have another twenty journeys around our star. Even if I have a million.

I don't pretend to know if something or someone is out there looking at us. Another me, prostrate on his drive, soaking up the last heat of the day, star gazing with pen (or iPad) in hand. Another me, ignorant of what he sees. Another me, tricked by the pinpricks in the night. Believing the light of our sun is just a blink away. Believing it to be infinite, eternal, when it could be gone before it reaches the eyes of another world.

Does my galactic clone-twin believe there is a God? Does he own some beautiful tale about his own star birthing all others out of love or desire for kinship in all that space? Does he believe the fire of all creation could be anything but love?

If so, what of the slaughter that occurs every moment? The collapsing of worlds under their own weary weight? Or the death of a child at a mother's dry breast?

Now I see a blinking star, a mere five miles from me, loosed from earth's grave hold by its own fire. Flying through the night from one name to another—not from Canis Majoris to Alpha Centauri, but from Dallas to Denver. Why it had to flash in the dark I do not know. Why it brought me from the mournful light of dying stars I do not know.

There will be other nights with phantom lights. Perchance I can watch without being pulled back from a dream by Delta Airlines.

After the Storms

He walked through his cornfield, careful not to trample the dead and dying stalks, though the funnel had leveled most of them. The radio said a wing of the courthouse was flattened. His house was spared. Only a few shingles were peeled from his roof, though his barn fared less well, the red behemoth now a heap of planks and beams, mournful in their silence.

He would rebuild, just as his daddy and grandpa had done after the black twisters chose this spot to ravage with their savage dance, their vengeful fall from the sky.

It was the foreign detritus which caught his eye: water bottles, white trash bags, and myriad papers littered his land, snatched from town, dropped on his fertile fields. The wife and he spent the gray day policing the acres most sullied by the trash, filling black bag after bag with rubbish until they bulged like bloated cows long dead on a sultry day.

He didn't long tarry at his task which was as wearisome as baling hay. At noon hour they rested, took light repast.

It was then he found it. Who would have thought a paper, filched from some drawer and sucked into the heavens, would find that spot, not fifty feet from where his boy slept until meningitis took him?

The document weathered the cyclone well—the writing still crisp, the edges not frayed. It proclaimed someone had passed, the date of death fresh.

He was his namesake, though they never called him Junior. When he read the words and saw his own name, for a moment he wondered if the dawn had been a dream, and it was he who was lost, yanked from the earth by some hand his son never saw, but one he witnessed with his own eyes and knew was black and without mercy.

We shared a Camel, after my thumb stopped you. I took the first drag before I handed it to you—you trusted my spit enough to share and my road look enough for me to be there, in your shining new Oldsmobile Eighty-Eight.

You had just come back, from there. I was on my way. I did not ask if that was why your right hand had only two fingers and a thumb, though you told me straight up of trying to close an armored personnel carrier hatch and the AK-47 round that kept you from doing magic tricks.

When our smoke was half gone, we passed the dying neon of a long dead bar, safe from its stench in your new smelling car. It was then you asked if I had "anything else to smoke," a line from our riddled anthem—one we sang like nursery rhyme.

I had my stash stuffed in my jeans since thumbs attracted cops as well as wounded warriors in shiny new rides. I piggy lit the joint with the Camel before I crushed the fag in your fresh ash tray. Now we were sharing our deepest breaths and whatever else we could not forget.

The weed was gone by the time we reached the last city lights. In our flying chariot, we zipped into the black desert night. It was then your demons began to howl. Maybe it was a full moon that called them out to ride on its beams into the starry sky where they could dance with other devils and gods who had forsaken them, and you.

I did not understand your moans, your tears, or the song you played on the eight track that chanted about freedom which could not be bought or sold or to whom you spoke when you wailed, you were sorry, sorry, again and again. I only knew they were ghost spirits likely kept at bay by the light of day, but there to haunt you in the dark.

"Reggie, Big Mike, and Cleveland" were all silent as you begged them to forgive you for some simmering sin I could not understand. (Not then in the desert dark, though one day I would beseech other ghosts to let me off the hook as well.)

Your cries did stop when you turned onto a rutted desert road, where you put the pedal to the floor and the rocks pocked the undercarriage like machine gun fire. You popped out the eight track and stopped a half mile from Highway 54. I lit another Camel in the synovial silence. Your tears kept streaming down your face, but you no longer called out to the ghosts, perhaps left resting behind you on that black highway. I don't know if they spoke to you when I handed you the smoke. You did look around, as if someone was there before reaching over to open my door…

I did not ask why you were leaving me with the moon and the stars and the sand, so far from the lights and sound, or why I could not feel my feet when they touched the ground. The last thing I saw was your dust filling the rumbling air and the orange glow of the Camel flying through the blue night.

Goodbye Charlie, Hello Vietnam

Nineteen. I was ten and nine. Two A.M. Landed in some muggy, putrid place. Between honor and complete disgrace. Smelled like that for sure. Issued tools of our trade. Heard the true sound of "rockets' red glare." Had us hunkering in bunkers all night. Pissing in our helmets. Holding our ears. Damn, the first night. Welcome to Vee-et-nam.

Morning. Sunshine and quiet. Except the rap from old timers. "Newbies". New jungle fatigues. Newbies. New M-16. Clean boots. All day the old timers, telling each other how these newbies had their cherry popped. First night in country and the biggest ass mortar attack they had ever seen. Heard. Heard, I said. Yeah. What, newbie? Now you have heard the real rockets' red glare. That's what you heard, Newbie.

I get it. Newbies are scum. We are scum and they aren't going to waste breath telling us anything. Watch. Watch and learn. I hope. Lines. Lines to get teeth rinsed with fluoride. Lines. To chow. To get shots. To in-country orientation. Lines. Memorize lines. Lines to get ammo. Lines to get orders.

No line at the outhouse. Gray three-seater. Heat roasting our dung. Old timer kicked the planks before he sat down beside me in the stench. I asked the question but only with my eyes. Kick the planks before you sit down so rats won't bite your balls off. Kick the planks to scare off the rats. Rats. The size of possum. Not an exaggeration. Possum rats. Rat possums. Who the hell knew? Just kick the planks. Save your balls.

More lines. Then darkness. Then more booms. Not incoming. Our own. 1-5-5s. Learn the difference newbie so you don't crap your drawers for nothing. That's the boys in that artillery firebase keeping Charlie awake for the night. Returning the favor. Charlie. Sounds like a name you would call someone who was a buddy doesn't it? Charlie. Victor Charlie. V C. Chink Charlie. Dink Charlie. Charlie this and Charlie that. Oh, Charlie would eat that rat.

My first duty. Guarding Charlie. Prisoner with leg blown off at the knee and cuffed to a bed in our clean smelling dispensary. MP and I assigned night shift. Keep each other awake. Looked at Charlie. Charlie looked at me. Smirk. Then spit. Landed on my boot. My newbie boot. Not a newbie boot anymore. Charlie squirms. Spits again and misses. MP gets up and threatens to bash Charlie in Charlie's little head. Medic comes and gives squirming, smirking, spitting Charlie shot of good drugs. Charlie doesn't spit on medic. Charlie gets drowsy. I get drowsy. MP falls asleep. I stand up. Newbie afraid to fall asleep on guard duty. I wake the MP before shift change. Charlie is up. Smirk, smirk. Thus spoke Charlie. The only conversation I ever had with Charlie.

Medic says Charlie getting on a bird to someplace. Can't remember where. Anyplace. Charlie leaving and me staying. Envy is a word I learned that day. Cost him part of a leg, medic says when I tell him I wish I was Charlie just then. Had heard tales about people shooting off their toes to get out of the 'nam. "Turd tales" I would call them, since I heard so many in those gray crappers. With rats. Possum rats and your balls. Balls or a limb? Did I really want to be him? I don't really remember. I didn't want to be there, somewhere between honor and complete disgrace. Goodbye Charlie. Hello Vietnam.

Memory Number Three

I found you, in a stack of photos: Albuquerque, 1967. The 2D you, I can't touch, taste or smell.

The first thing that came to mind was sharing a joint with you and spilling the chocolate ice cream cone on your skin-tight white shorts and sneaking into the Woolworth bathroom, and our freaked frenzied scrubbing of fabric with nimble fingers and pink powdered hand soap. And how we couldn't stop laughing until a woman older than time caught us before we could consummate.

Which we did after running the entire 200 yards to my van, wet white shorts in your hand, with me looking over my shoulder for imagined narcs, cops, and other freedom snatchers.

When we finished, we shared my last Winston, blowing smoke rings in the gathering gloom. Your shorts were dry, and our high had worn off. You didn't kiss me goodbye when I dropped you off.

Between your pad and mine, I hit a black mongrel pup wandering on the dark asphalt. I scooped him off the road with my hands. Lifeless, light he was.

I found you, in that stack of ancient photos—that was the day we conceived a son, one you had shredded in a doctor's office for $300 in illegal tender. I see the messy ice cream, your naked nineteen-year-old flesh, smoke rings disappearing, the poor mutt dying, and, though not for lack of trying, I can't see the child you had executed in utero—without trial, judge or jury, or reason, save an elusive dream of freedom.

Will was drawn to that spot. Spirits or not, something-somebody pulled him there like a mystic magnet that attracts flesh. And flesh he found in that grove, between a stubborn hackberry and twisted oak: mother and newborn, their blood soaking the prairie grasses.

He walked the hard mile to the pay phone, passing but one unfriendly ranch house on the way—a growling cur keeping him at bay. The operator connected him with the sheriff who collected his one deputy and was there in half an hour.

Lord Almighty, Lord Almighty, the deputy kept saying, his words like incantations hanging in the hot air above the bodies. The sheriff checked for pulses, his khaki pants painted round red at the knees for he was too old to squat. Neither knew the girl, who couldn't have been age of consent, but the baby looked pink, strong, though still as stone.

The ambulance couldn't make it to the grove. The driver and deputy carried them out on one stretcher, both commenting how light their fated cargo was and how it was a shame they perished in that old copse.

Will knew that was meant to be when he found them, the little one first clinging to a dark warm sea inside, forced out by time, the young mother's helpless heaving, and some invisible hand that took part in all matters of flesh, spirit and bone—the same hand that did not cradle them, but at least found them shade, a cool but cruel reprieve from their terse time in the sun.

Sweetwater, Texas, 1959

Francisco was thirteen. He had climbed the mountain west of his hamlet many times. Usually, he went with friends, but if they were playing ball or working, Francisco would go alone.

The day after his grandmother was buried, Francisco put on his new Keds and went across the desert towards the mountain. The previous five days, he had been at home, in church, and finally at the cemetery. Francisco was eager to get out—his friends hadn't come around since his grandmother passed and he knew they would wait a few days before returning. Junior High boys were not fond of the polite quietude that followed death in most households.

The thermometer on his porch read 97—normal for late July. He left without water, but he and his friends never carried water. In far west Texas, in 1963, the word dehydration was not part of anyone's lexicon and water was for pussies. At least that is what his coaches told them when they complained of being thirsty in practice.

A few blessed clouds followed him the first half of his mile trek to the mountain. When they moved east, Francisco was protected from the sun by only his Los Angeles Dodgers hat.

At the base of the mountain, Francisco sat on a large boulder and looked back at the arroyo that led to his house. Above him, he saw one whiff of cloud surrounded by a blue desert sky. There were days when the sky was white, and his grandmother had said a white sky meant God was cleansing the heavens. Grandmother knew nothing of Raleigh Scattering or the electromagnetic spectrum (and neither did Francisco), but he had begun to question his grandmother's mythology before he finished elementary school.

Directly above him, Francisco saw four buzzards circling. Francisco was always amazed by the flight of birds, especially raptors who seemed to move effortlessly. He looked around for a carcass and breathed through his nose. Many times, he and his friends had seen a circling kettle and had smelled the dead before they saw them. Mostly they came upon a steer or javelina. Once the vultures led them to a dead doe down from the mountains.

Francisco could not find any carrion and yet the birds circled directly above. They continued above him as climbed the mountain. Maybe there was something on top, he thought.

Francisco felt tired during his hike up the mountain, but he had not slept much since his grandmother had died. She had lived with his family his entire life. Each night, before retiring, she would ask him if he had said his prayers. Of late, she would ask him to pray for her, though she had not been sick. She died suddenly of a heart attack while sweeping the porch. She was fifty-eight. Too young to die, all the adults had been saying. She did not seem young to Francisco, though he had a great grandfather on his father's side and he was ninety. Francisco did wonder why Great Grandfather was still driving around in his truck, working in his garden and going to mass when his mother's mother was in the ground. Each night since her passing, Francisco would feel something, not an emptiness—more like a steel rod that went from the back of his eyes to his gut. This feeling kept him awake later than usual, and even though it was summer, Francisco found himself waking early, before the sun, and thinking of his grandmother.

He stopped to rest more than he usually did; each time, the buzzards were there, gliding on the currents. Francisco continued to scan the mountain and desert for the dead, but he saw nothing, even when he reached the top and could see in every direction. The vultures were still there, a tighter circle now, though no closer to the earth even though Francisco was closer to the heavens.

Francisco felt light-headed. He placed his hands on his knees and took a deep breath. He did not recall ever feeling like this. The heaviest of all his friends, Roberto, would complain of this when they hiked up the mountain, but Roberto was "gordo." In fact, that was what the older boys called Roberto.

Francisco was thirsty and felt as if he were going to throw up. It had been four hours since he had eaten and then only two small tortillas and two eggs. When he began hiking down, the sun was nearly overhead. The buzzards still were as well, making their casual circle. When Francisco reached the bottom, he sat again on the same large boulder and watched the birds, black against a now all white sky. Francisco thought of his grandmother's words and wondered what God was cleansing—if there was a God.

He looked at the arroyo that led to his back yard. A small canyon that became a river when rare heavy rains fell. Today, it was only a line of green slithering through a blanched desert. Francisco wished it would rain. He still felt nauseous and now very hot—he had perspired all the way up the mountain but little on top or during his descent.

Francisco's legs began to ache and three or four times he stopped in the shade of mesquites along the arroyo. Each time, he saw the kettle—now they were closer. His arm also started to hurt as he climbed from the arroyo to the small trail that led to the stone wall in his backyard. He opened the gate and fell to the ground. Above him, he saw the four vultures, still gliding on currents, closer now though not menacing—merely a quartet of silent raptors performing their ballet on an ethereal stage. Francisco tried to breathe but could not. His eyes were open. His heart stopped. The buzzards would soon reap the benefits of their prescience and their day's lofty labor.

And Not One Sparrow Falls*

Wedded that day, on their way to El Paso, for two nights in a grand motel with TV and AC. They would splurge, for profligacy was not a sin at such times, and a fat steer was sacrificed for it. The radio filled the cab of the pickup with Tammy "Why-not" singing D-I-V-O-R-C-E. The newlywed couple sang along, changing the letters to M-A-R-R-I-E-D, creating a cheerful cacophony in their shared space.

When the next tune started, he hit: a greasy buzzard, wingspan wide as a fence post was tall and black as an oil slick. The old windshield was no match for the vulture, and it was a vengeful one that crashed into Ronny. Glass, bone, feather and flesh tore into his sweet face like a chainsaw, his blood blinding him.

Ronny turned so hard on that wheel the truck rolled, twice, landing them on the passenger side in an arroyo, where he lay on top of her, gasping, his blood dripping generously on her.

Ronny, Ronny...

Her legs were numb, and she felt a warm liquid crawling down her back, blood she knew was from her own head, which smacked the roof so hard she was surprised her skull hadn't popped.

Or maybe it had, for she saw double: two steering wheels; two setting suns; two mangled birds and two crimson faced Ronnys, who then had stopped gasping. Only slow breaths came from him, like a warm whisper on her cheeks—but only until the song ended. And she knew, he was gone. Old verse came to her, from Psalms, or from Matthew, and she knew, she was sure, someone would find them, and make her whole, and resurrect Ronny for the good Lord would not do this to them, on this hopeful highway, before they consummated.

She harbored such a notion until her own eyes closed, and other dark birds came to find them, still, under her God's closed eye.

1968, north of Marfa, Texas

*The title is an allusion to a verse (from Matthew) about not one bird falling without God knowing. In the early 70s, I had a landlord whose daughter's face was mangled by a buzzard that crashed through her truck windshield.

The Character Actor's Son. The Soldier's Son.

Last week, an actor died. He had been in over a hundred films. I recognized the pic someone posted on Facebook. His son, Tom, from whom he had been estranged for decades, lives on my block. We speak now and then but are not close friends. The afternoon after his dad passed, Tom was walking his dog and saw me retrieving my trash bin from the curb. I said sorry about your dad. He asked how I knew. Facebook, of course, I said.

Tom stood in front of me, silent for quite some time, dog tugging on its leash. Then he told me the following. The night before, Tom said, he had a dream in which he was walking in a park. The foliage on the trees was thick, but then a breeze came. The leaves began drifting slowly to the ground. The wind picked up, with gusts ripping the leaves from the branches. All the leaves were falling directly to the ground, as if they were invisibly weighted. Laws of physics suspended in dreams, of course. At first the leaves were green, but then they became yellow, gold, and finally russet. The wind blew until all the leaves had been stripped from the branches, leaving the trees apocalyptically barren with their naked arms reaching out to the sky which had turned from blue to icy white.

Tom continued walking, now through leaves piled so deep he had to take high steps one would if walking through snow drifts. He came upon a pond that was uniformly covered with the leaves—equal spaces between each leaf like they had been placed there by hand rather than cast there by a tempest. But the pond was black, and the leaves were white. The pond was surrounded by trees. The tops of the trees were reflected in this black water. The branches looked ultraviolet on the pond. But what reflects off black?

Then Tom came to the edge of woods so dense they formed a dark impenetrable place. The wall of foliage seemed to be all around him. The pond was gone, the leaves gone as well. The ground was gray and barren. Two graves had been dug at the edge of the woods.

For years, Tom said, he had successfully blocked his father out of his mind, but lately he had been thinking about his dad often. Maybe it was knowing his Dad was eighty-five and had some heart issues his sister said the docs were unable to treat. Maybe it was turning sixty, Tom thought.

Tom reminded me he and his dad became estranged when his father left his mother for a younger woman. Tom's mom was an alcoholic and Tom didn't blame his dad for leaving her. Tom did blame him for not being there when his mom got breast cancer and died less than a year after his father left. Tom also blamed him for squandering his college fund on a flop of a flick he and some others tried to produce.

Tom said he guessed that was all water under the bridge now—all that baggage way down stream. Now he had to decide whether to attend the service.

I asked if he was really considering going. It was eight hundred miles to LA where his dad was to be interred. Tom said he would only go because of his sister. She had remained close to their dad.

My neighbor did go to the service. When he returned yesterday, he came to my house. I was surprised to see him and asked how the service went. Tom said it went well and he recognized some of his dad's friends from seeing them in films or on TV. Tom's sis was very glad he came, and Tom said he was too.

Tom said he came to talk to me because he had told me about the dream. He asked if I remembered. I told him I was surprised he told me to begin with, but I certainly remembered. Tom said he'd told only two people about the dream—me and his wife when she was driving him to the airport. When he got to LA, he didn't tell his sister. And, based on what his sister told Tom, he was not sure he was going to tell her.

Before Tom made the decision to go, his sister had only told him his father had a heart attack and died the night before. The details she fleshed out when Tom got to LA. His sister said his dad and wife, the woman for whom he had left Tom's mother, had been walking in the park. A storm approached, and they hurried back to the car. Tom's dad complained of chest pains and being lightheaded. His wife immediately took him to the ER where he coded. The ER staff revived him, and he was transferred to cardiac intensive care. As the on-call cardiologist was examining him, Tom's dad had another heart attack. They could not revive him. His father's wife called Tom's sister about two in the morning, but his sister chose to wait to until later in the morning to call Tom. He was told only a few hours before he talked to me about the dream.

Tom said he was a bit spooked he had a dream about the park and the storm the night his dad died. What was even more disconcerting he said, was the fact that he saw two graves in the park. I was about to ask why when he told me his father's wife had a heart attack herself the evening after his dad's service. The live-in housekeeper said the woman came home, sat on the couch, said she was tired and asked the housekeeper for some coffee. When the housekeeper returned with the beverage, the woman was keeled over, dead. The EMTs arrived quickly and worked on her for a long time—she was only sixty-nine and appeared to be healthy—but they never could get her heart beating again.

So, the two graves in the dream I said. But why hadn't he told his sister about the dream? Tom said his sister believed dreams could reveal things that were going to happen. Tom said even after this, he wasn't sure it was anything but coincidence. He asked what I thought. I paused before answering and said I didn't know for sure if dreams could be prescient but what happened to him was quite a coincidence. I don't know why I did not tell him, the night before my father died, I had a dream I saw a soldier leaning over my mother and handing her a folded flag, exactly the way it occurred at the VA Cemetery only a week later.

The Silence of the Street in the Morning

Through her window, Estrella watched sun shafts through the trees, a transient tapestry on her potholed lane. A half dozen eggs sat beside her bowl ready to be beat for the scramble--a half dozen hours after her street was alight with noise.

First the pernicious pop of the zip guns. Then the cops' .38s. Then the waling of the sirens and the howling of the survivors. Mostly Chico's mama and sister who watched Chico gunned down and tried to plug his half dozen holes with their hands.

The street doesn't remember, Estrella thought, even with a biography of black blood dried in its cracks and crevices. If it did, surely it would protest, or make a solemn sound when the dawn shed all that honest light on dark death. Estrella cracked the eggs, put them in the hot lard, not bothering with the bowl, breaking yolks blindly in the black skillet, her eyes yet on the silent street. The street will not remember, Estrella thought.

Spanish Harlem, September 1960

Tony Lama in the Kitchen

February 2017

I am now sixty-five. Tony Lama was born sixty-five years before I was. In 1970, I delivered groceries to him in his stucco home off Rim Road in El Paso. He greeted me warmly when I came through the back door with a box of groceries in my arms. It may have been forty-seven years ago today.

He made boots. Millions of them.

Many people make things. Some make boots, some make boats, some make bombs. Tony made things people pulled on their feet every morning. Some wore them to their office. Some on their ranch. Some to school. And some were buried in them.

By the time I met Mr. Lama in his kitchen, he had long passed the torch to others to make boots that bore his name. Standing there, all eighteen self-absorbed years of me, I wonder if I imagined when he had made his last boot. If I had the wisdom of years, which I did not, I would have asked him when he cut his last piece of leather, when he made his last stitch. I would have asked if he knew on that very day others would carry on, that his time of molding calfskin into his art was over.

I would have asked him those things. And I would have asked when he made his first pair of boots. Did he recall who wore them? If I had any sense, I would have asked if the time he made his first cut until the time he made his last had, as it seems to for me, passed like a sleepless night, with morning light dimmer than he expected.

I would have asked all those things. The answers may have meant little at the time. But tonight, a million boots and steps later, I could say I truly knew the man, not for his name and fame, but for our common humanity. Whatever that means.

I made nothing. I chose to be a healer of sorts, and not too good of one by my reckoning. I can live with that. It's a dirty job, but someone must do it. For others, the art of counseling is a noble calling. For me, it's all I know to do. I try to help others make sense of the chaos. That's on a good day. On a bad one, I try to keep someone from destroying himself and those around him. It's a dirty job, but someone must do it.

Most days, I wish I could rewind the clock and be side by side with Tony at the birth of the twentieth century, cutting and stitching along with him. Perhaps all I would have seen were the tools and calfskin in front of me. I suspect many craftsmen are so focused on the task at hand. Maybe, just maybe, my imagination would have soared, and I would have envisioned the boots with spurs on a bucking bronco, or a man slipping them off after a hard day's work, placing them at his bedside, close, ready to be pulled on another day.

But let's get back to the kitchen, the one I stood in forty-seven years ago (or just yesterday?) The place where I saw an old man, done with his labors, his legacy in place. But he took the time to smile and greet me. To make me feel welcome, though I was but an itinerant servant, stacking cans on a counter. I would never make anything. I would not have a name stamped on a million feet. And maybe he saw that in my eyes.

Perhaps he knew my hand would wield pens and not shears. Maybe he didn't give me a second thought after that smile. Perhaps he was back on the factory floor, dreaming while awake, the drone of the machines a symphony to him. I wish I would have asked. Though perhaps he was thinking only of whether I brought the salt pork for his beans, the peaches for his pie.

The Sea Glass Collector

The jagged edges which gashed the boy's bare feet on the trash trove of shore by his trailer slashed the folds of his memory as well. He chooses to tell no tales of that hungry, motherless time—sharp years when he prayed his dad would be passed out when he got home. And usually he was, there on the cat piss sofa, splayed out like some beached whale while the boy scavenged for food and old pop bottles.

A lifetime now since those foul filled days, he is a continent away, yet living on the shore, with a fat portfolio and thin wife, who both protect him from "intrusive thoughts." Though he still hunts for treasures on the sands, not the nickel returns which once bought his daily bread.

Instead, he seeks more ancient relics. Now the boy-man hunts for glass made smooth by the round chisel of time—soft, cool, full of color, with no recollection of the fire that forged it.

Raining in Manhattan

My actress, who sweated blood on Broadway each night—off Broadway too—said, on a long stroll through Central Park, she was successful because she did not like herself. On the stage, she proclaimed, she was never herself, and she fell in love with every character she portrayed. Every script was a better bio than her own, and the playwrights knew her better than she knew herself.

And when our walk was curtailed by a downpour, she dragged me into a crowded café, where she knew half the patrons and the wait staff, and they all knew the different personas she had owned on the dry stage. Rain now forced her to choose which selves to keep, and which to lose while she sipped scalding tea.

I had to wonder, which persona was with me on a grey wet afternoon, only hours before she would again be under the spell of hot lights and verses from the pens of prophets and poets: those who purloined her soul for the price of admission but took her to a place without self-loathing.

Along Fence Lines

Many of his posts tilted, like trees tired of the wind. Barbed wire sagged, red rusted, but still jabbed the errant cow when duty called.

Three quarters a century he rode the same trail. Of late, he had gone afoot, the saddle too heavy for him to heft. Walking, he reconnoitered the tracks with more care—hooves of his myriad steers, a few equine signs of the farrier's labor still there, fast fading. His boot prints were more numerous now, and sometimes tamped down by the few beasts left in his herd.

Across the line lay his dead neighbor's pastures, peppered with mesquite and pocked by fire ant holes. No livestock grazed, but the giant turbine blades whined, white whipsaws slashing not timber, but blue sky, driven by the relentless winds. They called to him, in chanted chorus, issuing a premonition: one day soon, your fence will fall, and the path you trod will bear no new tracks for other souls to read.

The Glass Cases at Schwarz's

Smudges on the display glass were wiped away each night by a mute custodian who found a biography in each set of prints he made disappear with clean cloth and vinegar. He could tell which ones were made by children, dragged there with promise of ice cream, later.

Oh, the young lovers' prints were unmistakable—eager tracks being led to more and more promising carats. And the thin marks left by the frail made him wonder if this would be their last precious purchase. A remorse? A reckoning?

The cases held diamonds, rubies by the score, but the silent sentinel saw only the surface. That was his world, one of cautious transparency and fickle reflections. He reluctantly erased these fingered tales, the marks life left anon and anon, for he knew it was his duty to wipe the slate clean, to allow resurrection, renewed vision of a bejeweled world for others to discover, just below his sight.

Math among the Markers

Inspired by a morning at the Fort Sill National Cemetery

I can never resist the urge to do the math when I visit the VA Cemetery. Today was no different. While my wife spent time in quiet contemplation at the headstone where her parents' ashes were placed, I wandered among the myriad markers, doing subtraction while I made tracks in the dew-covered manicured grass.

The VA is meticulous about the grass at this place. The turf they lay, water, and cut is an egalitarian blanket for all it covers. Colonel Thaddeus W, silver star, who lived to be an octogenarian, or buck Private Desmond D, who had no chance to be a hero, dying anonymously of exposure in his cardboard box the week he turned 49.

I come upon a stone with the star of David. This man, Jacob W, was born on Armistice Day and lived until 2018. Ninety-nine times he rode this rock around the sun. Purple Heart is inscribed on his headstone. I have decided he earned this at Anzio where he was a young lieutenant peppered with shrapnel. Not before he saved Jesse S who has a marker in an older section of the Cemetery. Jacob has a crisp inscription. Jesse, who fell in the battle with the bottle, succumbed to cirrhosis in 1984 when he was only 60. His remains were transferred here when the Cemetery opened in 2002. The carvings, still legible, have begun to show the ravages of time. The strong indifferent winds, the blistering sun, and the heavy but infrequent rains on the southern plains have already worn a bit the words, "He Served Proudly." Does time dull such sentiments the way it wears the marble?

On either side of Jesse S are Vietnam vets, both born only a year before I, but both gone by 2007. Am I on borrowed time, having lived a decade longer than my brothers in arms?

Carlos G, whose remains lay to the right of Jesse, I have decided, had cancer greedily consume him three dozen years after he was drenched by dioxins over and over in Tay Ninh Province. To Jesse's left? James B. He killed himself with a vintage 45 pistol a week before Carlos died. James did this in his garage apartment, two blocks from where Carlos made his last stand in the Oklahoma City VA Medical Center.

By the way, James practiced law two decades. What lawyer spends his last days in a $250 a month garage apartment? One who couldn't drink enough to blot out the image of the three VC he killed one rainy day near Kontum when he was eighteen. The VC James killed looked younger than he. James shot them at close range. One he hit in the eye, making the victim a strange asymmetrical Cyclops. It was the one-eyed phantom child who haunted his dreams the most. Perhaps James' bullet went through his own eye.

Two rows back, Robert Z. 1927 to 2002. USMC. Beloved Husband, the marker reads. The habit of smoking unfiltered fags he began on the ship to Iwo Jima never left him. Two packs a day from February 1945 until his diagnosis in December 2001. Had died six months later, asking the Hospice staff for a smoke in his final days. He remarked to a nurse, "Smoking never really calmed me, but I guess it killed me." Oh, Beloved Husband Robert Z's wife, like many others, is interred with him. Her inscription is Devoted Wife. If the math means anything, she was devoted; she died only 28 days after Robert did.

Three markers from Robert is Bernard T, also a marine whose drill sergeant was none other than Robert Z. Bernard never took up smoking, but during basic training, he met a Texan who introduced him to his sister, LaDonna. When Bernard returned from his tour in 'nam, he married LaDonna. They didn't live happily ever after. LaDonna had a fling with Rex. Bernard caught them in the act and shot them both, though he killed neither.

Bernard did eight years at the Oklahoma State Reformatory in Granite. There, he met a Chaplain who convinced him to be reborn in Christ. When Bernard was paroled, he began his own ministry. He was killed during a thunderstorm in an auto accident after visiting his old Drill Sergeant, Robert Z, at Hospice. Robert had encouraged him to leave before the storm came, but Bernard wanted to say just one more prayer with his old DI. Sans the prayer, Bernard would have left two minutes sooner, thereby avoiding the driver who, temporarily blinded by a bolt of lightning, ran a stop sign in his Ford F350 and demolished the Hyundai Accent in which Bernard took his final breaths. The power of prayer?

The last marker I read before my wife signaled me she was ready to go was Hiroshi T. His family was placed in an internment camp in WW2. They were loyal Americans living in LA. Hiroshi was permitted to join the military and fight against the Axis Forces in Europe. After being hit in the chest and arm with shrapnel, Hiroshi still managed to drag three of his fallen buddies from the line of fire.

When Hiroshi went to get a fourth wounded member of his platoon, he had to jump into a ditch to avoid heavy fire. In the ditch was a young German soldier, four feet from Hiroshi; the German had his rifle pointing directly at him. Hiroshi, ambivalent about a Christian god, closed his eyes and prayed. After a minute of fervent imploring to a being he was not sure existed, he opened his eyes. The German was still there. The German took his right hand from his weapon and raised his index finger to his mouth. Quiet, he said in English. Hiroshi closed his eyes once more. When he opened them, the German was gone.

I would like to be able to say the young German who granted Hiroshi his reprieve went on to live a full life...a wife, a family, a job teaching ethics or philosophy at a university. No such fate waited for the German who was shot in back only seconds after leaving Hiroshi in the ditch. This is the way of things in war. No moral symmetry can truly be achieved. Small acts of benevolence are balanced against man's horrific inhumanity to man.

After all that math, I was tired. My wife drove, and I lay back in the seat to nap. I didn't sleep. All those stones and numbers were still there, though gaining distance from me. The sky, cloud shrouded all morning, began to clear. Shafts of sunlight hit the highway in front of us. Behind, in the place of the dead, I believe there was yet a quiet, gray mist.

The Stoning of Stuart Manor

Dirt clods, actually. There were few stones big enough for throwing in the creek that separated their apartments from ours. A creek, and income gap even we, barely double digits old, could see as clearly as the stream between our worlds.

In our battles, I missed on purpose, as did most of the Manor marines—never did a clod or rock hit me. Our general, Rex, connected often, inviting obscenities from our opponents, but never did they cross the creek

If they had, it would have been for naught, for we had won the war before the skirmishes began. Our two pools, tennis courts, and club were the arsenals that gave us the edge, and the Stuart Manor soldiers knew this, but chunked the dirt valiantly all the same.

On the Thames, Tuesdays

His mate fancied himself Dr. Watson, or even Holmes, in a past life. But with the name, Jamsheed Razavizadeh, his friends, who chopped the proud appellation to J-Razz, laughed at such grand notions. Not Phillip, whose one brother had drowned last Hallows Eve, and this made Phillip a believer in all things.

From school, his mates walked the same lane past the spot, where his mother still lay wreaths every Monday morn, the vicar giving her the tired ones each Sabbath. Mondays Phillip took the long way home, not wanting to see the flowers, on their own eve of wilting—a pitiable reminder fresh things don't last. J-Razz was the only one who walked the long route with him, his own brother in the loam near Tehran, drowned himself by fire, not water.

Each week, the wreath lay but a day, and the two sons from different mothers would again take the shorter path, where they would find slight solace in silence, their journey home often in merciful miasma near river's edge.

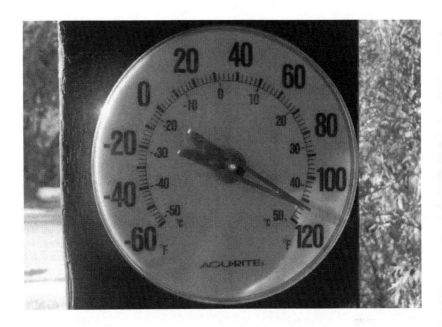

Out Yonder, West

The old man from across the street comes to me when I am in the yard, doing things we do in the yard after four years of record heat and half our annual rainfall. He's lived here ten years, but until last year, he still farmed. Lots of folks keep their acreage once they move to town. Some lease out for cattle grazing or allow drillers to have at it, that black gold still more lucrative than what they get for the grasses that come and go. Lately, those monster white turbines have popped up. The old man won't have any of that. Says it's not right to get paid for what is given for free on these prairies. He figures his sons will barter for those big windmills once he is gone.

We talk about weather mostly, like people do in times like these. His old arm points west, so weighted with years, his crooked finger aims toward the cracked ground more than to the setting sun. Thrice in eighty plantings, he's seen these droughts drench the thirsty earth with white fire, but this one, he swears upon creation, is the worst.

Holy houses fill with prayers for rain. The man says this is in vain. Though the good Lord hears all entreaties, he has always been miserly with his mercies. The old man stopped going to church regularly when a stroke took his wife and he hasn't set foot in one since cancer took his granddaughter—all of ten and gone with that leukemia. He doesn't curse the Almighty, but he can't put much stock in one who asks for prayers but doesn't ever seem to answer them. Yes, miserly with his mercies. But the old man says he guesses we're all guilty of something. Just not such grand promises. And he says all the kneeling saints and sinners combined aren't going to cloud this white-hot sky.

He helps me scoop water from the rain barrels to keep my young trees and shrubs alive. He never planted anything but Bermuda grass which he claims is obstinate enough to stay alive without any help from us. When we finish our few chores, we sit on my porch bench. Sometimes we watch the thermometer I keep on one of the support beams. One hundred and ten degrees at seven PM. He says this ninety day stretch of hitting the century mark is a record. We are quiet a while. Too many years separate us for our chat to marry, but the weather has kept the courtship alive. This weather at least.

We watch a sun, weary from its relentless burning, sink in the field behind our houses. The old man predicts the builders will put up more houses soon, and we won't have this view. Hell of a view he says. This too shall pass he avers, but he doubts he will see another warm summer rain—his baptismal to come as wind from the scorched plains, one that scatters but dry seed for tomorrow's harvest moons.

Birdsong

Gulls cawed, so loud their calls echoed off the cliffs behind us. A ghost flock answering, though not shrill enough to rouse us. Nothing was.

They flew crisscross patterns and dove into the surf, but not one landed on the carrion strewn across the sands. Not like the vultures of my youth, ravenous black hawks that began their devouring at the first scent of death, or a moment before.

No, these creatures merely called to one another, a curious conversing about the carnage below. Perhaps their strange song was our dirge, as they swooped to and fro, wings slicing the currents carrying our souls.

Omaha Beach, June 6, 1944

The Honor

Somewhere, in the folds of our collective memory, between honor and disgrace, lies that place—Vietnam.

A wet October left stock tanks full. From the commuter jet, at sunset, the tanks looked like a thousand sparkling pools.

When he saw these, Hank always had the urge to yank open the emergency exit and free fall, imagining he would land in one of the golden reflections on an otherwise russet sea of prairie.

But Hank wouldn't do this. He wouldn't leave his first-class seat he felt guilty for purchasing and take the plunge. It's not that Hank never had thoughts of suicide. His method would be in his garage in his BMW (another purchase he felt guilty making). Hank would go out with a belly full of valium VA docs gave him like candy and his lungs filled with carbon monoxide fumes. The VA docs would give him anything he wanted. Hank was part of that club. The ones who had to endure the brief time with the President who hung a heavy weight around their neck.

In truth, he wouldn't take himself out. The garage, the overdose (which would not kill him but would give him Morpheus's gift while the fumes did their work), the pushing the button to start the motor's mesmerizing hum—these were only fleeting thoughts, gone in the time it took for a traffic light to turn from red to green.

Still, during descent, for a moment that November dusk, Hank imagined opening the hatch and the flight through the graying Texas sky, his arms outstretched, reaching for something beyond the horizon, the stock tanks below waiting for him, patient as they had learned to be since the rain was so parsimonious on these plains. Before Hank hit the surface, the jet made its bumpy landing.

Hank grabbed burritos at a food truck on the way home. He got one for Deidre also. Deidre and Hank had been together thirty-six years but never married. They had met on the tenth anniversary of his return from 'nam. Hank and his cellist lover, Margaret, attended an exhibition and Deidre was one of the featured artists. Hank was so attracted to Deidre, he asked for Deidre's number and called her the next day. Margaret wasn't a fan of monogamy and would never love a man as much as her cello, but Hank still felt guilty. Hank felt guilty about many things. Mostly being alive.

When Hank arrived home, Deidre was sitting in her favorite chair with tea and a drawing pad she always kept by her side. Hank glanced at her sketch.

Two men carrying another on a sling stretcher? Hank asked.

No, Deidre said. A man in a hammock.

Deidre and Hank ate their burritos at the breakfast room table. Veggie for her and carnitas for him. Deidre was a vegetarian but not a fanatic. Cellist Margaret had been one also. And his last lover before Margaret, Nina, too. Nina, like the cellist and Deidre, was an artist—pottery, sculpture, anything to get her hands dirty. All artists. All vegetarians. It was a joke between Diedre and Hank. Deidre said Hank had to pick artists because he had not one artistic inclination in his soul. He had only gone to the exhibition where they met to appease Margaret.

Hank had inherited his father's two medical supply companies the year Hank finished his degree in biology. Hank had applied and been accepted into med school, and his father was willing to foot the bill, but his father had a fatal heart attack the month after Hank graduated.

Hank's mother had encouraged him to continue with his plans for med school—the managers and she could handle the companies, she said. Hank changed course, feeling guilty about his mother paying for four years at UT Med School. That guilt again. Hank, an only child. Hank who used his GI Bill for all his undergraduate studies. Hank who knew the money was there, still felt bad about taking it. He became one of the managers of the two stores.

When Deidre met Hank in 1980, he was driving the same 1972 Corolla he bought in college. He was living in a small rental owned by his mother. Diedre had been married to an oil man's son who left her when he discovered she could not have children. In the divorce settlement, she was given a spacious cottage in the Country Club. Had it not been for that, Deidre believed Hank would still be living in one of his mother's rentals.

When his mother died in 2001, Hank gave her four rentals to an interdenominational charitable group. He claimed he didn't want the headache of old houses, but Deidre read something else into it: the same old guilt for being so blessed, and for being alive he would acknowledge to her, though he would never explain why. Deidre felt it had something to do with the war, but in thirty-six years, Deidre knew only three things about Hank's Vietnam experience. He was a combat medic. He had received the Medal of Honor, and one of the people he saved was his platoon commander who happened to be a Congressman's favorite nephew.

This night, after Hank returned from the funeral of Lieutenant Billy Parker, Hank would finally tell her more. Deidre had a cousin who had been a 'nam vet who was the poster child for PTSD. He had drunk himself to death at age 50. This, and Hank's reticence to talk about his experience kept Deidre from pressing the issue. This night, as Hank finished his burrito, he said, I am going to tell you something I haven't told anyone.

Deidre poured glasses of wine and took Hank by the hand to the patio where she started a fire in the pit. Hank was taciturn briefly before he told Deidre he had a twin who had died at birth.

Jesus, Hank. Together thirty-six years and you are telling me this only now? Your mother too kept this a secret?

Yes, for whatever reason, when she first told me—when I was ten—I knew it was something we would never talk about. I remember my teacher, Mrs. Lincoln, telling my mother I had begun acting differently after my mom told me. I only remember feeling different. Feeling like someone was there with me, but at the same time feeling like I was missing something.

I had felt this way before Mom told me I had a twin. We were certain my brother, Harold, was my identical twin. When he came out, nine minutes after I did, the only difference between us was I was pink, and he was cyanotic. We came from not only the same mom but also the same egg. Always felt him there but not there at the same time. I have wondered if other surviving twins have had the same experience, but I never met one.

Diedre was silent and looked into Hank's eyes. Hank paused and then continued when Diedre gently squeezed his hand.

I am also going to tell you what happened in 'nam. I did save Billy Parker's life, and I was under fire, and I was bleeding from shrapnel that hit my right arm in that firefight. But do you know how many times I was in combat in five months? Twice. I spent part of my time as a ward medic at the 93rd Evac in Long Binh. We would alternate with another platoon going out on patrol. Four times.

Anyway, the second time we were on patrol, snipers opened up on us and hit a kid from California, Denny Baggett, in the leg—nicked an artery so I couldn't stop the bleeding with direct pressure and had to use a tourniquet. Billy and I were buds, so he wrote it the daily reports to make it look like I worked on Denny while under fire. Technically that was true. We were still getting heavy VC fire, but I had pulled Denny behind a termite mound and the snipers couldn't see us. I don't think a round came within fifty feet of me once I had Denny behind the mound. For that, I got the bronze star.

The other time we got hit was our fourth time out. There were probably a dozen VC spraying us with AK fire from what had to be the thickest jungle I saw my time in country. They first hit us with several mortar rounds and that is how I caught shrapnel in my upper arm. I bled like a pig but wasn't in much pain. Two guys were hit—one on either side of me. As I applied dressings, I could hear AK rounds zipping by. My hands were shaking, and I was expecting to get zapped. The VC liked to kill medics.

After I took care of the two beside me, I saw Billy go down. He was hit in the shoulder and the leg. I ran across the field to get to him. I have no idea why I didn't crawl. You are taught to low crawl fast when under fire, but I just ran. I felt more like I was running *away* from something rather than *to* something. I could "feel" rounds zipping past me when I was running but I got to him with nothing but the wound on my arm.

Like Denny, the Billy's leg wound was going to bleed out, so I applied a tourniquet. I was on my knees and Billy kept saying, get down Hank, get down. I didn't answer but told him later I could work better and faster on my knees than I could prostrate. As soon as I got the tourniquet on him, two VC came from the bush. I grabbed Billy's .45 and fired it three times in the direction of the VC. I say in their direction because I didn't aim. I was too scared to aim. I hit both. One square in the abdomen and the other in the throat. I then started working on Billy's shoulder.

After that, I zipped across the field again to help Tiny from Dallas. Tiny was six foot three and about two forty. He was hit in the foot. I remember how hard it was to get his jungle boot off because my hands were shaking. I could hear fire, but I didn't know if it was our platoon or the VC. While I was working on Tiny, another round grazed his face.

That was it. My total experience in the bush. When Billy was stable, they Medevac'd him to a hospital in Japan. There he was able to make a call directly to his uncle. I remember, later, Billy telling me his uncle had said, Make the report sound good. Typical politician, Billy noted.

A couple of weeks later, when I was recuperating at the 6th Convalescent Center, a young captain found me and told me I was being recommended for the "Big One." That captain was more excited about it than I was—of course, he thought I must have done something heroic.

You did, Deidre said.

Deidre, there were guys who humped the bush 200 days in a year. There were guys who got their legs blown off. There were guys who saw buddies die in front of them. I wasn't a hero. I was lucky. I have always been lucky.

You were drenched in your own blood and running through enemy fire to save a friend. You saved how many lives? Sounds to me like three or four, without regard for your own safety. I'd say that is worthy of something.

Yes, but the "Big One?" I got it because Billy Parker, who died of cancer the day before his 70th birthday, had an uncle who was a Congressman.

Deidre fired back. And because you saved lives. And because you risked yours. You and this guilt thing have been friends way too long Hank. What made you decide to tell me the story now? The funeral?

Indirectly, yes. Not the service itself, but a conversation I had with Billy's wife, Patty. She said Billy talked about the 'nam a lot in his last few months. When they first married, Billy had told her the story of me saving him. But weeks before he died, he told her the whole story of our time there. How he often felt guilty for surviving. How little he had really done. Without saying it, how little I had done.

Patty said he was always grateful I saved him, but there was something in the way she told me that led me to believe Billy knew he and I got off easy, relatively speaking. He went home early because of a shattered shoulder which healed and I because the week after I was told I was being recommended for the Medal of Honor, I got transferred to

Fort Hood. Spent my last eighteen months working weekend shifts as a ward medic at Darnall Army Hospital, four hours from home. I worked only two eight-hour shifts Friday and Saturday nights every other weekend. I don't know if it was the Medal of Honor or Billy's uncle, but I had little duty. Again, lucky me.

Deidre said, Yes, I guess you did have it pretty good. But what's wrong with that? You did what you were told. I'm sure you wouldn't have complained if you were working double shifts all week.

Who knows Deidre? I have never been unlucky. I was the lucky one who lived.

Like you had some choice over that? You had choice over being a surviving twin?

No, but it doesn't seem like I have much choice about feeling guilty for surviving.

Deidre and Hank said little else while the logs became embers in the pit. That night, Deidre initiated love making—the first time in weeks. In the post coital calm, they agreed it was the nicest experience they had in recent memory.

A week after Hank returned from Billy's services, Hank got a package from Patty. It was the Dan Fogelberg and Tim Weisberg CD, Twin Sons of Different Mothers. Patty had included a note that said the following:

Hank, Billy bought this CD years ago. Said it reminded him of the two of you. I don't think Billy ever told you. He had an identical twin who died at birth. He never talked much about it, but he had a thing about twins. Anyway, I thought he would want you to have it. Best wishes, Patty.

Hank went directly to the garage and popped the CD into his BMW's player. He turned on the engine, revved it a time or two, then used the remote to open the garage. Hank drove on the highway for hours, the moon roof open even though it was a chill November day. Hank listened to the CD three times. When he stopped for gas, he bought a large chocolate bar. Hank ate this as he drove down the highway, cruising a steady eighty-five, wind in his hair, feeling very much alive.

When he turned to head home, the sun was setting. The stock tanks were again reflecting gold. He swerved to avoid a deer crossing the highway and ran his car off the road. The doe had trotted up a small hill and stopped. It looked back at Hank in the gathering dusk. It was not in her ken to comprehend Hank had risked his life to save her. Hank sat still in the car for some time—until the blanket of night was full on him and the doe had long since disappeared, her lips lapping from the tanks that were yet full but had lost the glow that had enchanted Hank from two miles high.

The Mystic's Morning Glories

White petals pepper his ivy. Some droop casually into the monkey grass. All volunteers, their conception unplanned.

After his early constitutional, he takes tea with them, and tells them life tales—content they listen, hear. First cautious with his revelations. No lugubrious life lessons he has learned, little of loss: his first kiss; his summer sojourns with Uncle Elliott; his favorite hiding spot at play.

Then, when they've heard of joy, he praises them for their comely countenance, their generous journey from seed. Later, when he returns at eventide, he dares tell them of Sophia, his beautiful bride who tended tulips before these interlopers came. He whispers, so he does not startle them, or perchance wake her, as he confesses, she lies beneath them, forever silent in their bed.

A century skipped from one soup line to the next. Never thought I would stand in one, a homeless octogenarian who doesn't like soup.

The library serves sandwiches. Eden's apples too, on Mondays, but gray Sundays they are closed, so here I am at a holy house that feeds beggars, bankers and whores, but only after servicing our souls with etudes on eternity and other hymns to which I am deaf.

Tomorrow I will visit the VA for my monthly meds, free potions to pacify me while I wait for a bed in the shiny new castle, forever being built. In the meantime, I get the shed behind the shack of another "brother" who tells me war stories, which can't be true, since he was but ten and two when the last bird chopped its way into the Saigon sky—the embassy below yet teeming with ghosts, and the screaming hordes, scurrying still in a conquered land, desperate victims of our proud command.

I don't tell him he does not speak the truth, for he takes even more potent pills than I to keep his demons at bay. I listen. An older brother should.

Today the broth has chicken and rice, and our platoon slurps in unison after another plaintive prayer to a god I never knew. Tomorrow, over my white bread and bologna, we will be able to sup in silence, in the calm cathedral of tomes, where I will try in vain to comprehend the mystic Kabbalah, or perhaps read The Grapes of Wrath to hoist healing hope of suckled redemption before my ancient eyes.

White Men Chewing Gum—A Family Dialogue

Alabama 1962, Mother to Son

Mother: They didn't have a sign. I didn't see a sign.

Son: We don't need a sign to see we are not wanted. Look at that man over there. He's looking at us like we came from the moon.

Mother: We did. Boston is the moon for these people. You heard Auntie Lucinda talk about these people. Monkeys. Moon monkeys. That is what they think we are.

Son: Look at that man chewing gum. And those two at the table over there. Chewing gum also. Everybody in Alabama chew gum?

Mother: Keep your eyes on your menu. Just read your menu.

Son: Not sure I want to eat here.

Mother: You see another place the last fifty miles? We don't know what there will be to eat when we get there. It's a funeral and they didn't say anything about afterwards. Just the church. They may not feed us at that church.

Son: Why are we here anyway? We didn't even know the man.

Mother: Because your grandmother knew him when she was a young girl. Remember, she lived here before she went off to Howard. She is too ill to come so we are here in her place. Thomas Williams was the only uncle she ever knew.

Son: Yes. I know all about it. First girl in our family to ever graduate high school. First to go to college. I know all that. Heard it a million times.

Mother: Well, you better appreciate it a million times. You grew up in a place where we weren't treated the same, but we weren't crapped on. And we sure didn't have separate water fountains.

Son: There is another one chewing gum. How do they eat with gum in their mouths?

Mother: Just read your menu and make sure you know what you want when the waitress comes.

Son: If she ever comes—we've been here five minutes and she isn't here yet.

Mother: It is busy and there are just two servers. She'll come soon.

Son: Here she comes now. Maybe she heard me complaining.

Mother: Hi, that meatloaf you have on your special looks very good. I sure would like that if you have some left. And a tall glass of tea would be nice.

Son: I'll have a hamburger and fries and a Pepsi.

Mother: Thank you ma'am.

Son: I sure would like that if you have some left. Thank you, ma'am? She should be saying that to you. And where did you come up with that accent? You sound like you came from Tupelo.

Mother: Nothing wrong with being polite.

Son: Gracious.

Mother: What is that?

Son: Gracious. You always taught me there was nothing wrong with being gracious. But you were obsequious.

Mother: I was polite.

Son: Admit it. You were overdoing it. You were being sycophantic.

Mother: You know where we are? You really know where we are?

Son: Sure, I do. I am not ignorant. We are not fifty miles from where Benny got his head bashed trying to register people to vote.

Mother: That is exactly where we are. You registered to vote last month. Anybody assault you?

Son: OK. I get it. I got to know my place.

Mother: Don't be condescending. You know I am not asking you to know your place. I am telling you to be aware of *this* place. Benny, as white as the hoods some of these people probably wear at night, was nearly killed for standing in a line trying to help colored people register to vote.

Son: Benny was a Jew. Some of these people hate them as much as they do blacks.

Mother: You think they knew he was a Jew? That curly red hair? He could have been an Irishman, but he was helping colored people obtain the rights you never had to think about until you went off to college. And even then, it wasn't because you were being deprived of them. It was because you spent your time talking about how others didn't get them. Well, you ain't in that student center drinking coffee and philosophizing with a bunch of white kids who think they are being "hip" because you are their friend.

Son: I know. I am not trying to give you a hard time. I know where we are. I just don't want to have to suck up to people. And they are my friends—not just because I am black.

Mother: You are right. I was wrong to insinuate that, but I think you got my point.

Son: Yes. I did. Looks like our food is coming. That was fast.

Mother: Thank you Miss. That sure looks good.

Son: Thanks. Could I get a straw please?

Mother: Now, did that hurt to be polite?

Son: A little.

Mother: You will recover from this temporary journey into the land of humility.

Son: I hope so. You said there probably won't be but one or two distant cousins at the service?

Mother: Yes. I won't recognize anyone, but I'm sure we will find out who they are.

Son: You said he had five kids. Didn't they have children?

Mother: Only one of them lived to be old enough to have children. Typhus, dysentery or pneumonia got the other four. The one who lived—Ezekiel—he fathered only one daughter before he went to one of the work farms. Died there of influenza when he was about my age.

Son: A sickly bunch.

Mother: They didn't have medical care. Your father is a doctor. You know nothing of what it was like.

Son: I do know, but still seems like they had particularly bad luck. But my great-great Uncle Thomas lived to be a hundred?

Mother: Yes. Born a slave in a cabin the year before the Emancipation Proclamation was signed. His mother had been violated by two men and her master didn't know who Thomas' father was, so he gave him his name. By all accounts, the master was a decent man, if you can say that about any person who had slaves.

Son: You can't.

Mother: I suppose not.

Son: And who taught Thomas to write? You said he wrote Granny Bell lots of letters before his eyesight went.

Mother: There were often one or two slaves in a group who could read and write. And they always had a bible. I suspect it was one of the people in his cabin.

Son: When do I get to read those letters?

Mother: When my mother says you can. Since when did you become interested in those?

Son: When you told me about the lynching. I heard Granny tell you Thomas had made a cross on an oak for every lynching he could remember.

Mother: Yes, that tree is near the church. And your reason for wanting to read the private letters your granny got from her uncle is a morbid one.

Son: We going to see the tree?

Mother: I can think of no decent reason to do so.

Son: History.

Mother: You were an accounting major and since when did you become interested in history? Our family's or anybody's for that matter? You look forward—not backwards, and that is probably best.

Son: I look forward to getting out of Alabama.

Mother: Soon. After the service. We'll drive as far north as we can.

Son: Sounds good to me. But I do want to see those letters someday.

Mother: Someday you will.

Alabama 2018, Grandfather to Grandson

Grandfather: Where that McDonalds sits was once a diner.

Grandson: How did you know about that? You said you'd only been to Alabama once.

Grandfather: My mother and I stopped there to eat when I was twenty-one.

Grandson: On your way to the oak?

Grandfather: On our way to a funeral. I told we didn't go to see the tree. My mother wouldn't tell me where it was and forbade me from looking for it.

Grandson: But we are going to see it today?

Grandfather: If it is still standing. Only the ruins of the church are there. I assume the tree is there, but it would be more than a century and a half old and who knows if we will be able to see where he made the carvings.

Grandson: You saw them before?

Grandfather: Yes, I disobeyed my mother and when she was visiting with her distant cousin Letty, I went across the field from the church and found the oak—middle sized southern live oak. Not as big as I had imagined.

Grandson: But you saw his carvings?

Grandfather: Yes. When we pass over these tracks, you will see some apartments on the left. Shanties were there in 1962.

Grandson: So there literally was a place on the "other side of the tracks?"

Grandfather: Oh yes. Railroad tracks were a clear line of demarcation for race and class all over the south. Other places too.

Grandson: Those apartments aren't bad. A lot of junk in the yards. Dad would have yelled at me for leaving my bike out. There is a lot of trash and what is that?

Grandfather: You had a two-car garage to store your bike. And curbside garbage pick-up twice a week. That dumpster we passed is likely the only place they have to dump their trash. You see how far it was from the last apartment building there by the tracks?

Grandson: But Grandpa, there were dirty diapers in one of those yards. How much time does it take to walk to the dumpster to stick dirty diapers there?

Grandfather: You don't measure time the same way many of these people do. Zips by when they are playing ball on that lot or having dinner with friends but drags on when they are waiting for a paycheck to get their cell phone turned back on or when they are waiting for their food stamps when their refrigerator is empty. OK—look at that hill off to the south.

Grandson: I see the hill, but I don't see anything on—oh wait, I can see part of a roof. No cross though.

Grandfather: They took it when they built the new church. Took the cross but left the graves.

Grandson: All black people, right.

Grandfather: Yes. But nobody has been put in the ground here in forty years. They bury them with the whites now on the other side of town.

Grandson: Death, the great equalizer.

Grandfather: That it is. And other things. Time. Time changes things. Time *has* changed things. Was a black mayor elected here last year.

Grandson: That a change in attitude or change in demographics? I googled this town. Exactly 50% black now.

Grandfather: Both. If I recall, it was almost half black back then. I googled it too. That black mayoral candidate got 60% of the vote. I suspect a few white people cast ballots for him. Here we are. My mother and I parked our 1961 Chevy Impala right here.

Grandson: I thought your mom had a 1962 Cadillac—kept it until 1980 you said.

Grandfather: Yes, she did, but she took my father's Chevy—didn't want to look too fancy.

Grandson: You mean "uppity."

Grandfather: Same concept but white people called that "uppity." We wouldn't have.

Grandson: That's the tree over there isn't it.

Grandfather: Yes, and I will really be interested in your response when you see it.

Grandson: Why?

Grandfather: You'll see.

Grandson: Why do old people always want to keep you in suspense?

Grandfather: Why do young people always want something right away?

Grandson: Because we get everything right away. Millennials. The world in our pockets.

Grandfather: I have had a cell phone in mine twenty years and I still have a little patience. Ok—here it is. Look closely at that patch there.

Grandson: I see some initials. E. W., Z. F., B. F. I can't make out many of the others but there must be ten sets of initials. Where are the crosses?

Grandfather: There is not one cross on this tree—never has been. Look carefully at the initials. E. W was Ezekiel Walker. I know that from Thomas's letters to my grandmother. But look at what is around each set of initials.

Grandson: Looks like a circle. A circle. A loop. Yes, a loop.

Grandfather: Look above the "loops."

Grandson: I see what looks like a line. I see a line on a lot of those circles.

Grandfather: You sure do. Those loops are nooses. Great Uncle Thomas made initials and placed them in the hangman's noose. He even did one set—the B. F. who was Benjamin Fuller—before the noose got him. In the letters, he told my grandmother Benjamin was in the jail awaiting trial for assaulting a white deputy. Benjamin had been back from Korea only a month and got good and drunk and beat the hell out of deputy who was calling him a nigger and trying to handcuff him. Thomas said the sheriff was a good man and made it clear to the folks in town there wasn't going be any lynching while he was sheriff. He knew the assault on a white man would land Ben a ten-year sentence easy. But another white deputy took twenty dollars from some Klansmen and let them take Ben and hang him. The sheriff fired the deputy, but Ben was still dead. Thomas made his noose the day before they hanged Thomas—said he knew the sheriff had to sleep sometime.

Grandson: Bastards. Drunk and disorderly meant a death sentence.

Grandfather: Well, that and being black and brazen enough to defend yourself against a white officer in Alabama in 1954.

Grandson: Guess I am lucky I was born in 1998.

Grandfather: You are lucky my grandmother went to college, moved to Boston, married a dentist, had a son who was a doctor and a grandson who was an accountant and a father who owns a business that pays for your tuition at BU.

Grandson: The history lecture. The five miles to school in the snow story.

Grandfather: Your stories wouldn't have been five miles in the snow—how about ten behind a mule in hell's heat for beggar's wages. But you didn't hear any of that. Just know where you came from.

Grandson: I do. We gonna stop at that McDonald's on the way back through town?

Grandfather: Sure.

Grandson: The one where the diner used to be? See, I was listening.

Grandfather: Yes, you were.

Grandson: I bet there is a story about that diner isn't there? I bet you remember what you ate.

Grandfather: A burger and fries and a Pepsi. And there is a story, but you don't have to hear it.

Grandson: I can take it Grandpa. I am tough.

Grandfather: Well, I had to drink the Pepsi without a straw. And watch out if you see any white men chewing gum.

Grandson: The horror. The horror!

Grandfather: You will never know.

Twenty-seven

Two tens and seven. The square root of 729. No matter how the numbers collude, they are there, just as I drift off, before I catch myself thinking of other numbers, like the age at which Jesus died.

Twenty-seven, my four-syllabled mantra, for that is the age you got the needle. I was not a witness, but your attorney was. How he did not weep, I will never understand. He knew they put you in a diaper before you took the final stroll. Twenty-seven, and during those final steps, your sins yet dragged behind you, like ball and chain, not severed by the axe of repentance, the chisel of remorse.

Where did the gods fail, taking you so fast from the dim lights of the b-ball courts and your dreams of being Michael or Magic to the dead afternoon when you strode up the cracked walk to that crack house and put two thirty-two rounds in the eye of your second cousin who came in first on your short list. All because of a hundred dollar slight and a spoonful of powder the world could mistake for simple sugar.

You didn't fight when they strapped you in, and your final testament to an uneven world, an insolent audience, was, "It is what it is." Did you feel the tug on your loins, from the raiment wrapped to hide your seeping shame? Did it take you back a quarter century, when a manic mama pampered you in pampers and kissed your tiny tummy more times than numbers could count, though not enough?

Did you, like I, in the moments between light and dark, between this world and one where you must sleep alone, see twenty and seven flash before your eyes and disappear before you could realize what the plaintive plungers and naked needle meant?

Seeking a Cure for Cancer While Contemplating the Virtues of Infidelity

Struck by lightning twice by twenty-four, this astronomical record was hers, Guinness proclaimed. This lady so famed, top of her class at Stanford, then Yale Med, and blissfully wed, to a surgeon who always came in second.

This did not matter at Cabo, or even in their first condo, but as her curriculum vitae grew faster than a Walmart receipt on Black Friday, he scrubbed up for one bloodletting after another, removing appendixes, and appendages, feeling her shadow grow heavy, even in the bright lights of his operating theater.

His first was, of course, a nurse, though at least her age. His second, a decade newer model, fixed his lattes at Starbucks. Number three was the neighbor with whom they shared nothing but a fence, and a few awkward stares.

Her hours in the lab with petri dishes grew, and she never let on she knew, that her clean-shaven number two was lying with others to stand himself. When he asked for a divorce—number four requiring more than liquid exchanges in hotel suites—she acquiesced and even let him have the Welsh Corgi, the cabin in Aspen, and half the 401K.

To this day, she recalls imagining his liaisons while she married menacing molecules to one another in tubes under faithful light, seeking answers to questions asked by the dying she would never meet. A lump would only grow in her throat if she thought his scalpel never sliced the heart of number four, for a number five.

His Encounter with Cygnus Olor*

Kayaking. On the same lake, since college, two score before. By the tiny bay ice fishermen swore was haunted—having lost one of their own, only last winter. If the dead man's spirit lingered, he hadn't heard or seen it, and the bay, though small, was deep, calm.

He rowed daily to this big cove, a treasure trove of quiet and color without a house or pier in sight. As the sun was sinking into the lake one August eve, he heard a hissing from the thick stands of pine.

Webbed feet, he did not imagine, could be as treacherous as talons, but they were. And the knobby beak of this mad mute swan felt like pliers when it yanked on his ear, ripping nearly half of it off.

It took but one sharp blow from his oar to thwart the attack, and the giant bird disappeared into the dusk. In its wake a pool of blood and pain he had not felt since hot shrapnel pierced his young leg in that crazy Asian war.

The battle lasted but a few manic moments, as is the case with most wars of the flesh. Long enough, though, to end his silent sojourns on this still blue glass, now shattered by flapping limbs of man and beast.

*Cygnus Olor is the more technical name for the mute swan, a large and aggressive bird not originally from North America but here in considerable numbers now.

Of Loons, Lakes, and Luck--Helen's husband, 1899-1983

When he was 84, he rarely recalled the Great War, though he left a finger somewhere in French soil. But on deep sleep nights, few and far between, that time would call him—a spectral image of gas dead faces, drifting through like sallow clouds in the charcoal sky.

His nephew was the only one left to fish these green waters with him, to court the steady trout the old man also saw in his dreams. All the others, even his own sons, were marching through the concrete squares of the cities, visiting now and then like peddlers hawking wares he could not understand. Soccer games and mutual funds, gourmet feasts at eateries with cryptic names.

The lake remained the same. The loons chatting, the waves lapping, but with his Helen gone, the fish he caught were usually granted reprieve, saved from his sharp gutting blade and her sizzling skillet. Without her beside him under her ancient quilts, the nights were not longer; for grief, he knew, did not stretch time, but only made its circle smaller.

Was a sun sated Saturday when the nephew had honey do's as good excuses and the old man was left alone, sitting by a black rotary phone, waiting for one of his old nine digits to dial the new nine and two ones. That is what they all would have expected, a cry for help, a long mute ambulance ride, them seeing him helpless with hoses and wires, delaying the funeral pyres, as was the custom in this post teen century.

Instead, though he felt the anvil on his chest, and sweat drenched his JC Penney work shirt, he moved not his feeble fingers to the phone, but his fated feet to the lake—once only a long a hop from the porch, now a mammoth journey, ten, twelve Sisyphus steps downhill. When he reached the water's edge, the fowl called him casually, their slow song on the currents. He sat in the fresh grass, watching the painted blue sky. The old man saw the fins of those he had set free, hoping that would count for something, when he curled in fetal repose, and closed his eyes by this lonely lake.

Lolo's

The old stone walls are still standing, though they no longer echo with sounds of cornball jokes, bottle caps popping off cokes and the happy humming of a repaired motor. The old man was there when the first car pulled in for gas. Twenty-eight cents a gallon, all fluids checked for free. Spotless windshield guaranteed.

He hired that Mexican boy because he was polite. Yessir, and was the best damn twenty-year-old grease monkey in the county—hell, the state. The boy had one leg shorter than the other and had a twin brother whose two fine legs carried him that place, somewhere between honor and complete disgrace, called Vee-et-nam. But those strong legs couldn't bring him home. He come back in a box, both his good legs blown clear off.

He hired Lolo the day before his brother come home. Was hot as Hades at that graveside, but he went and stood by the boy, his sobbing mama, his sober father and the hot hole in the caliche where Lolo's brother was gonna spend forever.

Business was good. The boy spent much of his time under the hood of Riley's '51 Ford, or Miss Sampson's Impala, (white 1962, with red interior, clean as the day she bought it).

Nixon beat that old boy from Minnesota and told everybody he would end that crazy Asian war the right way. But the old man had been in those foul trenches in France, killin' krauts when he was 18, and he knew there was no "right" way.

He and the boy had many a good day with the register cling-clanging, mechanical mysteries being solved and a good hot lunch now and then when the boy's mama brought fresh tortillas and asada or the old man would spring for chicken fried steak sandwiches from the café.

Yes, many a good day, until that hot July afternoon the day after we landed on the moon, when "they" came not from some lunar rock but from an El Paso shithole where graffiti were their psalms and switchblade knives their toys. "They" came, parked their idling '57 Chevy in front of the bay, and bust through the front door with a gun and a ball bat. Both had hair slicked back with what looked like 30 weight oil. "They" smiled and smelled of beer and sweat.

Dame el dinero! Give us the money! Give us the money old man, cabron!

The old man glared at them and the bat came down and grazed his head, cracked his shoulder. "They" did not see the boy with the wrench who laid the bad ass batter out with one righteous swing. The one with the gun did not aim but pulled the trigger three times. Two of those hot speeding streams sliced through the boy's throat.

The shooter was through the door and burning rubber while Lolo lay bleeding red blood on the green linoleum floor. The old man knelt over him, helpless. He saw Lolo's eyes close a final time, while the sting of the burned rubber was still in his nose, and the hellish screech of the tires still in his ears.

The old man had seen the dead before, piled in heaps in the dung and mud of those trenches, faces bloated with their last gasps from the nightmare gas. But he hadn't shed a tear in the pale pall of the dead until that hot July day, with a man on the moon, all those miles away, and the best boy with a wrench in the whole state, Lolo, silent on the floor in front of him.

They caught the shooter and sent him to Huntsville for a permanent vacation. The one Lolo laid out with a wrench died on the way to Thomason Hospital in El Paso. The ambulance driver was Lolo's cousin, and he may have been driving a bit slow.

Lolo was buried the day the astronauts came back from the moon, right beside his brother in that ancient caliche. His mother sobbed softly, "mi hijos, mi hijos." Both boys now cut down, her left with prayers and memories: the boys at the ballpark, their first communions, the grandchildren she would not have and the gray graves where they would return to dust.

The Saturday after, the old man turned 69. When he flipped his "Open" sign to "Closed" that day, he climbed the ladder slowly, painted over his store-bought sign with new white wash, and red lettered it with "Lolo's." Not a person asked about him using the dead boy's name, and things would never be the same.

The old man lasted another nine years until the convenience store started sellin' gas (they wouldn't even pump). His hands were stiff with arthritis and his shoulder stilled ached from the crack of the bat. He closed on a windy winter Friday. Yet he painted the sign a final time that very day, nearly falling, as he made the last red "S." But he made it down the ladder and saw the boy's name in his rear view as he drove into the winter dusk.

Windy Sunday, 2005

Cyclones of russet leaves doing devilish dances in her yard, while she read, sipped chamomile, and listened to the cat's warm hum by her feet, the neighbor's Harley on her street. The default ring tone she never changed, interrupted her mid paragraph, between the writer's deft description of a noisy bar, and an anonymous couple walking to the car to find something they lost long before that night. The words she heard when she answered became part of her own novel, lines scribed in a book she would carry with her forever, words she read over and over as she ran to the car, "Your husband is in the ER," "Your husband is in the ER," "Your husband…"

He had gone for cat food, asparagus, and likely some beer, or Chablis if he remembered they were having chicken Milan that very night. And he did, because the bottle was yet on the floor board of his Honda Accord, after…

Two officers met her at the sliding ER door. The eyes of one, puffy with compassion, required they say no more than her name—this also now written in her own book since half of it was his.

His parents arrived at 2:56 AM the next day, two hours late from JFK. First class only meant more mournful space around them they could not fill.

Her own mother handled all the arrangements, being a master at such, having buried her father, the last pilot downed in that crazy Asian war, and putting her older brother in the ground when white blood cancer took him before he made it to double digits.

Services, closed casket, were on a thick Thursday, delayed a day while they waited for their priest to return from his own mother's wake in some other world.

All friends and family gone by Saturday, leaving her to listen for the cat's hum (but he was hiding), the neighbor's rude roaring machine, and more ring tones. More sound that also would become indelible lines in her timeless tome, which began on a windy Sunday.

The Casket Maker's Wife

His wife brings him tea, a piece of cheese late morn, for he has been toiling since dawn. His plane shaving the wood reverently. The old oak speaking, though not complaining, in a language the man does not understand. A coughing code for loss, forbearance, acceptance, redemption, he hopes, for the boys keep coming—first from Ypres, the Verdun, now the Marne.

Before, he heaved hewn planks for the hopeful homes, built their pantries to be filled with the bread, the kind milk. Now the sawn boards are for those who once watched his labors, but no longer hear the simple sounds of sanding, sawing...or anything at all.

Most of the lads do not come home. Their souls and bodies left to rot on the blood sullied grass or buried shallow, naked in the French soil. But each gets a fine coffin, thanks to the carpenter's wife, whose babe was the first to fall, and demands for them all, a holy horizontal home to be built, and, empty or not, placed gently in Anglican ground.

She Would Be Eighty-Six

She would be eighty-six, or eighty-six plus one. Ten and eight my senior. Her name was Eve. She had me when I was a bucking young mountain man only weeks back from that crazy Asian war.

Now, I am a prisoner of the prairie. Its harsh daylight douses my waking dreams of her, dispersing them downwind, with other wafting memories. I yet hear her British tongue, see her bobbed blonde hair against her finest silk pillow, and feel the warmth of her huge fireplace and her slender fingers on my shoulders.

Then, twenty-eight years younger than I am today, what would she say I saw her now? Would we lie with each other, or to each other? What if she has passed, and all that keeps her here is the faint fire behind me, the embers speaking in red whispers, of Eve, of yesterday, and of soft dances in nights of naked forgetting.

April's Ants

I forgot you were there, hiding under winter's slow, grisly grip. Only ten days into spring you made your return, myriad mounds pocking my pastures.

Dead center, in one of your proudest heaps, I teased you with sweet pear, just to see your red raiding industry, though a tiny roach occupied half your tugging army, its only crimes being live birth and waddling through your battalions. Yes, I forgot you were hunkered in the wet, wormed soil, patient, until ninety and one degrees brought you to the desiccating ground.

You had not forgotten me, had you? For you sent a special sentry from your brigades to find my ankle and welt it with an unwelcome black kiss. Tomorrows from now, after the soldier's scratching, martyred memory fades, I will forget again, though winter never does.

The Lordsburg Cafe, 1945

You barely touched the cherry pie I ordered for you, and I stopped eating half way through my roast beef and mashed potatoes, the special for the day. You got up when I put my fork and knife down. I left you while you were in the water closet. I got on the bus, handed the driver my last twenty before I even asked where the bus was going.

As the bus pulled away, puffing diesel fumes in its wake, I saw you in the café window. I saw you, side by side with the red reflection of a weathered Apache squaw who hunkered outside in the fading veil of bus smoke. Like a mocking twin she shared the glass and light with you, a young white princess with ruby lips, a purse full of treasured trash and more words I did not want to hear, waiting to spill from your mouth. Sorry. You were sorry. That meant something else. I could not find the word. So, I stopped looking.

I had been gone two years in the flying fortresses, deafened by the din of their moaning motors, the machine gun fire and the nightmare fighters sent to the blind skies to escort us to hell. I counted the desperate days and the missions I had yet to fly until my feet could touch ground for good and my eyes could see the light of you. When our crippled B29 landed in a green English pasture, and we did not burn in the fire, I didn't kiss the grass like our tail gunner did, but the first thing I did was thank the good Lord I would get to see you again. Through eight more black missions, I saw your face whenever I closed my eyes in the fuselage.

Then your letters. They said less and less but I kept them folded in my leather coat two miles from earth, like the parchment talisman I once dreamed them to be. You had left me before I even left you, and I knew, but it was easier to chew a quiet lie than to swallow a screaming truth. I did wonder if you walked into the street and if you asked the Mescalero lady if she saw me leave. I did not look back once as the bus passed Lordsburg's lone light, nor did I long for you any more in the dreadful night.

The Bullfighter, from Juarez

I do not know why you moved to this side, to El Paso, long before your city became a killing zone. Perhaps you knew something I did not. You knew many things I did not, which I discovered when you politely corrected my grammar, though it was my native tongue, and one you learned reading our newspapers, watching our televisions—listening, more carefully than most, to what the gringos said.

You told me tales of the arena, usually after dinner, on your back porch when the shadow of the mountain covered our houses like a quiet blanket, blocking out the blistering heat of the desert day. Always, you would offer me a soda, before my questions began. Your civility was strange to me at first, for the adults in my family barked and cackled. Your words rolled out like sweet liquid and left me wanting more. I never asked why you had no woman, though you were as handsome as any man I knew. Years later, years of name calling later, I understood, perhaps that was why you left your home. Though the blind blood of bigotry ran freely on both sides of the Rio Grande.

And I knew you to be courageous, for when you told me the stories, as the desert sky became violet and cool, and the few cicadas began their song, you boasted not of your dangerous dance in the hard-packed dirt of the ring, but of the art it took to slay the beast. You spoke not of your sharp sword, but of the lost look in the bull's red rum eyes, and the silent sadness you felt as the crowd cheered another beautiful death.

The Eve of May

Just another day, this eve of May, with April's abnegation of her title, the queen of time. Just another day, when the mother marked an "X" on the calendar, holding her breath with hope, her coffee in one hand and the red pen in the other, the hand she used to make two slashes to bring your boy a fraction closer to home.

He was to arrive alive and well in a fortnight, neatly packaged, like a belated mother's-day gift. A reasonable thing to expect, the eve of May, since you, his father, had arrived the same way, after her same hand, younger, more dream driven, had brought you home with the same crosses.

But you, the man for whom she waited all those eves ago, were wrapped neatly only long enough to see April's thirty crosses, May's eager ambitious start, and you came unwrapped, leaving your uniform on the bedroom floor in a heavy heap you said reminded you of what you left behind. Not in the steaming stench of Mekong's paddies, but in the quiet lanes of your hometown—in the high school where you met her, the church where you married and where you were sure you would be buried.

Your eve of May passed, along with thirty-five more, though you were there, walking the same streets. To you, the crumpled green garments were still in a heap on the floor, even though she had buried them in a drawer, years before. You did not mark off the days, for they made you wonder if their end meant your homecoming and not his, an infidelity you felt.

You watched the hand make the X's, and April finally relent, when "they" came to the door, neatly packaged themselves, erect and filled with well-formed words. You did not hear them, though you saw their lips move, and you watched your wife walk past, to the ancient kitchen, the kingdom of the calendar, and make a final "X" this eve of May. Just another day, when another mother's son who was crucified in the desert would become a mystic memory.

The Eve of September

They are erecting a 49-story skyscraper one block east of my flat. A nine-floor hotel was there from the beginning of the century until 1992, the year Rachel passed.

Many mornings, Rachel and I would take our coffee and watch the sun rise through our kitchen window. The new building is almost finished, and I can't see the sun until noon unless I walk a block to the park and watch it creep up between the new scraper and another one, the same height, completed just before 9/11.

But many days, I don't have the energy to walk to the park, especially if it's cold. So, most days I have to wait until lunch time to see the sun and appreciate its warmth through the window—its "worthy light," Rachel would say. She loved to paint and often did her art mornings, in that light. Water colors, mostly. Incandescent light bulbs never pleased her eye. I guess it's best she isn't here to see the sun blotted out by all that concrete, steel and glass.

Paul, the little boy who lives next door and goes to the market for me, told me the men at the site said they were taking Labor Day weekend off since they were ahead of schedule.

This morning, a peculiar thought came to me. I guess strange notions go hand in hand with old age. For whatever reason, I was feeling particularly irritated about that big bastard going up and thinking how much Rachel would have hated it, and I wondered if I could build a bomb big enough to bring the whole building down.

Mind you, I haven't killed anyone since Korea and never even had a thought like that before. I won't rule out the possibility I am losing my marbles. I am 89, and George, the rabbi from across the street, is 4 years younger and his wife says he has the Alzheimer's so bad he can't remember how to brush his teeth or tie his shoes. Funny though, she says, when he is asleep, he recites long passages from the Tanakh.

George's wife claims I am still "sharp as a tack," and Paul is always telling me how impressed he is with how I am with numbers, giving him the exact sum for shopping and his tip without using a calculator. I tell little Paul it's because I don't own a calculator--never have. Then he shows me the one on my cell phone. I only use my cell phone for long distance, I explain to him. Paul thinks that is peculiar, but he doesn't press the subject.

So, I guess I ought to get back to my idea to raze that building with a bomb. In the Korean "Conflict," I was taught how to make and detonate explosives. We destroyed a few bridges and even a Korean officer bunker. No telling how many souls were crushed or burned to death when that blast went off. That is what my team and I did. I was never supposed to talk about that, but I don't suppose it matters 65 years after the fact.

Now, here I am, an old wannabe anarchist, looking on the internet for instructions on how to build a bomb powerful enough to bring down a structure the size of a city block. I think I got it figured out. I think I have the know-how, but the logistics would be beyond my ability.

I did think about recruiting Rudy, the fella who lives in the place next to Paul. Rudy has done time for assault, attempted murder, and robbing a liquor store. He has spent more than half his 45 years behind bars. Believe it or not, Rudy is an affable man, but he is renowned for his temper. He also hates his job at the hardware store. I figured I could clean out most of my 401k and pay Rudy to do the job. For him, it wouldn't be a matter of conscience, just his calculating whether he could get away with it.

I even called Rudy while the notion was still rumbling around in my head. He didn't answer. Maybe that was a message from whatever god there is left in this forsaken world that I wasn't meant to do such a terrible thing. Still, the idea is there, straddling that line between curiosity and desire.

I suspect if I went through with it, it would take my flat along with it when it came down…mine, the Rabbi George's, Paul's, and a half dozen renovated lofts they now say are part of gentrification. If I didn't know its meaning, I would think that word was a multi-syllabic version of theft or lie.

I have been thinking about this since this morning. Now, the sun is almost down. I don't have to look west to watch its descent. On the new glass of the scraper, every cloudless sunset, I see that bright orange ball of fire. The reflection is so pristine, I think I am seeing the sun itself. So bright, I must put on the sunglasses they gave me after I had my cataract surgery. I could blot it out with the Venetian blinds, but I don't. I don't want to miss sunsets, no matter how impertinent.

When darkness finally comes, I will not likely be entertaining that crazy idea of conflagration. I will, however, probably fall asleep wondering if I am truly a madman.

In the morning, when Paul comes to empty my garbage and get my grocery list, I will give him an extra $5. I might ask him to find Rudy for me.

There was a Crooked House

From the road...

Susan turned sixty-six on 9/11/2001. The trip was a birthday present from Kamiko who likely wanted a break from San Francisco more than she wanted to travel to the great southwest with her best friend. They had intended to fly to Albuquerque, rent a car and hit Taos, Santa Fe and Abiquiu of Georgia O'Keefe fame. When the attack occurred, plans changed. They drove instead.

When Kamiko first saw the old house from the window of her Mercedes, she said, there was a crooked man, and he walked a crooked mile. True, the house was now tilting after a century on the New Mexico high plains, but the Mother Goose rhyme was flippant to Susan. To her, the house, though listing more than the tower of Pisa, was a place of memory, a place of sorrow—the type of sorrow that carves deep crevices in the heart. For all the time blood flows, those canyons shadow and channel the life force.

The winds that thrashed the place on these prairies were calm when Susan got out of the car to walk to the house. The sky was a deep uninterrupted sea of blue save some cumulus clouds gathering above the Sangre de Cristo Mountains far to the west. To anyone else, it would be a nice stroll to a curious site.

To Susan, it was a journey into the past, with each step conjuring a vison from her childhood. The first, the back seat of a 1940 Ford her father drove from Los Angeles to Susan's grandparents' home on December 9, 1941. Two days before, not only had the Japanese attacked Pearl Harbor, but also Susan's mother had slit her wrists and bled to death on her back porch while Susan cut out paper dolls and her father listened to the news on the radio. The last time Susan saw her mother was two hours before she killed herself when her mother placed two ham sandwiches and two bowls of tinned peaches on the breakfast room table and said, you two eat without me, I am not hungry. Susan and her father watched her mother walk out the screen door to the porch where her mother often watched the sun set on the Pacific. Susan's father later discovered her lifeless body, called the ambulance and told Susan to stay in her room.

A step later, a step closer to the old house, and Susan recalled her grandfather, gone now twenty-seven years (dying of a heart attack the day Nixon resigned), walking towards the car as they pulled up to the house. Susan remembered the way her grandfather leaned into the stiff, dust filled wind as he approached the car. Her grandparents had no phone, and the telegram informing them Susan and her father were coming arrived only an hour before.

Another step in the tall grass, and she was sitting at the old wooden table, her grandmother pouring her milk and placing a cherry pie on the sturdy structure her father and grandfather had built the month before her father had gone off to fight in the Great War. Another step, a glance at the bedroom window behind which Susan had lain and stared at the star rich sky while listening to her father and grandfather speak of the war and of her mother. Had there been any signs? Surely her mother didn't take her life simply because she was of Japanese descent and came to this country from Yokohama as child? Do you want another cup of coffee, son? How is Susan taking all this? Questions. More questions. Susan fell asleep hearing questions without answers.

More footsteps, more visions. Behind her, Kamiko saying something Susan did not hear. Her grandfather's old truck and her first day of school in Springer, New Mexico—the students speaking to her in Spanish, a little of which she had learned growing up in Los Angeles. As an Amerasian, she had often been told she looked like a Mexican. When Susan said she was not Mexican, an older boy said what are you? The teacher, Miss Binswanger, told the class this was Susan Ward and she was from California and they were to make her feel welcome. When they later discovered Susan's mother had been Japanese, her name changed from Susan, or "California girl," to "Jap," or "Slant Eye."

Another step, Easter (Christmas, only two weeks after her arrival, completely absent in her memory), and her grandmother and Susan boiling eggs—dozens of them to take to the church for the children to paint. Another step, and her gaze focused on the steep roof she remembered her grandfather patching after a brutal hail storm, and the neighbor named Benito who came to help and gave her agave candy.

Another footfall and she found herself close enough to see a spiderweb in the window frame and that brought to mind the tarantula Susan thought was a creature from hell—especially when her grandmother smashed it with a broom, leaving a red stain on the wooden floor. And Susan remembered, years later, her father had never let her see the place where her mother had done her bloodletting, and how much blood must have been left there on the concrete. In fact, Susan's father sold the house only weeks after her mother's death and Susan had only driven by it as an adult, moved by some strange curiosity. Always, when passing on the street, she would think of the back porch, the crimson blood on the concrete and whether her mother had seen the sun set on the Pacific that night.

Inside and beyond the walls...

The midday sun cast good light through the old window frames and doors. Inside, Kamiko said the house seemed bigger than it appeared from outside. It is empty, Susan said. Even with furniture, it seemed big to her as a child, she reflected. There was a loft that served as her grandparents' bedroom until her grandmother, in 1945, broke her ankle stepping off the front stoop. This was the year Susan's father returned from Washington where he had spent the years of the war.

For the summer of '45, Susan, then nearly ten, slept in the loft; she remembered the sun coming through the window and waking her each morning. On the 4th of July, there was no sun, only gray sheets of rain. The damaged roof her grandfather and Benito repaired leaked in one spot only, directly above her bed. She was awakened by the feel of the wet blanket on her shoulders. She tried to move the big bed by herself but had to ask her grandfather for help. He placed a bucket on the floor beneath the leak and it filled itself like clockwork every hour. All day, she hauled the bucket to and from the loft, up and down the steep stairs.

The storm did not stop until the following day and not before lightning struck one of grandfather's steers, which survived but was blinded it seems. Grandfather put it down and had it butchered. On the same day, July 5, 1945, a telegram came informing Grandmother her elder and only sister, Millie, was afflicted with some mysterious malady that had taken her sight the day before. Millie's son had admitted her to the hospital in Colorado Springs and the doctors believed she had a stroke though the only symptom had been her sudden loss of eyesight. Late that evening, Susan and her grandparents drove north to Colorado. By the time they arrived Millie had passed, apparently suffering another stroke in the night. Susan recalled Millie was sixty-six, the same age Susan was now.

Susan and her grandparents stayed in a hotel until the funeral services were held in Manitou Springs two days later. Susan recalled the snow on Pikes Peak, there and glistening in mid-summer. The preacher referred to Millie now being in a place more glorious than all God's earthly creations, and Susan, though nearly four years after the fact, recalled how little the priest had said at her mother's funeral. Susan's mother had converted from Shinto to Catholicism—now no priest could claim she was in a grander place. And Susan knew she wasn't.

On their return, Grandfather's truck had a flat tire going over Raton Pass and nearly careened off the side of the mountain. Grandfather was able to pull into a small pasture of tall grass. Only minutes after they pulled off the road, a man in a 1940 Ford like the one Susan's father drove stopped and offered to help. As he and Grandfather changed the flat, the man revealed he was from Denver (where he too had been at a funeral), but was going to Alamogordo, New Mexico. He said only that he worked for the government and had been in Los Alamos for a couple of years.

When the spare was on the truck and the man was about to leave, he introduced himself—he was Warren Simmons. When Grandfather told him his name, Bill Ward, the same as Susan's father, the man froze. Warren said the whole time he had been helping with the tire, he was wondering why Grandfather looked familiar. Warren asked if

Grandfather had a son who worked in Washington, DC. Why yes, Grandfather said, he was called there shortly after the war broke out. Warren said he had met Susan's father several times. Susan's father had visited them only four times since he left her at the house on the high New Mexico grasslands. Each time, her father would say only he had business in northern New Mexico.

After the war Susan would learn Warren Simmons was part of the Manhattan Project and was headed to Alamogordo for the testing of the first atomic bomb that was detonated a week after they encountered the man on the road. Warren Simmons was a physicist who worked for Robert Oppenheimer. Her father had also worked on the Project but in a different capacity in the War Department. For whatever reason, being married to a former Japanese national did not keep him from being part of the top-secret project. In his later years, he reflected to Susan he believed her mother's suicide on the day we were attacked was part of the reason he was permitted such high clearance.

The September following the funeral the war ended and her father came to get her. They did not return to Los Angeles but instead moved to San Francisco. It was there she met Kamiko her senior year in high school. Kamiko and her family had been in internment camps the very same time—almost to the day—Susan had been in her own exile in Northern New Mexico. They attended Stanford together and had remained close friends since then. Both had been fine arts majors, both had been married and childless and both had husbands who left them for younger women.

Kamiko and Susan spent only twenty minutes in the old house. Both said it would likely collapse upon them if they spoke too loudly. There was little to see—the memories there belonged to Susan and the dead. Susan told the story of the funeral and the chance meeting with Warren Simmons. Kamiko recounted her own woeful tale from that time—not of the interment she and her family suffered but of the incineration of her own grandparents in the city of Hiroshima on August 6, 1945. Both remembered hearing of the event on the radio. Kamiko recalled her stoic father's silence and her mother's wailing when they realized their family members had vanished in a ball of fire. Susan recalled her grandparents saying, thank goodness, now maybe this terrible war will end soon.

Back in the Mercedes, both women were silent for a time. As the afternoon shadows grew long and the city of Santa Fe came into view, Kamiko and Susan turned the radio on and searched for a station. They wanted news of the 9/11 attacks, now only 48 hours old. They both knew their wistful recollections would, perforce, be supplanted by the shock of the present—the planes crashing into tall buildings and grassy knolls, the images on the big screen, the new day of the dead, all far from their afternoon walking slowly through the past and the from that December day of infamy that wove their lives together so long ago.

What Blossoms Survived

Two legged beasts choked in afternoon's haze. Days all rated like pain, one to ten. Three's admonitions were to the elderly, the infirm; lucky seven still said all but necessary travel was verboten. Nine was malign enough for the bug-eyed masks, and even indoor tasks were advised with caution.

Double digits meant doom, stay in your room, with equal measures of oxygen and prayer. Outside if the scale really read the ominous ten, fears were of fire igniting in the skies. But some days were yet a two, when masses moved about enjoying a respite from wrath. Though one was remembered as if a dream, with skies a strange hue; most thought it was once called blue.

Plants, trees, were taxed without exemption, mixing molecules, a chemical marriage in silence, their birthing of atoms, our salvation. And there were those who ventured far enough into the fields who vouchsafed they had yet seen daffodils, wilted but alive.

The Washerwoman

Those folks hired white help, maybe a Mex to tend to the yards, but they let old lady Latty wash their soiled sheets, bath towels and undergarments. They sent out their fine clothes for that new process called dry cleaning, a magic Latty would never fathom—how you gonna clean anything without steaming water, lye and labor of love?

But Latty knew those folks whose shit-stained drawers she was scrubbing had more secrets than money, and she knew to keep lips God gave her closed.

For nobody need know about the joy juice that was on the sheets when the man of the house was gone, and the towels covered with the seed weren't none of Latty's business. She said not a word about what sins were seepin' under the cracks of those fine wood doors, or what other rich as Croesus gents were walking softly on the polished floors.

Latty was off Mondays, but not on the Sabbath, for it was often the eve of that holy day when the most soiling was done, and that didn't bother her none. For Sundays the folks was mostly gone to church, and whatever sinning was to be done took its rest like the Lord did, unless sitting in a pew with a man you never loved counts as such.

Tulsa, 1908

The Quickening

Two miscarriages. God's abortions her curse. The third time not a charm, though with a marriage of joy and alarm, she feels a flutter. More wings than feet taking flight amniotic.

She lies still and waits for another, the expectant mother. She is not disappointed; it moves again to her delight. Climbing closer to the light, wet wings flapping slowly, this web fingered, big-brained swimmer-flyer son-daughter-carrier of the eternal flame.

Who will be to blame if its eyes never see the sun? What God would will such a denial? The one who gifts all things life yet has been but a fickle teaser with her. She lies very still, holding the breath of life, hoping its exhalation will be the current on which new wings take flight.

Coyote yelping helps. The winds, too, distract him from the now. The Comanche who put the arrow in his back lies beside him. Gone before him. That is condign comfort to him.

He cannot speak, nor move his tongue, but he smells the Comanche, the creosote. He sees the clouds, stingy white whiffs in a hot summer sky. As good a day to die as any he reckons, and he feels no pain.

Again, the yelping. Closer now—are they talking about him? Will they beat the buzzards to his body? Would they begin their feast while his eyes are yet open? He closes them; the flapping of the wings does not arouse him. He knows they are on the Comanche. Beaks and talons at work.

He lets himself drift, content the vultures are choosing the dead, but they fly off. The coyote pack approaches. The pads of their paws patter on the hard caliche.

He lets himself drift, dreaming now of sweet green grass and good water. And the coyotes begin their work: the Indian and he now a solitary offering for the ravenous dogs.

A Revolution of Uranus

He sat bedside with his great grandmother, stroking a hand laced with what he saw as tiny blue rivers, flowing from a thin wrist dammed by ancient knuckles. Boulders chiseled by eighty-four years.

He read from his book while Mommy dozed in the chair, and nurses squeaked in and out, all with half smiles he could not decipher, for Grammy was sick. And when his mother was awake, she cried.

He hadn't seen his mother's tears before. He tried not to look, preferring his book with its pictures of the sun, orbiting planets and mazy moons. And spaces in between where heaven might hide.

He understood most of its words, and none were of heavens— unless noxious gasses and swirling clouds of dust were the winds which whipped through the pearly gates. But his seven wise years knew that was not so.

When he turned to the page of the penultimate planet from the sun, YOU-ruh-nuss, he discovered it took four score and four years to orbit our star once. Math's mystery may have eluded him. Though coincidence was not yet in his lexicon, and now he knew Grammy had her times around the sun, her eighty-four, equaling one for the great tilting Uranus.

East of Eavesdropping

At the first Missouri rest stop on I-44, I stopped to pee, to walk, and to listen to strangers. This had been my habit of late, of late being the last ten years, since I lost her, and sojourned solo.

On the move, I would catch snippets: a "this potato salad is stale," complaint, or a "I don't want to drive" protest. On this June day, summer solstice, I got lucky, for a couple spoke loudly and I was hidden behind a fat oak.

"I'm not going to have this child."

"You don't get to decide alone. It's my—"

"No, it's not and it's my body!"

Then he jumped up from the table and marched mad steps to his Mercedes. It was a royal red. And the hue matters not to most, but it figures clearly in my rear view.

Headed east again after I heard what I was not intended to hear, I could yet see them just behind my eyes. He, trying in vain to explain that a few cells mattered—she, muscularly clinging to a convenient cleansing. Their words echoed in my head and in the blood red coach that carried them east to uncharted malaise.

One Gallon of Gas

One gallon. 31 miles or so the EPA guesstimated. 163,680 feet. 54,560 steps if he walked.

He avoided the major "arteries," damnable euphemisms for interstates, for what lifeblood did they carry and what did one see at 110 feet a second, 1.25 miles a minute.

At mile 3, he spotted a cur crossing the asphalt, or perhaps it was a coyote; and until mile 12 he wondered why he wanted to know where it had come from, rather than where it was going, because aren't road trips about getting somewhere?

At mile 15, he saw a farmhouse abandoned before time, or maybe when a feeble old man died in a sagging bed, the month after he put his wife in the cold ground, and told his progeny if their homestead was good enough to bring them into the world, and for her to depart, it was fine enough for him to do the same.

At mile 21, he traversed a bridge over Red Bluff Creek, and he knew there wasn't a bluff within a hundred miles. Perhaps it was got its colored appellation after a poker player named Red, known for his bluffing.

At mile 30, he had a blowout. No, he didn't careen off the old road into a ditch, but slowly rolled to an impotent stop atop the only hill in 50 miles. A man in overalls with an ancient pick up stopped and offered aid in a drawl thick enough to slow time. Together they put on the donut from the trunk. The man wouldn't take a ten but said take care.

And our traveler decided his helper had to have been kin to the old man in the abandoned shack, and perhaps he had been there in the end, watching the wheel spin on a tick tock clock, noting the precise minute the old man passed—to write this time in a family bible.

Because that is how it should be. Of all those things he would see: beasts going nowhere; mythic rivers from everywhere; and behind ghost painted walls, men dying. Men whose sons would stop to render aid to strangers and help conjure the imagined tales infinitely available from a gallon of fossil fuel.

Strip Mall

In John Gibson's last fall, a strip mall was constructed where the county hospital sat for eight decades, The hospital was built the year John was born, bricks and mortar courtesy of his uncle, who passed there, along with John's mother, father, and Wendell Haney, the only man John killed in his long tenure as sheriff.

John stood bedside with all four, watched and waited until their last breaths came—even the one his own gun put there. Maybe that was the hardest, seeing the young man die, unnatural in the order of things. A man, not half John's age, who, after killing his own father, pointed a rifle at one of John's deputies, Willie Bishop. John went over this a hundred times and would have done the same thing again: his gun; his decision; his words imploring Wendell to put the gun down. Yes, John would have done it again, because sometimes, he thought, one must play God. Sometimes one must choose, and John chose to save Willie, his youngest deputy who had an infant son at home. If John had not pulled the trigger, Willie wouldn't have been there, ten years later, to see his son pitch a no hitter. Perhaps, John thought, there wouldn't have been a no hitter.

The night he shot Wendell, John didn't think of Willie's infant son. John thought only of how a boy had grown so wild to kill his own father. Those thoughts didn't last longer than the few minutes the doc and nurses worked on Wendell. When they pronounced him dead, John quit wondering why, but held the image of Wendell's blank eyes. And he pondered what, if anything, the young man saw on the bright ceiling above him his last seconds of life.

This same hospital was where John's sons made their entrance into this life. His elder son, Junior, drove him now to the courthouse, past the shiny new mall—steel, stucco and glass. John could still see the old building, a place he imagined would go gracefully to ruin, still strong in its abandon, perhaps creeping ivy cradling the old brown brick walls.

The county had different ideas. A new hospital was more cost effective than renovations and the real estate value of the property was high. The wrecking ball did its job; an out of town company got the contract to remove the rubble. A thousand bricks were left for anybody who wanted a souvenir. John got two for his boys. The new hospital sat by the new high school, land for both donated by the county's biggest oil company, with the proviso a wing of the hospital bear the name of the owner's daughter who perished when she crashed her new Corvette, a week past her sixteenth birthday.

The courthouse was busy. Their business took longer than expected. Junior suggested they take lunch at Chipotle's at the new mall. John and he arrived at noon on the nose and found a crowd. In the line in front of them were two young ladies who had to be twins. Dressed differently; one's hair bobbed and short, and the other shoulder length— but they were definitely twins. Junior greeted them. John nudged him and with his eyes asked who they were. Junior had just retired as junior high school principal. After thirty years in the business, he recognized every other person they saw. Twins he was sure to remember. He answered he did not know.

From where John and Junior sat, John could see the young ladies, two tables over. Their blonde hair, their big blue eyes—pretty girls John thought, but at his age, comely countenances held his attention only briefly. There was something about them John couldn't decipher. Whatever the notion was, it settled somewhere between his throat and his belly, making it harder to swallow his bites of burrito.

At eighty, John had survived prostate and lung cancer. His wind was still good; they had caught the cancers early and the radiation did the trick. His hearing was going, but that was to be expected, though John's vision was still sharp. And, after being a lawman forty-five years—not retiring until he was seventy—the habit of scrutinizing everything around him had never faded. John had noticed the emaciated boy preparing their burritos had tracks on his arms. The heavyset cashier had a bruise on her face she tried to disguise with makeup. She was soft spoken, and jittery, and John figured her for someone whose husband or cracker boyfriend beat.

Ten years earlier, in his last days as sheriff, John would have let the boy know where he could go for treatment, and he would have handed the young woman the card he kept with the number of the County Woman's Shelter. Now, John kept no such card, and though the inclination was there, John said nothing. His time was short he surmised, and John had done what he could to leave the face of the county, the country, and the fate of mankind better. John was never sure he had been successful but fretted over it little. Less and less each day as John took longer to walk to his mailbox to get his paper and the ubiquitous junk that came with his few bills and letters.

John saw the man enter and kept his gaze on him. Junior had been talking about Mom and how it was good John kept her petunia beds up, even two seasons after she passed (keeled over on a Saturday morning while she was digging in those same beds). Truth be told, it wasn't sentiment that kept the beds fresh, but boredom. John no longer spent nine hours a day on the job, he read little but the small-town paper, and had no hobbies. John listened politely as Junior said he'd pick some of the flowers when he dropped him off that afternoon, but John kept his eyes on the man who entered. Hispanic. Shaved head. Tat barely visible on his neck. Overcoat though probably sixty-five degrees outside. Overcoat. Black.

John rose to his feet. Junior stared at him. "Dad." John walked towards the man. "Dad." The man pulled an AR15 from his coat—exactly the gun the old sheriff thought the man would be carrying a decade into this new century. He fired first at the scrawny boy who had made their burritos. The boy went down, fast—a round to the head.

John knew by the look, by the carry, it wasn't over. The shooter turned the weapon on the customers and fired again, hitting an older woman in the back and then shooting the woman across from her. His next targets were the twins. John put himself between the gunman and the girls. The shooter looked surprised: an old man with nothing but a tuft of white hair and skin as aged as Methuselah coming straight at him. The man fired, but not until John grabbed the muzzle and pulled downward enough for the shot to hit John low abdomen, dropping him, but John didn't release his grip on the gun. Junior and two other men were on the assailant by then. Junior wrenched the rifle from the shooter's hands and hit the man in the face with the butt of the weapon. The other men held the man down as Junior hit him two more times, making sure he was out. Junior then turned to his father. John was looking at the twins, trying to remember, trying to understand. "Dad." Junior leaned down and pressed a wad of napkins on John's bleeding gut. John's vision was clouding; he felt dizzy. The last thing he recalled seeing while on the floor of the restaurant was the ancient oak outside the window. Then John remembered. Then he understood. Then things went black.

John woke in the ER with Junior and John's younger son, Josh, flanking him. The lights were bright, but John's vision was yet blurry. Each son held a hand. Josh told his father the docs said he'd lost a great deal of blood but had a fighting chance. John saw the tubes running from his arm. He remembered the tubes running into Wendell Haney's arms—Wendell who died in the old hospital. The sturdy structure that was demolished for a strip mall. The strip mall where John had been shot. The one where he put himself between two girls and another killer. The place where John saved the lives of the Wendell Haney's twin daughters. The place progress forgot to gobble up an old oak tree. A tree against which, a quarter century before, John had leaned and sought refuge from the hot sun and from the nagging vision of the young father taking his last breaths.

4:30 AM in the City

It's cold in this motel. All the paisley carpet in the world won't make the halls warm. A faux fire is burning in the lobby. The clerk is long numb to it and to the rest of the world, it appears. No guest has disturbed him for hours

I don't want to go upstairs, to a room where my only daughter waits, curled in the cover like chrysalis in cocoon. Eyes dried from crying all the tears eyes can make. Still she dry sobs. Still she aches for a mother she believes abandoned her, in a motel, like this one, a lifetime ago.

We will attend the service early today—too late for a reconciliation between mother and daughter, the tether torn a decade past. I will hold my daughter close; her eyes will dart around the room, wondering who the mourners are, how they knew the mother she did not.

Until then, I will sit a while longer by this timid flicker of light. Before I don the black suit. Before I knot my tie in the mirror and see the face of the man who could not forgive a transgression, a human misstep, and robbed a girl of her mother, until today, when words will spill from strangers' mouths, the only biography my daughter will ever have of her. And I will wish for short epitaphs, a quick return to the earth, while those words and truths haunt my soul.

Winter's White Grip

The boy had never seen a rabbit so still. Only its fur moved in the cruel wind. He pulled an arrow from his quiver and took aim at the cottontail. The boy's hands shook from the cold, but the arrow struck its mark—almost. The shaft lodged itself in the creature's hind leg.

Now the rabbit hobbled in the deep snow, leaving a thin red trail on the white blanket until the boy caught his prey and snapped its neck. Fresh hot meat for the night's meal. His father would be proud.

Nearly back to the village, the boy spotted the wolf—white, almost invisible in the drifts. He drew another arrow, but then remembered what the elders had said: a white wolf in winter may not be harmed, and a gift must be proffered.

The boy sheathed his arrow and lay the rabbit in the snow, the animal's blood still warm. The wolf and the boy watched each other, and a great gust swelled. The boy turned away from the blast, the wolf.

Behind him he heard the howls. A synchronicity. The wail of the wolf wedded to the wind. A marriage of flesh and the elements. The two were one in the boy's ears, until he found his lodge and warmed his hands with fire's gift.

Moon on the Path*

When the moon was full, grandpa and I would stay in town past sunset. The road home good, with few ruts, the pastures soft silver in all that lunar light.

His team was old, slow, but grandpa knew no haste, even getting to the cellar when great twisters came. Born the week Lincoln freed the slaves. He not once drove a car, though he lived to read of Sputnik in the Gazette and died when JFK was elected.

Summers lasted a long time with grandpa. I still see him. giving reins a gentle shake, reminding his horses to pull us home, whistling to them, telling me tales.

On a July night, the year of the Crash he put his gaze on the fat orb, barely waning, and proclaimed, "One day we'll put a man up there." But I thought he was pulling my leg. "Have to put him in a cannon like, enclosed in some hard shell, otherwise we'd blow him all to hell, gettin' enough power to loose the bounds of God's earth."

Grandpa didn't live to hear Neil's famous words, two score after that summer night. Though I yet hear the shod hooves plodding, the wagon wheels rolling, and his words soothsaying, whenever I gaze at a white moon's face.

*Based on a true story, told to me by Bill E. Bill lived from 1919 to 2004 and recounted this story to me the last years of his life.

Crown Victoria

The old cruiser sat in his drive. Tires as tired as time, the whole car speckled with droppings from the sparrows and mourning doves in his oak. The back seat still the same: blood dried black from the boy's brief ride.

Justified use of force the grandest grand jury decreed. Still they made him put up his sword and shield. The sullied car was part of his severance. His Crown Vic replaced by a fat SUV, and he replaced by his own deputy.

He knew it less was a blessing than a curse, the cruiser turned hearse gifted to him. The men had tried it scrub it clean, but the boy he felled was eighteen. The young man's blood copious, stubborn, and a condign reminder of the sheriff's last night as the law—of his frenzied, futile attempt to save the boy, the "deceased," whose last testament was forever scrawled in the bowels of the car that now sat still as stone, alone with its red written tale.

The Scar on the Stranger's Chin

Paler than her skin, was the scar on her chin, a two-inch memory phantom at a forty-five-degree angle. That, I recall most of all. The lady beside me at the deli, the Saturday before my daughter was born. I know I looked at her twice in the flash of time it took to order, two pastramis on rye, both of which went to ruin since my wife went into labor the moment we sat to eat.

We made it to the hospital in twenty minutes, though I don't remember the ride. My hands on the wheel, the traffic lights. We missed every single one, my wife said. Yellow then red, and those were perhaps a portent, an omen of what was to come: thirty hours of breathing, heaving, fetal distress, a caesarean section, and a beautiful daughter, who lived thirty minutes.

I can't usually see her face, except when I close my eyes to sleep, and then as a small circle floating above our bed. Her visage smooth, baby pink, full of light, though it lingers but a moment, before I see the scar on the woman's chin, the meal uneaten.

October's Thirst

Judicious July, two inches. Auspicious August three. September sunk to half an inch and leaped to record heat for the month.

October first, he was at the bank, hat in hand and pride somewhere deep inside, after he swallowed it two droughts ago. The banker would know. This time he would not bother to ask. This time the reaping now would be from blood, not soil. The blood of his ancestors who fed a nation. Anonymous plodders who plowed the sod where they were now buried.

He was the last. He would have to move fast to get dollars for his dirt, before the loans came due. Before the wife, the children knew they would soon be town dwellers. October would be the month "Farm for Sale" signs would hang from his fences like mocking scoreboards. And the month he would feel like he had drowned in drought, leaving no doubt he had failed his father, and his sons.

First Freeze and other Prognostications

Jimmy's local CBS affiliate hosted a first freeze contest every year. The person who came closest to guessing the exact time the station's weather recorded 32 degrees won a prize. Jimmy never participated in the contest, but in October 2000, Jimmy wrote down 2:46 AM, November 10 as the predicted time. Jimmy left the piece of paper on which he had written the time and date on his coffee table.

There the paper sat, along with two National Geographic magazines and a Civil War book until November 10, when they announced the winner, Mrs. Verna Wood, who had guessed 3:01 AM on that day, fifteen minutes after the first freeze. She won a new big screen TV.

Jimmy did not know how he chose the exact time of the first freeze. He also didn't know why he had done the same thing with the "Triple Digits" contest. In that one, you had to guess the date and time the temp would hit the century mark in his Texas city.

Jimmy's peculiar prescience was not restricted to weather. He also predicted the precise minute the first baby of the year would born in his city. No contest was hosted for that event, but the local news always reported it. Jimmy had predicted that two consecutive years.

Jimmy could not guess when an event would occur when asked. These numbers simply "came to him." When he thought about the process, he wasn't sure he "heard" the numbers or "saw" them. Maybe neither. Maybe both.

Jimmy didn't reveal this unusual talent to anyone but his brother, Phil, who didn't believe Jimmy at first, but the second baby guess proved it to Phil. Jimmy had called Phil at the annual New Year's Eve party Phil hosted (and Jimmy never attended) and said, It's 11:31 PM, right? In exactly two hours, the first baby of the new year will be born.

Phil said, yeah, yeah, let me get back to my party. If you are right, I'll give you a thousand bucks. The next night, after watching the local news, Phil called and said, I owe you a grand.

Jimmy said he didn't want the money. That week, a new television was delivered to Jimmy's apartment. Jimmy called Phil and said, Hey Phil, it wasn't a bet. I just wanted to prove to you these things happen to me.

Phil could never see Jimmy as a victim. Phil believed this clairvoyance was a gift—an underused one like Jimmy's other talents. Jimmy had a degree in Electrical Engineering, yet he worked at Radio Shack.

Once Phil discovered his younger brother's "gift," he began asking when stocks would peak. Jimmy explained repeatedly his precognition wasn't something that could be summoned on command. Phil tried another tactic to use Jimmy's ability to divine the future. Phil would simply give Jimmy a range of numbers and ask Jimmy to randomly select one. Pick a number between 34 and 40, Phil would say.

Jimmy played along, giving Phil the first number that would pop into his head. After Jimmy did this a few times, he assumed, accurately, Phil was attempting to get numbers where a stock would peak for the day or week. Phil said the four times he had asked Jimmy, Jimmy had gotten it right. Then Phil did the same thing to determine when a stock would reach its nadir before jumping back up. Jimmy nailed those numbers also. Phil told Jimmy his portfolio was probably twenty thousand bucks fatter because of Jimmy's "gift."

This meant little to Jimmy. Money meant little to Jimmy. Jimmy and Phil's parents had perished in a head on collision with a semi when they were toddlers and their Uncle Barlow had taken them in—oil rich Uncle Barlow who had no children of his own. Both Phil and Jimmy had modest trusts. Phil had become an investor and turned his trust into a fortune long before Jimmy revealed his gift to him. Jimmy was content to work part time for nine dollars an hour. The trust was enough to pay the rent and keep his camper van running.

Jimmy took a vacation to northern New Mexico in early September 2001. The afternoon before he was to return to Texas, Jimmy sat at his small table, ate refried beans and tortillas and looked at clouds form over the Sangre de Cristo Mountains.

Two distinct rock formations sat at the foot of the mountains to the west of Jimmy. His eyes fixated on one of them. Jimmy opened the book he had been reading, *The Seven Pillars of Wisdom*, and wrote 6:46 AM, Mountain Time, 9/11. Though it was a warm day, Jimmy felt a chill. The remainder of the afternoon, Jimmy watched the clouds become darker and more billowed. From his vantage point, he watched rain fall first on one rock formation and then the other.

Jimmy slept fitfully that night and dreamed of Phil. Phil and he were on a dark field, throwing a ball to one another. The ball always landed short. Jimmy told Phil to throw harder. Phil was silent. Then the ball became the shape of a ring—a life preserver. The brothers kept throwing the object, but it always fell short. Jimmy felt his arms stretching to catch the ring. Still, he could not. Jimmy threw the preserver harder towards Phil. Then Phil was gone. Jimmy was alone in the dark.

Jimmy woke at 6:42 AM, just before sunrise. He threw off his blanket and put on his Nikes. Jimmy had no appetite and decided to immediately head home. By 6:44, he was pulling away from the Mills Canyon rim campground where he'd spent the night. In all his previous experiences of clairvoyance, Jimmy had never felt any emotion. In this case, while looking at the clock turn 6:46, he felt the same electric chill he had when he wrote the time in his book the previous afternoon. Jimmy also had an uneasy feeling in his gut.

Jimmy did not know at the precise moment he was looking at the clock, over 1700 miles to the east, a plane was crashing into one of the World Trade Center towers. Jimmy would not discover this until later in the morning when a cashier at a convenience store told him about the attacks. Jimmy had never shaken the feeling in his gut. By the time he pulled away from the store, he felt like an iron bar was running from the back of his eyes to his bowels. Jimmy thought of Phil. He felt the need to talk to his brother. Jimmy pulled to the side of the road and called Phil on his cell. No answer.

Jimmy was not aware his brother was on first plane to hit the World Trade Center that morning. Jimmy had no idea Phil had been in Boston the night before. Jimmy's mind returned to writing in his book the previous afternoon: 6:46 Mountain Time—8:46 Eastern Time—which Jimmy had been told was the time the plane crashed into the skyscraper. This was why Jimmy was not surprised when he called Jimmy's cohabitant, April, and she told him Phil may have been on American Airlines Flight 11 from Boston to Los Angeles where she was to meet him the next day. Late morning on 9/12/01 Jimmy and April got confirmation Phil had been on the fateful flight.

Jimmy's grim prescience continued after Phil's death: 11:11 PM, 9/27/05, Uncle Barlow's death; 2:22 PM, 4/14/11, a Cessna hitting the side of a foggy Kentucky hill, killing a family of four Jimmy knew well;

3:33 PM, 11/01/14, the discovery of a ten-year old's body after the child had gone missing while trick or treating the night before. Finally, 6/13/17, the day Jimmy fell to his death while rock climbing in Utah. When April, to whom he had remained close after Phil's death, was going through Jimmy's apartment after his demise, she found a note on his coffee table. 2:01 PM, 6/13/17. The Park Service report indicated Jimmy was seen falling to his death at 2:02 PM.

Forgetting

My daughter bought me one of those extensions for my cellphone. To take selfies so I wouldn't forget who I was, as if looking at a "me" in the face of my phone would remind me: I am John Smith, I am 73.

She wants me to remember I had been an engineer at a missile range for 45 years and two months, that I had lost a finger in Vietnam and my wife died in an automobile accident three years ago. And her name was Emma.

But my daughter says I never called her mother anything but "M" and now, whenever I read, hear, say or write the letter M, I get a lump in my throat. It does not last.

My daughter has notes taped on every surface of my house, reminding me to eat and take my meds. She placed a big one on the door: DON'T GO OUTSIDE. But I wouldn't anyway. I like it here, where I think I have been a long time, and this place is filled with things my daughter calls memories and photos of a lady I don't recognize with a sticky note on each one.

The notes are all yellow and have an "M" on them. I get that lump in my throat when I see them, and sometimes water comes from my eyes, though I don't know why, because Emma didn't look like that.

Gwyll, on her Shore

I visited her cottage each month, never staying the night. Through her window by the oak table we watched the surf. On days when the sea was angry, we could hear the waves crack against earth's spare spine. Those times I liked, for she would hold my hand, tightly, like I was her tether to the wild world.

Each visit, I would leave as the sun set, the moment a million gold sparkles vanished from the waters. When I found her, I pretended she was sleeping. Her eyes were open and still, staring it seemed through the same window. I sat with her and rubbed her cold hand.

I stayed until the sun sank into the same salty sea, wondering if the old tales were true...if a billion tears had flowed into the blue depths making a soulful brine. I know mine fell on the soggy sand, disappearing in the deepening dark that swallowed my tracks.

Man and Beast. Beast and Man.

That hot stretch of highway saw few cars. The interstate ran parallel a few miles north. Unlike the big highway, which willed its way to the ocean, this road appeared to have a barren mountain on the horizon as its terminus. Through my truck windshield, the asphalt, center marks long ago vanished, made a line to the base of a craggy peak. If vegetation grew on that rocky mountain, I couldn't see it. Surely a few cacti hid in crevices with the snakes and Gila monsters.

Off the road, I saw cattle bones and wondered who ever tried to graze this land. If Dante had imagined another level on the surface of this third rock from the sun, this would have been it. The few cacti I saw along the highway appeared bleached under a white sky and looked to be begging the gods for rain.

That was twenty years ago. I was fifty. I was broke. I had been thrown out by my third wife. That was before my liver rebelled from all those years I fed it whatever poisons my wallet would allow. Now my yellow eyes tell the world my biography. Part of it. Soon, that story will be engraved in stone. At some VA cemetery. My name, rank and some numbers that require only simple subtraction to measure a man's life.

In my pick up, I had a gallon of water and a twelve pack of warm beer. I was sipping from each. I wore only a pair of Adidas and jeans. My shirt I left in a convenience store bathroom where I had given myself a sponge bath the night before. My first attempt at hygiene in the fifty hours since she kicked me out. And told me not to return. And told me she wasn't even going to forward my VA checks to me.

Wouldn't have mattered at that point. I didn't know where I was going. Guess she thought I was headed to hell. From the looks of things around me that day, she was right.

Today, in this bed in this cool, quiet place, I am not sure I know what regret is. Remorse, repentance, disappointment. Those are not part of my lexicon from my brief seven decades here. When I ask myself if I would have done anything different, I don't know the answer.

But that day on the highway, I know I would have changed nothing. Hungover, reeking of ammonia sweat, rejected by a woman I thought I loved, disowned by my son, desperately alone, I did what I had to do.

I had stopped dead center of my lane at what had to be an eternal high noon. I got out to piss. I was the only person on the planet I thought. But I wasn't. Before I got my zipper up, the pearl black BMW flew by, driver's hand glued to the horn as they swerved into the other lane to avoid rear ending me. The passenger flipped me the bird. I returned the salute with both hands. I saw the brake lights come on, briefly, but the bastard downshifted and sped up. Up yours. Come on back.

But they didn't. I watched them until they melted into the heat waves on the horizon. I imagined them crashing into the mountain. But they wouldn't.

What they did was mow down a coyote a mile down the road. I came upon him, pulling himself along the asphalt with his front legs, dragging blood drenched hindquarters. I saw where the tires left a crimson tread mark. Not one bit of rubber on the hot road. They didn't even brake. I took my .38—the same one I had in my mouth two nights before—and got out. I walked along beside the brush wolf, as big as any I had ever seen and in a pain trance. Moving as slowly as the tarantula I saw in the middle of the highway a few feet from us. An arachnid escort for this canine's final journey.

I moved to a spot in front of the coyote, not three feet from its snout. The blood trail in its wake was close to ten meters. You are a strong one I thought. I walked backwards, rewinding a clock, my gaze fixed on the beast—its eyes, its sagging tongue, its bloody hindquarters. When I stopped, it did also.

The coyote looked into my eyes. I knew that look. The sky above me turned from white to blue, the dry heat turned to steam, and the coyote's gold irises turned dark brown. Its face underwent a transfiguration to become a man-child. I aimed my .38 at a spot between the boy's eyes. I cocked the hammer but did not feel myself pull the trigger. But I did. Now the boy was dead. And before the blood from the blast hit the ground, the creature was a coyote again. I was no longer five clicks from the DMZ, standing above a VC who had his short legs shredded by M 60 fire. His eyes and mine locked in a marriage soon to be annulled. He nodded when I pointed my M16 at his face. He whispered something I did not understand. I did not feel myself pull the trigger that day either.

The sky was white again as I walked back to my truck. I drove past the coyote carcass. The tarantula had not moved. A faithful spectator in a wake.

Another mile down the road I saw the BMW flipped over. Neither driver nor passenger was in the car. They were not far though. Both had been thrown from the vehicle. Of course, they were not wearing seatbelts. That would have saved them. That would have kept them from their assigned fate on a line that cut through hell.

I stopped and walked up to the body closest to the highway. The driver. Thirty something. Blond. Tanned. A white polo shirt turned red. Dead. A dozen feet from him, the passenger. The bird thrower. Blond also. A woman with hair cropped short. A baby blue polo. Alive. She looked at me and asked a question with her eyes. Was she asking to die or asking for help? Which would be her salvation, I wondered.

I did feel the pull of the trigger then. But I shot above her head. Disappointment or relief? I don't know what I saw in her eyes. Baby blue finger thrower whispered something I did not understand. But I had already ended the suffering of one beast that day. I had done the same in the jungle thirty years before. What else was required of me on this hell bound highway?

Once Met Hears Without Ears

Our old truck had a flat at the foot of the Sangre de Cristo mountains, on a rutted brown road, by a singing stream, swollen from snow melt. The sagging bridge across looked too tired to handle our load. We replaced the bald tire with one equally hairless.

We were washing the grit and grease from our hands in the rushing waters, when we saw him, so small we were surprised he could walk, and her, at the other end of life's long string, so old she moved like a question mark down the bank, a bucket in one sinewy hand, the tiny boy's paw in the other. We crossed to greet them, though neither of us knew why. But we were under an infinite blue sky and on four wheels again. What else was there to do but cross the baptismal waters to meet strangers by a strange road?

The little one spoke, with words so small they disappeared by the time they reached our ears. How we knew what he was saying we would never recall, though we did as he commanded, taking off our shoes, placing our feet in the cold current, following his lead in this dance on a nameless road. The ancient one never uttered a word, but gestured to us, to the sky, to the blue green peaks, and to the waters at our feet, and told us, with skin and bone, that the blood of everyman flowed from the high country and washed our tangled toes and simple soles.

Florida Fireflies*

In this pasture, one hundred days past, scores cheered as the current coursed through Bundy's body. This evening, I am here, solitaire, except for my spaniel, the cattle, and the fireflies sprinkled against the night.

My bitch nips at the flies, but they are quick, eluding her jaws to perform a brilliant alchemy again. Amidst this spectacle, cows chew their cud, unaware it appears, magical lightning comes without thunder from these creatures. Ted too was a creature, beyond comprehension—beyond redemption it would seem.

The bovines don't scatter as I walk among them. Perhaps they've forgotten those revelers here on a crisp winter night, eager to celebrate an extinguishing of light.

*Serial killer Ted Bundy was executed in Florida in January 1989. Across the road from the prison was a cow pasture where hundreds celebrated during and immediately following his electrocution.

The Full Mailbox

One day, some automaton called a mailman will be driving down his street, flipping and flapping those boxes open and shut, loading them with opportunity, sadness, joy, reminders, colorful half-truths that attempt to sell or soothe. And he will notice one isn't empty, and he won't even think, "Old guy must be out of town."

The postman will come again, flipping and flapping those doors, and he'll notice again, that one isn't empty, and if his eyes are half open, he may think, "The old guy may be out of town," and again, flipping and flapping another day, until he again comes to the same box that is now nearly full—of even more anonymous half-truths—and he may say, "Gotta ask the neighbor when he's coming back."

A flip and flap away, he leaves his truck for the first time that day. Knock, ring, ding. "How ya doin'? Old guy next door out of town?"

"His daughter lives in Dallas, but he's too old to drive down."

The automaton and neighbor walk to the house of the full box. One looks in the garage while the other checks the locks. Ding dong, ding dong, loud bells for ancient ears. But no one hears. And the black car is still in the garage. And inside the house, in cool darkness and starkly alone, the old man with the full mailbox has forgotten the opportunities, half-truths, the sadness and the joy. While others flip and flap and knock in vain, he has passed quietly into the eternity of night. With a full mailbox.

While Asleep

You check on me many times a day. With my antique ears, I hear your squeaking shoes on these vinyl floors someone laid for those who came before, like passengers on a stalled bus with windows that allowed only one view.

I know you and I wait for the same thing. For you to check on the passenger who replaces me. He will be no different. A few more hairs—perhaps a few less stares. You will gently place your hand on his wrist, write in his chart, and maybe glance at the date of birth, do the mindless math and wonder without wonder if my replacement will have a bigger number than I.

But I am still here. I am still here gazing at your angled glances while you count the beats, which slow a little each day, waiting for you to say, without words, how long will this one last? Don't fret, squeaking vinyl floor walker. When my drum stops pounding, I will try to make sure it happens one someone else's shift.

A Place Among the Thorns

(Chapter one: discovering the dead)

On the trail through the mesquite, I found a calf—a bloated victim of chemistry, bovine eyes still open, though not ravaged by scavengers. This very spot, I once found a felled feral piglet, and another time, a lifeless coyote pup. Both molested by the elements when I came upon them, several hot suns after they died, but neither devoured by birds of prey.

What killed the beasts in this field of timothy grass, mesquite, hot winds, and a godless sky, and why did the vultures not feast upon them? Perhaps I had found a place where the dead played a trick on the living, here among the thorny mesquite.

(Chapter two: the old man)

The rancher who owns this piece of ground is barely 70, but the weather in this harsh place has aged him beyond his years. The weather and perhaps some grief he chooses not to share.

His name is Charles Sullivan and he is the fourth generation bearing that name to keep stock on this land. He will be the last—his only son, Thomas, chose to live in the city. An accountant, a keeper of other's money, Charles says. Thomas was my neighbor. Years ago, he introduced me to Charles when we hunted quail on his ranch. Thomas moved to Dallas and no longer came home, but Charles granted me permission to hunt on his land.

Charles is a widower, but he is not alone. His daughter, Patricia, palsied since birth, lives with him in the century old ranch house. Patricia is wheelchair bound and Charles seems to be the only one who can understand much of what she says. He takes care of Patricia by himself and has since his wife passed ten years ago, at which time he sold his herd and gave up ranching.

(Chapter three: seeking answers)

I'd said nothing to Charles when I found the feral piglet and the coyote. When I found the calf, I asked him why a calf would be there. Every now and then a stray comes across a cattle guard onto his place, Charles explained. When I told him where I had come upon all three animals, Charles asked me to sit with him at the dining table. He poured us each iced tea and asked if I was certain about the spot on the trail. Yes, I told him, it was the place where the trail split into two, one path going to the stock tank and the other to a stand of hackberry. At that very fork? Charles asked again.

Charles asked if I knew Comanche had been a menace in this part of the country. Yes, I said, I had read about that. Well, Charles said, I never read a word about it, but my granddaddy told me all I needed to know.

(Chapter four: a cursed place)

Charles took a long sip from his glass, looked over at Patricia, in her chair, watching the old TV in the living room, and told me the following:

In 1898, my grandfather was thirty and my father, Robert, was ten. My Aunt Priscilla was only eight. My grandmother had died the year before, thrown from a horse. At the very same spot on the trail.

(Chapter five: evil among men)

In that same year, a renegade band of five Comanche killed a Texas Ranger, a settler, and the settler's young daughter in Archer County, due east of the county where our ranch is. All the ranchers were on the lookout for the renegades and children were told to stay within earshot of home.

(Chapter six: the tempest)

A week after the murders, my grandfather broke two ribs when a steer battered him against the side of a pen. While he was recuperating, a fierce summer storm hit, lighting up the prairies and turning the gullies to freshets. Though still ailing, Grandfather got up from his sickbed and saddled his horse to check on a cow he was sure would drop a calf that night. He ordered my father and Priscilla to stay in the house.

The children knew calving was sometimes an all-night affair, but after Grandfather was gone two hours, they began to fret, their worries no doubt heightened by nature's ferocious display of its power—the lightning was still striking near and at frequent intervals several hours after the storm began. The explosive sound of the thunder had Dad and Priscilla shaking in their boots.

My dad and Priscilla were obedient children—all kids were back then. But this was different, my dad decided. His father was out there alone, injured and trying to work in a terrible storm. Dad saddled a colt and he and Priscilla headed to where they believed their father would be, not far south of the fork in the trail.

(Chapter seven: the assassins in the night)

As soon as Dad and Priscilla were on their way, the rains stopped, but not before Dad and Priscilla were drenched and shivering. Where the trail split, they saw them—five men on horseback. Five Comanches. Dad booted the colt and it took to a gallop; Priscilla fell off, not a dozen steps from where her mother had broken her neck when she fell from her horse the year before. Dad tried to stop the colt, but it kept running, leaving Aunt Priscilla sitting on the prairie.

(Chapter eight: a salvation)

Though the dead of night, with the distant lightning and a gibbous moon shining through breaks in the clouds, Aunt Priscilla could see the five mounted figures, still as statues not twenty paces from her. Priscilla was towheaded and wearing a white frock. The Comanches had to see her. She was frozen to that spot on the trail. Where could she run?

The renegades began moving in her direction, not stopping when they came upon her, the hooves of their horses nearly stepping on her. They spoke among themselves as they rode by, but not one of them looked down at her. In recalling the incident, Aunt Priscilla swore again and again she believed she was invisible to them. Some benevolent force of the night had made the murderers blind to her presence. The girl they murdered only a week earlier was seven. Why would they spare her?

(Chapter nine: a reckoning)

The morning after, Texas Rangers and soldiers from Fort Richardson encountered the Comanches and killed all of them. Only one Ranger was lost in the skirmish.

(Chapter ten: much is mystery)

Grandfather came home to an empty house that night, not having seen the Comanches but he heard the story when Priscilla and my father (who had gotten control of the colt and returned to the place Priscilla fell off) came in together. My grandfather scolded them for leaving, but he was so happy they were alive, he chose not to take a switch to them.

My father told me Grandfather had Priscilla tell him exactly what happened several times before they finally went to sleep that night. Priscilla asked him over and over why they had not seen her. Grandfather was, of course, skeptical and told me he had wondered if the Comanches were blind drunk or simply didn't feel like any more blood that night. Never in his ninety-seven years did he say he was sure they didn't see her. Never in Aunt Priscilla's eighty-nine years did she waiver from the notion she was invisible that night on the prairie. Aunt Priscilla did say she heard grandfather talking to Pastor James about it, and she recalled something about the spirit of her dead mother protecting her in the place her mother's soul had left her body. Priscilla felt this may have made sense to the Reverend James, and maybe even grandfather, but she claimed she never understood what saved her. If it had been a benevolent spirit, she never could fathom it was her mother's.

(Chapter 11: is there more to the story?)

Charles finished telling me about the events that occurred in 1898. I asked him if he had any other experiences at that fork in the trail. He said the year his grandfather died, Charles' father and he found a steer in the mesquite only a few yards from the place. The steer's throat had been slashed and its blood had already gone from crimson to black on the grass by the time they found it. By then, his father was 77, but he still remembered the stormy night vividly. His father only said, this place, this world, these are things I will never understand. Charles said his father had also wondered aloud if Patricia's cerebral palsy was a curse from this land where so many peculiar things had happened.

(Chapter twelve: back on the trail)

After our conversation, I walked back to the spot on the trail where, not two hours before, I had found the calf. It was still there, swollen and rank, but no raptor had touched it. I saw vultures riding currents in the blue sky above the pastures to the south. I saw others to the north, circling tight, waiting for some beast to draw its last breath. Perhaps another calf. Not the one at this junction in the trail, this place surrounded by thorns.

It is good to be grateful...

The storyteller wishes to thank Raymond S for being the great brother in arms he chose to be and for his support of this project. He would also like express his appreciation to Guy T, not only for providing financial support for this collection, but also for being a better friend than the storyteller believes he deserves. He is sorry he had Guy die in the first short story in the collection, but that is just how the story unfolded. Guy's dog, Taylor, lives on, chasing those dumb beasts along the Cimarron.

The author would also like to express appreciation to Professor Jim Hoggard, scholar of distinction, and former Poet Laureate of Texas, whose graduate class, Contemporary Literature, changed not only the way the storyteller viewed literature but also the storyteller's understanding of the human condition. Amazing how far the words, "communicate the texture of experience," can go when one is watching the reels roll behind one's eyes. Jim's class influenced the storyteller's world view more than all his psychology and counseling classes for his undergraduate and graduate degrees.

I would like to thank David Larkin for granting me permission to use his painting, "Scarborough Sea Breeze." David's melodic, wistful painting was the inspiration for the story, "Sea Breeze." I would also like to express appreciation to Dana Newman McCartney for her photo of the 1957 Brother Atlas which inspired the story of that title. Finally, I would be remiss if I did not thank Rebecca G, AKA "Reba," for sending me her late husband's poignant photographs which included the image of the woman on the front cover. RIP Everett—your artist's eye was a gift I am glad you shared.

About the Storyteller

Jim Cunningham lives in a small city on the prairies of north Texas. The prairies and the desert where he spent some of his formative years provide the backdrop for some of his stories, although his tales also take the reader to battlefields on beaches and in jungles and to other cities on the plain.

Jim is the grandson of a spy—being perilously curious is part of his DNA. Jim lived on three continents by the time he was eleven. After dropping out of high school, he joined the United States Army, volunteered for and served in Vietnam.

Jim found higher education more appealing than the public schools and obtained undergraduate and graduate degrees from Midwestern State University. Ironically, despite his abysmal lack of success as a student in public education, he spent his career as a public-school teacher, counselor and administrator.

In retirement, he works part time with handicapped students in the school district from which he retired. He hikes, reads, travels, watches reruns, and writes stories as they are revealed to him.

Jim has also written under the names J Donovan Carrasco and spysgrandson. Image on back cover, "The Limited Gravity of Masks," was created by the storyteller.